PIERCED

LUCIEN & LIA

New York Times Best Selling Author

SYDNEY LANDON

PIERCED

Lucian and Lia Trilogy

Book One

Copyright © 2014 Sydney Landon

Graphic Content Warning:
This novel contains depictions of violence, sexual abuse and child abuse.

Cover Design and Interior format by The Killion Group
http://thekilliongroupinc.com

ALSO BY SYDNEY LANDON

The Danvers Novels

Weekends Required

Not Planning on You

Fall For Me

Fighting For You

Betting on You (A Danvers Novella)

No Denying You (Coming 12/3/2014)

Always Loving You (Coming 2/15/15)

CHAPTER ONE

Lucian

"If I don't have a date with me tonight, Monique will have her hand on my cock before the first course is finished." My friend and employee, Aidan Spencer, tries unsuccessfully to hide the smirk on his face at my prediction. Unfortunately, or fortunately, whichever way you want to look at it, we both know I'm right. Monique Chandler is always on the prowl and right now, her sights are set on me...again. Fucking her was one of the biggest mistakes I've made recently. No pussy is worth that kind of Hell, especially when it was a sub-par fuck, at best.

"Yeah, that must be a tough problem to have. I guess I could run interference for you. Do you think she would have her hand on my dick by the end of the evening?"

I laugh saying, "Be careful what you wish for. That is one bed-hop you might want to rethink. She's a fucking viper. As much as I want to discuss your future sexual conquests, right now I need a date."

"Maybe you should have thought about that before you dumped Laurie last week. You couldn't put that off until after dinner tonight?"

I prop my legs on the desk, crossing them at the ankles. "No, Laurie punched her own ticket when she laid down the ultimatum. I grant you, the timing was less than perfect, but I have never caved to threats, and I'm not going to start now. The only thing she gave a damn about anyway was the balance in my bank account.

"Well, at least you didn't have to waste a lot of time moving her out of your place. Did she ever actually see the inside of it?"

I stare at my friend before answering, "You know better."

Aidan shakes his head. "I don't understand that, Luc."

"What's to understand? My home is mine. I don't intend to spend my life with any of these women, so why complicate things?" Shooting him a smirk, I add, "You're not exactly playing 'happy home' with any of your women, either, so why bust my balls?"

"There's a difference between me and you, my friend," Aidan says. "I've actually had women in my home and in my bed. You dated Laurie for months, and she never even walked through your place? Fuck man, how did you even explain that to her?"

I raise a brow at the question. "I don't explain myself to anyone, Laurie included. She will have someone else on the hook by the end of the month, anyway."

Aidan rocks back in his chair smiling. "I think you are giving yourself too much credit, my man; she will have someone else by the end of the week. Of course, he will probably be well-advanced in years, but if the money is there, I'm sure Laurie can overlook everything else."

Smiling at his accurate assessment of Laurie, I nod in agreement because it's more than fucking true. I mentally brace myself. Damn, this next question is going to hurt. "I really hate to ask, but do you know anyone who would be available to accompany me tonight and not think I'm going to be picking out china with them next week?"

Aidan looks surprised but recovers quickly. "I know I'm going to catch Hell for this, but I do know someone. Well, not really a specific someone, but I know a place that can help."

Another of Aidan's whores, just perfect. They are strictly women you keep behind closed doors. "Do explain that statement. If this involves anything that's going to get me five-to-ten years, I'd rather pass."

"Please reserve your judgment until I'm finished. I...um, have on occasion had the need of a date at the last minute. A friend of mine recommended a service that provides dates for executives. It's mostly college students. I have never had a problem with them."

I'm momentarily speechless, which doesn't happen often. "You mean an escort service, don't you?" Has he lost his mind?

"Yes, but it's not what you think. There is nothing illegal about it. They don't provide lap dances or sex; it is strictly business. Although, I wouldn't object to the other things if they wanted to throw that in."

"I can just see how this would look if word got out that I had to resort to hiring my dates. Surely, you know of someone else? You go on a different date every night, man." Now I know where all the dates were coming from. When did he start buying women, for fuck's sake?

"Yeah, I know a lot of women Luc, but none who won't chase you for months after the date. You just got rid of Laurie; I don't think you want to jump right back in the shark-infested waters so soon. I'm telling you, this is the perfect solution for tonight. I'll even set it up if you want."

I run my hand through my hair, wanting to growl in frustration. Has my life gotten to the point where I am seriously considering Aidan's suggestion? Recalling the last dinner I attended where Monique cornered me outside the men's room, practically sticking her tongue down my throat, makes me look at Aidan and say, "Do it. Get an address for me to pick her up. I don't want to spend all evening hunting a stranger in the parking lot of the restaurant. If this turns out bad, you're fired."

Aidan smiles, knowing my threat doesn't hold substance. We have been friends for most of our lives and always have each other's backs. We first met back in elementary school. He was getting his first-grade ass kicked by a third grader when I jumped onto the back of his tormentor. I grabbed Aidan's hand and jerked him to his feet, and we proceeded to deliver a few kicks of our own to the bully before we were pulled into the principal's office. From that moment on, we were inseparable. I'd never admitted to Aidan that I almost pissed my fucking pants that day when I jumped on that asshole for him. I'd been scared out of my mind and was grateful the bastard had tripped from the surprise attack and done most of the work for me.

Aidan had grown up with the standard house, dog, and white picket fence. He was an only child whose parents doted on him. I lived with my Aunt Fae; my parents died in a car accident when I was five, so my dad's sister had taken custody of me. When I reached twenty-one, I took the sizable inheritance from my parents and bought my first company, an ailing software firm that was operating in the red. Within a year, I had turned it around, and Quinn Software was born. Back when the other kids were reading comic books, I was reading *Business Week* and the *Wall Street Journal*. At twenty-nine, I was at the top and everyone wanted a piece of me, especially the women. With the weight of responsibility I carried, sometimes twenty-nine had never felt so damn old.

Our brotherhood had taken a small shift the day Cassie Wyatt moved into the neighborhood and enrolled in our school. Like us, Cassie-or Cass, as we soon started to call her-had been a social outcast and easy-pickings for the mean girls. She had taken to following us around on her bike even when we tried to shoo her away. After a while, her sheer determination to make friends had won both of us over, and she was officially in the club. Her father, who tended to drink too much and work too little, had raised Cass. She always put off going home until the last possible minute. As a teenager, she would fall into what I later would recognize as a manic-depressive state where she would cycle from off-the-chart highs to almost-suicidal lows.

Aidan had been in love with her for most of our childhood and all of his teenage years. Cass, though, only ever had eyes for me. Sure, she loved him as a friend, but as we grew older, she saw more in me, and eventually I returned her feelings. If I hadn't been such a competitive bastard, I would have backed off and hoped she turned to Aidan. Would it have changed anything? That question had haunted me for years. We dated through high school and were still together in college until one night changed all of us forever. Shaking off the feelings that threatened to choke me, I tune back into Aidan's taunting.

"For you, my friend, I will request the best they have. Maybe a nice, chubby blonde?" Aidan jokes.

At that moment, my assistant comes in to let me know my next appointment has arrived. "Thanks, Cindy. How about dragging Aidan out of my office so I can stay on schedule?" I sit back in my chair and smile as Cindy-always a sucker for punctuality-literally removes Aidan from his chair and hustles him out the door. God, I love that woman, and she deserves a bonus just for putting up with my moody ass every day.

She is in her mid-fifties and has been with me for five years. After her two sons left home for college, she returned to the workforce, and I am grateful to have her. She runs my office like an army sergeant, and I suspect she has moved me firmly into the role of another son. She is a good judge of character and had never liked Laurie; I caught her rolling her eyes behind Laurie's back on more than one occasion. As she ushers in my next appointment, I have to wonder just what in the hell I am getting myself into, letting Aidan hire a date for me from an escort service. I imagine some bubble-gum-chewing Barbie doll showing up tonight. Knowing Aidan, she will have huge tits and very little upstairs. If it keeps Monique off me for the evening, though, who cares if the only current events the woman knows are the words to the latest Britney Spears song.

Lia

I walk into my apartment and promptly fall down onto the couch. My roommate Rose looks up from the book she is buried in, asking, "Bad day, kid?"

"Ugh, yeah. I barely slept at all last night thanks to this cold, and now I have an assignment tonight from *Date Night*." Rose grimaces as I blow my nose and settle back against the cushions.

"Why did you take the job when you feel like shit?"

"Why do I ever? I need the money. At least this one is just for some dinner meeting. God, I hope he's not a playboy like the last one. He kept thinking he could buy his way into my panties if he offered enough. What is so hard to understand about "escort?" Nowhere in that word does it insinuate stripper or hooker."

Rose throws her head back and laughs. "I'm sure it's a common misconception. You're lucky that most of the men know the rules and abide by them. I don't care what your occupation is; you always have some butthead who thinks he is special. A guy came in the coffee shop last night and pinched my ass when I handed him his espresso. When did men start thinking it was okay to feel their server up? If it weren't for Jake freaking out, I would take a job with you in a minute." Jake was Rose's boyfriend of two years, and Lia knew he would indeed freak if the love of his life was out escorting other men around town.

I am in my fourth and final year at St. Claire's University, located in Asheville, North Carolina. St. Claire's is a smaller school and, therefore, very hard to gain admittance to. The tuition is steep, and the scholarships hard to come by, but the level of education is second to none. When I got accepted, I was over the moon... until I started trying to figure out how to pay for it.

At eighteen, my mother had packed my bags and pointed to the door. After years of doing anything I could to avoid my stepfather's unwanted advances, it was almost a relief to leave.

I never knew my father; my mother was neglectful at best and crazy angry at her worst. To say I am unlucky in the parental department is a real understatement. When my mother married Jim Dawson, though, things went from bad to oh-so-much worse. Oh, I never had broken bones like some who are abused; my mother always preferred slapping and backhanding. Occasionally, she would throw in a belt when she was really mad.

Sadly, Jim's arrival made me long for the days when I just had my mother to fear. I was fifteen and, as Jim was constantly pointing out, well-developed for my age. It started with lingering, seemingly-innocent touches and quickly escalated. He started coming into my room at night.

He would twist my arm behind my back until I agreed to remove my top. He would sit or lay beside me, pinching my nipples painfully while masturbating. After a while, my breasts weren't enough, and he wanted me completely naked. The first time, I fought him until he put a hand around my throat, cutting off my air supply until I blacked out. I woke to find one of his hands fondling my sex while he jacked-off. Each night he went further, taking more and more. I feared that soon he would no longer be content to just touch me. I knew without a doubt that my mother was aware of what was happening; I tried to talk to her more than once, and she would either walk away or backhand me until I shut up.

After having to endure his touch at every available opportunity, I heard him say something that saved me from certain rape. He was ranting to my mother about how she had better not gain any more weight because he hated heavy women. That night, I started eating everything I could hold without puking, and by the end of the month, I was fifteen pounds heavier. This continued until I gained almost fifty pounds. It was obvious my size was a complete turn-off to Jim. He stopped touching me and instead insulted me at every turn, but I didn't care if it meant he no longer snuck into my bedroom at night.

I had no real friends in school, and my size made me the target of constant taunting. The upside of being a social outcast was I had a lot of time to study and graduated from high school at the top of my class. Even having no idea how I would afford it, I applied to every local college, desperate to escape the Hell I was living in. The day I received an acceptance letter from St. Claire's was also the day my mother kicked me out. I should have been brave enough to leave before then; she would have never looked for me.

On my last night at home, I was in the laundry room ironing clothes when my mother stomped in, looking pissed at the world. Jim followed closely behind her. As they argued, I sat the iron down and tried to slink out the door without being noticed. When Jim suddenly yelled, "Fuck," my spine stiffened and I looked over my shoulder to see him shaking his hand and pointing to the iron. "Look what the fuck you did, you fat ass! You left the iron sitting right in the middle of the floor and caused me to burn my hand. I bet you did it on purpose, you conniving bitch!"

I closed my eyes, feeling tears prickle behind the lids. "I...I'm sorry." Suddenly, Jim's anger switched from my mother to me. I was terrified and started trying to back away from him.

"Where the fuck you think you're going?" As Jim advanced on me, my mother slid by and out the door, never looking back. I knew there would be no help from her. When had there ever been?

When Jim grabbed the bottom of my t-shirt, he jerked so hard I felt the thin cotton tear. As I tried to hold the shirt together, he ripped it from my body; snapping my neck painfully. I crossed my arms over my bra, repeating over and over, "I'm sorry, I'm sorry."

"You're not sorry, you lying cow. You intentionally left that iron there, hoping I'd burn myself." Spittle flew onto my face as he spat the words at me. When a cruel smile turned up the corners of his mouth, my blood ran cold. Oh, God, I knew that smile. My arms tightened around my breasts, trying to cover myself as I shook in fear. "Don't you worry about me touching those big tits; you disgust me. What I'm gonna give you, girl, is a reminder of what happens when you fuck with me. You want to burn me and think you can get away with it? It's time you learned a lesson you'll never forget." He turned me away from him, keeping a strong arm around my waist before leaning over to pick something up. He jerked my long ponytail aside, making my scalp sting. Suddenly, my back between the shoulder blades was on fire. I gasped in agony, trying to pull away. The smell of something horrible stung my nose, and as the room started spinning, it hit me; he was burning me with the iron. As oblivion rose, I heard him whisper in my ear, "Cows are always branded so they know who they belong to, and you'll always belong to me." I never felt my body make contact with the floor, and when I woke later, my back was still on fire, and I was alone. The bastard had marked me, and the years would never remove his brand from my body or my mind.

I slept in the park the first night I was on my own, and it was the best night I could remember having; I figured the odds of me being attacked were less than they would have been at home. I used the few dollars I managed to take from my mother's purse to buy Tylenol. Luckily, the store also had a water fountain, and I downed four of them, hoping I wasn't overdosing. My back was still in agony from the iron. The next day, I applied for a waitress job, and the owner Debra took pity on me and hired me. She also agreed to let me make payments to her weekly on the old Honda she had for sale. Finally, I had somewhere to sleep until school started in the fall. Debra also let me have my meals for free; I suspected it was because she knew I was homeless but never asked. Debra mentioned casually on my second day of employment that the truck stop down the street had showers for the truckers. Her boyfriend Martin owned the place, and she got me a voucher to use their facilities whenever I needed to. Between the truck stop and the laundromat, I had somewhere to spend time other than my car.

I had carefully avoided looking at my back and tried
to keep water off it in the shower; a month went by
and it no longer stung. On my break one day, I used
the restroom at work and finally got brave enough to
raise my shirt and turn my back to the mirror. "Oh,
my God," someone whispered behind me. I jerked
around to find Debra standing there with murder in
her eyes and her hand over her mouth. I pulled my
shirt down, cursing myself for not hearing the door
open. Debra walked over, pulling me against her.
"Who did that to you, Lia?"

Tears started to seep down my cheeks. I wasn't used
to concern or affection, and the sorrow in Debra's voice
was enough to undo me. "It doesn't matter," I
whispered back. "It's over now."

"Oh, baby girl," Debra said. "It matters because I
want to kick someone's ass. You tell me who did this to
you, and Martin and I will do the same damn thing to
them." When she pulled back, I could tell by the look
on her face that Debra was deadly serious. In the time
I had worked at the restaurant, I had bonded with the
outspoken redhead and her boyfriend Martin. She
studied my closed expression before releasing an angry
breath. "You're not going to tell me, are you?" When I
shook my head, Debra raised a hand to wipe away a
stray tear from my face. "Is anyone after you now,
baby girl?"

"No," I whispered. "I'm on my own."

"All right then," Debra answered. "If anyone bothers
you, or whoever the hell did this to you shows up, you
tell me or Martin, okay?" I hugged Debra in way of
reply and thanked God I had met her; I finally had
someone in my life that cared whether I lived or died,
and I'd never forget it. As we walked back out into the
restaurant and I returned to my job, I tried to block
out what I had seen in the bathroom. As promised, Jim
had indeed branded me, and the horribly scarred flesh
on my back would always be a reminder of a Hell I had

barely escaped. Only my dreams would haunt me now because I vowed to never let him close to me again.

Working and being away from Jim had also allowed me to return to my normal eating habits, and the extra weight I had gained for protection had fallen away, leaving a girl I hardly recognized staring back in the mirror. I was slowly returning to the petite size I had always been and was grateful I didn't appear to have done long-term damage to my body. It was a sad testament to my former life that now, even homeless, I was the happiest I'd ever been. Debra had tried to convince me to move in with her and Martin, but I had refused; I didn't want to be a burden to them, and I was getting by. I worked mostly nights, so sleeping in my car seemed much safer during daytime hours. I also caught naps in the break room at the restaurant some days.

I hoped I could save enough money by the time school started for living expenses, since my grades won me a full scholarship. God, how naive I had been. My small amount of savings was gone by the end of the first semester, and I had no idea what I was going to do.

St. Claire's requires that all students live on campus for the first two years. Unfortunately, that wasn't part of my scholarship; neither was transportation, the cost of books, and other fees. The small, two-bedroom apartment I shared with Megan for a year, and now with Rose, was much cheaper than most apartments, but still expensive. Money had trickled through my hands like water.

I had given up and was planning to drop out of college. Even working two part-time jobs, I couldn't swing my expenses. Debra had offered to loan me the money, but I couldn't do it; it was important I make it on my own. My then-roommate Megan had told me she worked for a company called *Date Night* and had offered to put in a good word for me. I had been so desperate to stay in school that I jumped at the chance. Now, three years later, I was just months away from having my degree in business and owed it all to Megan and *Date Night*. As Rose said, there were jerks to deal with in any job, and I considered myself lucky that it was rare in mine. Working for *Date Night* had allowed me to quit my other part-time jobs, which had given me more time for school. I missed Debra terribly but still hung out at the restaurant whenever I had a free day.

Looking at my watch, I blow my nose once more and force myself to stand and head toward my bedroom. After a loud sneeze, I look over my shoulder at Rose and say, "This is one night I would gladly change places if I could. I don't know if it's possible for makeup to tone down the Rudolph nose I'm rocking right now." Looking at my bed longingly, I grumble, "You better tip well, Lucian Quinn, because I would much rather be in my warm bed watching a chick-flick than out with a bunch of rich snobs, drinking wine I would never be able to afford on my own."

CHAPTER TWO

Lia

Checking my reflection in the mirror, I groan at the disaster looking back at me. The last rounds of sneezing and nose-blowing have done a number on my makeup. I pull my compact out and once again powder my nose. My eyes look glassy from the cold medicine I took before leaving home, making me look more like a crack-whore than someone's paid escort. This is a really bad idea. I take a hairbrush from my handbag and pull it through my wavy, blonde hair. Ugh, I desperately need a trim, but with my hair so long, I mostly keep it pulled back in a ponytail. On date nights, though, my dates prefer something a little less 'look at me, I'm a college student.' Shit, even the brush makes my stuffy head ache. If not for the expensive books I need to purchase, I would have skipped tonight and lived on Ramen Noodles and water for a while.

I step out of my old Honda Civic and look around the parking lot. It's probably too much to hope that some lonely man is holding up a sign with my name on it. Maybe it would have been a good idea to ask what type of car Mr. Quinn would be driving. Why had I been so damn stubborn about riding in his car? Oh, yeah, I didn't want to be locked in his trunk, taken to some deserted road and killed. I've watched enough Lifetime movies to know all about 'stranger danger'. Since there still doesn't appear to be anyone looking for me, I decide to walk to the entrance and check with the valets. I have just stepped on the sidewalk when a sleek, black Mercedes purrs to a stop at the curb and a tall, middle-aged man steps from the driver's side and walks around the car. I am almost even with the car when the driver opens the back door. A man inside the car closes a laptop and steps out onto the sidewalk.

Holy shit, he's beautiful. Rose would die because he has the fuck-me style of tousled hair she just loves on men. His hair is as black as the night surrounding us and looks as if he-or someone else-has run their hands through it several times. His suit is obviously expensive and drapes perfectly over his muscular body; my heartbeat escalates as I imagine what that suit must be covering. He's tall, powerful, and looks like something straight out of a wet dream. I've given myself countless orgasms picturing a man like him.

I can only blame my next action on Nyquil intoxication. Thinking only of sharing the visual pleasure of this male God with my friend, I grab my cell phone and snap his picture. When he turns to speak with his driver, I giggle as I snap another of his ass. I stand oblivious as I start texting the pictures to Rose. When I finish, I look up, still smiling to find the male God in question standing directly in front of me, a smirk pulling at the corners of his kissable mouth. "Did you get what you needed, Miss...?"

Before I think better of it, I murmur, "Adams."

"Lia Adams?" he asks.

Surprised, I can only stare at him for a moment. "Um...yeah. How did you know?"

He takes my arm and pulls me to the side. "I'm Lucian Quinn; I believe you are here for me?"

"No way! You're a god!" I slap my hand over my mouth in horror. Did I actually just say that aloud?

He grins, obviously highly entertained by my slip of the tongue. "Why, thank you, Miss Adams; that is very flattering. Is there any particular reason that has led you to that conclusion?"

Mortified, I squeeze my eyes shut, trying to block out those sexy lips I'm sure are still smirking at me. "I...ur, sorry about that. You're just so beautiful." Fuck, someone shut me up! When the silence continues, I open my eyes and stick out a hand, determined to change the subject. "Hi, I'm Lia Adams, your date for the evening."

He leaves my hand hanging in the air for a moment longer before firmly grasping it between his. Heat races through my body at his touch; I can't remember ever having this kind of instant response to a man before. "Lucian Quinn and it is certainly a pleasure to meet you, Miss Adams." He continues to hold onto my hand until I finally tug it away. He studies me intently for what seems like minutes, but is probably mere seconds. To be the sole focus of that kind of intensity is disarming, at best. Was it my imagination or does he almost look shocked? Crap, do I look that bad tonight? No doubt, the answer to that question is a resounding yes.

Squaring my shoulders, I ask in my most professional voice, "Is there anything I need to know before we go inside?"

He seems to shake off whatever thoughts had taken over his mind. Amusement lurks in his eyes as if he knows I'm grappling for composure. "I don't believe so. I assume you understand that to anyone else, you are my date for the evening and not a paid escort. I would like to keep that bit of information private."

"Of course," I reply. "I'll just follow your lead." He takes my hand and settles it into the crook of his arm. He steers us effortlessly through the crowded lobby and to the hostess stand.

A perky blonde with fake breasts beams as if she has just been handed her Christmas and birthday present at once. "Mr. Quinn, how great to see you again!"

"Good evening, Mindy. How have you been?"

As Mindy and Lucian continue to converse, I fight the urge to stick my finger down my throat and gag dramatically. It's like watching a real-life Barbie and Ken meeting play out. Lucian seems to know he is giving Mindy the thrill of a lifetime by talking to her longer than required. I wouldn't be surprised to see phone numbers exchanging hands. I want to poke him in the ribs and whisper that he can do better, but it's none of my business; I am just the hired help for the evening. When Lucian puts his hand in the small of my back in an attempt to move me forward, I stumble before catching myself. A face-plant right in front of Barbie and Ken would be a freaking nightmare.

He leads me toward a quiet corner of the restaurant where several other couples are seated. The men rise to their feet as Lucian pulls a chair out for me. I am happy to sit by an older couple. For some reason, everyone over the age of fifty seems to love me. Other than Rose and a few other classmates, I rarely spend time with people my own age; I learned early on that people can be petty and mean. Debra always tells me that I have an old soul.

Lucian seats himself beside me and begins making the introductions. The couple to our right is Margaret and Howard Sterling, and as I had hoped, they greet me with warm smiles. I can barely remember the rest of the names with the exception of the woman on Lucian's other side, Monique Chandler. She has long, dark hair and is wearing a form-fitting, emerald green sleeveless dress. She is attractive, but to me, it's all artificial...almost hard. The smile that she greets me with is calculating and cold. Lucian is polite but doesn't seem overjoyed to be sitting next to her. I am just thankful I will likely never see these people again after tonight; I have a few regulars I have accompanied more than once, but venues change each time and, generally, so do the people.

After everyone has placed their drink orders, Monique leans around Lucian and asks, "So Lucy, how do you know Lucian?"

Before I can answer, Lucian says, "It's Lia, and we met through mutual friends."

I am grateful for his quick response. I am even happier when the server places the red wine Lucian ordered in front of me; liquid courage is just what I need.

It is hard to miss Monique's red nails trailing down Lucian's chest and the possessive smile she shoots my way before turning back to him. If he were actually my man, I would be ready to knock her on her ass. Luckily, Margaret is indeed friendly, and I tell her honestly that I am attending St. Claire's. Surely, that's not something that needs to be kept secret.

When the dinner course arrives, the prime rib is big enough to cover my plate. Lucian ordered for us, but I was expecting something a little more…manageable. I have gotten even drowsier from my cold medicine and trying to cut the steak is going to be tricky. Taking a deep breath, I pick up the knife and fork and look for the easiest place to start. When Lucian speaks near my ear, I jerk around, almost stabbing his arm. "Whoa," he mutters. "Do you need some help there?"

"Yeah, couldn't you have ordered something easier? My Dayquil or Nyquil or whatever is making this hard." Holding the silver knife closer, I study the elegant pattern on the handle. "It is pretty, though, isn't it? Hey look, I can see my reflection in it." Oh, dear Lord, did I just say that?

Lucian looks momentarily speechless before taking the knife gingerly from my hand. "Let me help you with that. I've never been stabbed at dinner before, and I don't want to start now." He pulls my plate closer to his and begins cutting the steak into small pieces.

I beam my approval at him, gushing, "You're my hero."

Monique notices what he's doing and sneers. "Luc, really, if you're going to bring a child to dinner, at least make sure she's table-trained."

"Monique," Lucian responds, a clear warning in his tone.

Monique curls what I have come to think of as her talons around his arm, purring, "I guarantee you won't have to baby me. I am fully capable of taking care of my needs...and yours."

I roll my eyes before whispering far too loudly in Lucian's ear, "Who invited Cruella? Oh, and her tits are totally fake. Rose and I can always spot those." I giggle to myself at how much Monique reminds me of Cruella Deville from the *101 Dalmatians* movie. I doubt Monique has ever seen the movie, so the insult is probably lost on her.

Lucian's shoulders are shaking and Monique is gaping at me. I shrug and turn to my plate as Lucian puts it back in front of me. Margaret puts an arm around my shoulders and pulls me in for a side hug. "Honey, that woman will probably kill you, but you have just officially become my new best friend. I haven't enjoyed one of these stuffy dinners this much... well, ever!"

"She's right, you know," Lucian says as he slides an arm around the back of my chair. "The viper will want to kill you." A shiver runs through my body as his fingertips caress the side of my arm. "Did you really take Nyquil?"

Nodding, I say, "I've got a cold and I couldn't stop sneezing. It's kind of zoned me out, though. We were out of Dayquil, and Rose said Nyquil is the same thing. Do you think it is?"

Lucian lets loose a panty-melting laugh. "I don't know, but you should have told me that before I poured you a glass of wine. You aren't supposed to mix cold medicine with alcohol."

"Whoops, my bad." He is so warm, and the air in the restaurant has grown chilly. "Mmm, you feel nice," I murmur against his side as I curl closer. His body heat feels better than a blanket. He smells amazing, and I fight the urge to put my nose against his skin and sniff...or even taste it.

I feel his body stiffen for a moment before he blows out a breath. "Eat your dinner, Lia." After that, the meal goes by at a fast pace. Lucian keeps a firm arm around me, anchoring me to his side. At one point in the evening, I catch Monique's eyes boring into me, and I childishly stick out my tongue at the other woman from behind my napkin. Take that, Cruella! When the evening is over, I say goodbye to my new friend Margaret and try to ignore the fact that Monique is giving Lucian a hug that borders on humping. God, the woman seriously lacks class.

As Lucian leads me toward his car, I jerk in surprise as he opens the door for me to precede him into the interior. Shaking my head, I say, "My car is in the parking lot, but thanks for the offer."

Lucian tightens his grip on my arm, looking down at me. "You aren't in any condition to drive yourself home, so I'll drop you. Leave me your keys, and I'll have your car delivered to your place later tonight." I resist as he tries once more to steer me into his car. Finally, clearly losing patience with me, he snaps, "Lia, get in the damn car, now!" I am so surprised by his tone that I jump to do his bidding, never questioning his authority until the door closes firmly behind him and he settles his thigh onto the seat next to mine.

"Your address?" I rattle it off, knowing it's useless to argue. Peeking at him from under my lashes, I wonder if he looks like a serial killer.

"I am perfectly fine, you know." For some reason, I feel the need to point that out to him, even though we both know it's not true; there is no way I should be driving myself home.

He turns to me, raising a brow. "I'm sure you are, Lia, but when I take a woman to dinner, I always make sure she arrives back home safely."

"Oh," I reply, his answer taking the fight out of me. It makes sense, right? He is just being a gentleman.

"I want you to call into work tomorrow and quit your job. I don't think you need to bother with notice; it's not likely you will ever use them for a future job reference."

I nod my head in agreement, fighting the sleep threatening to claim me when his words finally hit me. What the hell? "Wh—What did you say?" Had I imagined the whole thing?

Without looking at me, he repeats his demand. I shake my head, completely confused. "What are you talking about? Why would I quit my job? Oh, no," I gasp in horror, "are you trying to get me fired because of tonight? It was just cold medicine!"

His eyes are glittering in the darkness. "Baby, if I wanted to have you fired, I would. I want to fuck you, but not when you're being paid to be my date."

Oh, shit. I know I am more than a little intoxicated when my first reaction is being flattered. How can a man like Lucian Quinn want to fuck me? I'm a struggling college student with none of the flash of a woman like Monique. What could he possibly see in me? What is the appropriate response when a man says he wants to fuck you? "Ummm...that's...thanks. I can't quit my job; I need the money for school." I reach over to pat his knee, adding, "You're so hot, and I'm sure you can find another woman to...fuck." There, that sounds good, right? I'm proud of my answer. I turned him down but also gave him a compliment. Way to think on your feet, Lia!

He puts his hand over mine, and I smile, thinking he appreciates my honesty. When he uses a firm grip to pull me closer to his side, I start to worry. Please tell me we aren't on a dirt road in the middle of nowhere. Does he resemble someone from *America's Most Wanted*? His breath is hot on my neck as he whispers against my ear, "I want you, and I always get what I want." He trails a finger down the side of my face before running the tip over my mouth. My lips part in surprise and before I think better of it, I touch his finger with the tip of my tongue. He inhales a breath, and I freeze, my eyes locking on his face.

I have no idea how long I've been staring at him when the driver clears his throat. I look out the window and recognize my apartment building. Lucian is still holding my hand as I turn to the door the driver is holding open. Lucian pulls me against him again, saying, "It wasn't a question, Lia. Do it." With those words, he releases me. I draw a ragged breath and stagger from the car. The driver insists on walking me to the door and waiting until I'm safely inside. Oh, God, he probably heard everything Lucian said to me, how embarrassing. No doubt, he is used to going home alone while his employer stays the night with whomever he is...fucking. Lucian Quinn is clearly a psycho. When the driver asks for my car key, I pull it from my ring and hand it over. I mutter a quick thank-you and dash inside.

Rose and Jake are sitting wrapped around each other on the couch. When I almost miss the chair

PIERCED   23

trying to sit, Jake smirks at me saying, "Whoa, girl, how much did you have to drink tonight?"

I flop back, groaning, "Not as much as you think. It's the damn Nyquil along with alcohol that did this. I'm lucky I didn't face-plant in the middle of the restaurant." I giggle as I imagine Lucian Quinn's face if that had happened. It would almost have been worth the embarrassment to fall all over his expensive shoes.

"So, other than your public intoxication, how was the evening? Old dude or young?" Rose asks.

I roll my eyes, saying, "Young, hot one, but a little on the weird side. Didn't you get the picture I sent you of him?"

"Shit! That was him? He was a total freaking..." Looking at Jake who is watching her, she quickly adds, "Um...okay. I mean, he was just okay. I'm glad you made it through the evening with him."

I smirk, knowing what Rose had been going to say; the man was a stud. "I'm not totally sure since I'm a little out of it, but I believe he might have ordered me to quit my job because he wants to fuck me." When the words leave my mouth, I slap my hand over my face. "God, I can't believe I just said that." I look over to see both Rose and Jake gaping at me.

"He said that to you?" Before I can answer, Rose sighs, "That's just so hot."

Jake looks at Rose then back to me. "You two seriously have problems. Lia, if some stranger said that shit to you, then you had better stay the hell away from him." Turning to his girlfriend, he says, "And you, I think it's time we went to your room and discussed some things." Rose snickers as Jake pulls her up from the couch, and they practically run to the bedroom. At the door, Jake stops, turning back toward me. "I'm serious, babe; you stay away from him. That's whacked that he said that to a stranger." He shuts the door behind him, and I hear Rose giggle. Ugh, I know I will be hearing too much through the paper-thin walls tonight.

I think about what Jake said and wonder if Lucian Quinn is dangerous. He certainly looked it when he was holding me against him in the car. I wasn't scared, though, not really. Thinking of him fucking me was exciting. I can feel the dampness of my panties and know it has everything to do with him.

Jake has been protective of me since his friend Jackson broke my heart last year. It was my first and last sexual experience. We had been going out for about a month before I finally caved to pressure and slept with him. What a mistake. It had hurt like Hell and was over before it had even started. Could I only have an orgasm at my own hands? Rose talked about sex with Jake as if it was earth-shaking, but for me, the earth hadn't moved. I got out of bed afterwards to use the bathroom, and he had gasped, "What the fuck?" When I turned to look at him, he was pointing to my back. "What's wrong with you? Shit, do you have something contagious?" He frantically threw his clothes on, acting like he had just had sex with someone with the clap.

"It's just a scar," I had replied before wrapping my arms around myself. He made me feel self-conscious and dirty. Jake was furious when he heard Jackson telling some of their friends that I 'was all messed up' under my clothes. He knew from Rose what my stepfather had done to me and almost physically came to blows with his friend over it. Since then, they barely spoke anymore. Jake was a good person and wouldn't tolerate anyone mistreating one of his friends. What would it be like to have a man like that to love and be loved by? Rose is damn lucky.

CHAPTER THREE

Lia

The rest of the week is a blur of too much studying and too little sleep. On the rare occasions when I find myself in bed at a decent time, the sexy Lucian Quinn haunts my dreams. I am munching on a muffin and drinking a huge cup of coffee at the campus coffee shop when my cellphone chimes. I pull it from my backpack, figuring it's Rose. It's a process of elimination, really; very few people have my number and even fewer of them actually call or text.

"Did you do as you were told?"

I study my phone in confusion, not recognizing the number. Finally, I type back:

"Wrong number, buddy."

Tossing my phone down on the table, I am surprised when it chimes again almost instantly.

"I don't think so, Lia."

"What the hell?" I look around as if expecting Rose to be hiding in the corner, laughing her ass off. No one seems to be paying me any attention, though, and there was no Rose nearby.

"Who is this?"

"I'm truly hurt. You've been on my mind for days, sweet Lia, but apparently, I haven't been on yours."

This is starting to get scary. Surely, Jackson isn't playing some type of nasty trick on me. He's an asshole, but I haven't heard from him in months.

"Listen, whoever you are; I'm busy, so unless you want to tell me who this is, piss off."

It isn't in my nature to be rude, but I don't want to encourage some weirdo.

"Wow, in just a few days, I've gone from being a God to you to being told to piss off. How the mighty have fallen."

I drop my phone as if I've been burned. "No way." Lucian Quinn is texting me? This has to be some kind of joke, but who else would know what he is saying? Tentatively, I type:

"Lucian?"

"Unless you've met another God this week."

Oh, my God! I try not to question the excitement coursing through my veins as my phone chimes again almost immediately.

"Now, back to my earlier question. Did you do what you were told?"

"Um...I have no idea what you're talking about, Mr. Quinn."

"It's Luc...and you know exactly what I'm talking about."

I lay my head on the table. He meant it. He really wanted me to quit my job so he could...fuck me. Oh, shit on a stick. The man is officially crazy. That actually explains a lot.

"Listen, MR. QUINN, I'm flattered you want to...you know, but I have no intention of quitting my job or doing...that."

I wait on pins and needles, both wanting and dreading his reply. What could a man like Lucian Quinn really want with an inexperienced college student? If he thinks I'm one of the *Girls Gone Wild* co-eds, he is sadly mistaken.

"Oh, Lia, you never challenge a man like me. I promise you; you'll do everything I want you to do and beg for more. I'll see you soon."

My face flushes and desire races through my body. My nipples harden into stiff peaks as I picture the scene in my head: the beautiful Lucian Quinn fucking me. I find myself more excited at just the thought than of my entire sexual experience with Jackson. A few words from Lucian...Luc, and I'm ready to go off. Surely, he is just playing with me. Regardless though, his face is firmly etched in my mind and his name on my lips later as I finger myself frantically into release.

"Are you working tonight, chick?" Rose asks as I walk into the living room dressed in my usual escort attire. Being a poor college student doesn't leave much room for variety. I have invested in a few outfits for my job, but the little black dress is the go-to choice.

"Yep, I'm meeting someone for a party at Valentino's. It looks like another business thing. At least those don't require much conversation."

Rose flips the television channel, before asking, "Is this someone new again?" She looks disappointed when I nod. "Oh, well, I guess you couldn't get lucky enough to have the God again, huh?"

Without understanding why, I decide not to mention Lucian's earlier text messages to her. What's the point, really? I doubt I'll hear from him again. Maybe he's some kind of weirdo that gets his kicks teasing women. A pang of disappointment pierces me at the thought of never seeing him again. How could someone I barely know have this type of effect on me? Rose reminds me to write the name of the restaurant and the person I'm meeting on the notepad in the kitchen. We started this routine on my first assignment with *Date Night*. Rose then joked about making it easy for the police to find my body if I don't make it home one night. There have been a few men over the years who wanted to test the boundaries, but none who haven't accepted the word no.

I look down at the name I write beside Valentino's. Aidan Spencer. He sounds harmless enough. With a goodbye wave to Rose, who is now firmly engrossed in a Lifetime movie, I set off for another long evening. Do I wish it was with Lucian Quinn and not Aidan Spencer? Unequivocally, yes.

CHAPTER FOUR

Lia

Walking into Valentino's, I look around in confusion. Aidan Spencer is supposed to be waiting at the bar. I'm grateful for that information because otherwise, I would have no hope of finding him in the crowd of people milling around. The bar is packed, but mainly with couples. Of course, he could be talking to someone. There is a dark-haired man sitting alone at one end watching football on the big-screen television above the bar. I straighten my dress and decide to try him first. Taking a deep breath, I tap him on the shoulder. "Mr. Spencer?" He takes his time sitting down the drink he is holding before swiveling around on the barstool. I jerk back in surprise, stuttering, "Luc—Lucian?" Shit, I know I sound like an idiot, but I can't control my shock at seeing him again. Dear Lord, he's hot.

"Lia," he purrs as his eyes run leisurely down my length; I'm absurdly grateful I haven't worn the same dress tonight. "You look beautiful."

"Th—thank you," I stammer. God, what is this man doing to me? I've lost the ability to carry on a simple conversation without tripping over my words. Clearing my throat, I ask, "What are you doing here?"

A smirk settles on his full lips as he answers, "I'm here for you."

I gape at him before deciding he is teasing me. No doubt, he is meeting someone just as beautiful as he is. I refuse to let him pass the time making fun of me. "Very funny. Unless your name is Mr. Spencer, you aren't here for me, and I'm not here for you."

His eyes dance as he says, "Just call me Aidan." Pulling out a chair beside him, he adds, "Have a seat; you look like you need a drink, Lia." Before I can object, he settles me next to his side and a glass of wine appears. "I trust you skipped the Nyquil tonight?"

Before answering, I pick up the glass and take a big gulp. "You tricked me. There is no Aidan Spencer, is there?"

His hand moves to my knee, rubbing circles against the tender skin before saying, "Oh, there is an Aidan, and he is here somewhere tonight. I just decided to hedge my bets and make sure you didn't turn me down. Even though I know you wanted to see me again as much as I wanted to see you, I knew you would deny it, even to yourself." His touch is doing crazy things to my body, and I'm fighting the urge to moan in pleasure. He leans closer and his lips settle near my ear, sending shivers down my spine. "You've been on my mind this week, Lia. I can't stop thinking about how you'll look when you come."

The drink of wine that I am in the process of swallowing is suddenly blowing from my mouth and nose. I try to catch my breath as I choke. Lucian removes his hand from my leg and pats my back gently until I can breathe again. Mortified, I take the napkins the bartender is holding out and try to dry up the mess I've made. Turning to the amused man beside me, I roll my eyes and say, "Please warn me next time before you say something like that."

"So, you agree there'll be a next time. I knew you were a realist, baby."

I raise a brow, loving the verbal wordplay despite myself. "Baby? Isn't that a little...personal for someone you barely know?"

His wandering hand returns to my knee before running lightly beneath the hem of my dress. "I'm ready to remedy that whenever you are...Lia." I can't ever remember being so turned on from just a conversation. Talking to Lucian is like word foreplay. My core throbs and I fight the urge to squeeze my legs together to assuage the ache there. This type of desire is foreign to me. I have the usual needs of a woman my age, but I easily take care of them myself. I've never been turned-on by a man to the point of misery before.

Looking around the room, I attempt to change the subject to something less stimulating. "So...um, why are we here tonight?" When he gives me a devilish smile, I rush on before he can comment. "I mean, is this business or pleasure?" Oh, shit. I want to drop my head and admit defeat. There is no way he is going to let the pleasure comment pass. At this rate, I'll drop my panties within ten minutes and beg him to fuck me on the counter while the bartender refills the peanuts beside my head.

Lucian grins, seeming to know what I'm expecting, so I'm surprised when he simply says, "It's business tonight. This is a celebratory party for the sales team. They closed a particularly big contract this week and deserve the recognition."

Curious, I ask, "Are you a salesman?" I had been so high from cold medicine at our last meeting that I scarcely remember the conversation from that evening.

Idly, he continues to twirl his finger on the delicate skin of my inner thigh as he answers. "No, baby, I'm not." Again with the 'baby', but it sounds too damn sexy for me to actually object. I like it...a lot, and he knows it. As I continue to wait for him to explain further, he blows out a breath and almost reluctantly admits, "I own the company."

I'm not surprised; truthfully, I would hardly expect anything less. It doesn't take an expert to realize his clothing isn't off the rack. The man has probably never stepped foot in Walmart before. I have a strange urge to giggle when I imagine what he would think if he knew my dress had been bought on sale at the mall for fifteen dollars. Just as his finger starts to wander into dangerous territory, someone claps a hand on his shoulder, causing him to jerk around in surprise. I immediately miss the loss of his warmth against me. "Luc, I was wondering where you were." Turning, I find a handsome man of about Lucian's age grinning at me. "And who is this?" Is it my imagination, or does Lucian suddenly look uncomfortable?

Lucian stands, helping me to my feet so we are facing the newcomer. "Lia, this is my friend and work associate, Aidan Spencer." Aidan is giving me a curious look as I gape back at him. "Aidan, this is Lia Adams, a friend of mine."

Aidan takes my hand in his, brushing his thumb against my palm. The move has probably sent many women straight into orgasm, and it might have worked on me were I not firmly captivated by Lucian. At this point, Aidan is just sloppy-Luc-seconds. Lucian slides a possessive arm around my waist, seeming pleased by my lack of reaction toward his friend. Outside of Lucian, Aidan is probably one of the best-looking men I have ever met, but he's not Lucian. "It's an honor to meet you, Lia. Are you here with Luc?"

Before I can answer, Lucian tightens his hold on me, saying, "Yes, she is. Where is your date, or are you flying solo?" I'm not sure if it's me or Lucian who groans when Monique walks toward us; she is one thing I remember vividly from our last evening together. "Who invited her?" Lucian asks, clearly unhappy.

Aidan smiles sheepishly. "That would be me, buddy." Lucian shoots him a look of amazement to which Aidan just shrugs. "Hey, one man's burger is another man's steak." The conversation ceases as Monique reaches us, going straight for Lucian.

"Luc...darling, there you are." She leans in, pressing a kiss to both cheeks. I have no doubt she would prefer his mouth, but he isn't offering. She then turns, looking me up and down before wrinkling her perfect nose. "Oh...Lucy, isn't it? You're Luc's little...friend." Great, she makes it sound as if I should be selling Girl Scout Cookies and playing hopscotch.

It's obvious she is trying to belittle me. I'd love nothing better than to run for the door and never look back, but some part of me I didn't know existed refuses to let her win. My dislike of her is stronger, and the need to get under her skin is even stronger. Without giving myself time to ponder the wisdom, I curve my body against Lucian's and stick out a hand to the other woman. Giving her my best innocent smile, I say, "It's Lia. I'm so happy to see you again, Mandy." There, take that, smart-ass. I know I've scored a direct hit when her possibly-botoxed mouth tightens, and her handshake is hard enough to sever my fingers. Lucian's arm tightens around my waist, and I have no idea if he is amused or pissed by our verbal bitch-slapping contest.

Unfortunately, Aidan appears almost intrigued with me now. As Monique settles back at his side, he asks, "So, Lia...how did you meet Luc? I've never heard him mention you before, so it must have been recent." What is the saying, if you're going to lie, add some elements of the truth to it? Since Lucian isn't rushing ahead with an explanation, and both Aidan and Monique are looking at me expectantly, I forge on. "It was quite by accident. Lucian texted my phone...thinking I was someone else." I smile, trying for a sexy grin. I have little practice in that area, so it probably looks more like I'm constipated. "It was a very enlightening conversation, to say the least." Far from being angry, Lucian chuckles beside me.

"It was certainly that, baby." There it is again, the warm feeling washing through my body at his easy use of the endearment. He's good; I have to give him that. Even I am taken in by the intimate tone of his voice.

Monique looks as if she could spit nails, and Aidan appears to be deep in thought as he studies Lucian and me. No doubt the poor sap is wondering how his handsome, powerful friend has ended up with an average, cheaply dressed schoolgirl. He ponders us another moment before directing his next question at me. "I believe Monique mentioned you were in school. Where do you attend?"

This was one question I am at least comfortable with. "I'm in my last year at St. Claire's."

Aidan looks suitably impressed; it's rare that anyone in Asheville hasn't heard of the prestigious school. "Wow, that's quite an accomplishment. What's your major?"

"Business Administration," I answer, suddenly shy at the attention focused on me. I thank God at that moment for the dreadful Public Speaking classes I have been forced to take. I am completely out of my element, and I damn well know it. Maybe it's just my imagination, but Lucian seems just as interested in my answers as his friends.

Monique, not one to be out of the spotlight for long, gives a yawn before covering her mouth as if it were an accident. "Oh, that is just so...interesting, Lucy. I'm sure you'll find a little job somewhere after you graduate. Now, since this is a party, shall we go have some fun?" I fight the urge to hold up one finger and yell, "Score one for Cruella," but manage to control the urge. She has effectively put me in my place and reminded everyone I'm not of their social class. The only advantage I still have over her is that firm grasp that Lucian continues to have on my waist; I know it's driving her out of her mind. With equal parts stupidity and bravery, I decide to press my advantage over her. Turning to Lucian, I let my hand rest on his broad chest and notice his eyes flare in surprise and something else...something exciting and possibly forbidden. I like it more than I care to admit.

"Luc, would you mind showing me around? I've never been here before, and it's beautiful." I hear Monique snort at my admission but ignore her. Lucian looks at me for a moment, humor dancing in his beautiful eyes.

"Of course, Lia." Without looking away from me, he says, "Aidan, Monique, I'm sure I'll see you later on." With that, we walk away, and I release the breath I've been holding. Lucian is stopped several times on our way across the crowded floor. He is polite but aloof. He is the boss here, and all these people know it; the men stand just a bit taller and the women glow when he acknowledges them. He is the force field everyone gravitates around. I find myself firmly under his spell as well; it's impossible not to be. Instead of pretending I don't exist, he introduces me to each person we meet. I'm surprised and oddly touched by this move. Most of my dates with *Date Night* use me as nothing more than an attractive prop to stand next to them all evening. A potted plant would likely fill the same purpose. Not Lucian, though essentially, we are a couple this evening. The curiosity that fills the air tells me this is rare for him.

We finally reach a quiet corner of the restaurant, and I'm enchanted by the lovely waterfall covering one wall. The sound soothes me, and it's easy to forget there are people only steps away. I trail a finger through the water while I try to look anywhere but at the man before me. He captivates me, and I'm so far out of my depth it's absurd. I should walk away now...no, I should run. He steps closer to me and

simply stares. He seems to feel the same inner conflict
I do. Maybe he will be strong for both of us and be the
one to leave. As the seconds turn into minutes, I start
when his hand is suddenly at my waist. The decision
has been made; neither of us is leaving. "You look
beautiful tonight." Just as I began to glow at his
compliment, he adds, "I've never wanted to fuck a
woman as badly as I want you right now; did you know
that, Lia?" I look up at him, mesmerized, and shake
my head. My God, what is he doing to me? My nipples
harden and push against the fabric of my dress as he
continues to study me. I want him to put his large
hands over them, to pinch the painfully hard peaks
that ache for him.

His head lowers slowly toward mine as he whispers
against my lips, "Would you like that, baby? Do you
want me to turn you to face the waterfall, hold your
hands against the wet rocks, and push my cock balls-
deep into your wet pussy?" His tongue trails over my
neck and I moan low in my throat before I can stop
myself. I want everything he just said and more. I've
never had a man talk to me like this, and I'm
surprised at how wanton I feel. He pulls my lower
body into closer contact with his, the weight of his
erection pressing into me. I'm not the only one lost in
the moment. Lucian is big and hard, and I sway
against his length, unable to help myself. He moans
and suddenly his hands move from my waist and dig
into the delicate skin of my ass. He grinds against me,
and I feel the big head of his cock nudge against my
entrance through the thin material separating us.

When his tongue enters my mouth, I'm lost. There is
nothing I wouldn't give him in this moment just to
continue feeling this way. I ride the leg he has inserted
between mine and feel the tension starting to build
within me. When his lips move to my neck, I moan his
name, completely caught up in all things him.
"Luc...ohhh." He seems to realize from the sound of my

voice that I'm close to coming just from his mouth, hands, and knee. At this point, I don't even need his cock inside me to find Heaven. When he starts to pull away, I whimper, needing him to ease the ache in my body.

"Shhh…baby, it's okay," he whispers as he continues to put distance between us. I stand there dumbly as he straightens my dress and hair. Almost matter-of-factly he says, "This is a public place, Lia, but I would fuck you here and now if you had done as I asked."

This statement cuts through my sexual fog. "Wh—what are you talking about? You haven't asked anything of me." I wrack my mind trying to figure out why I'm being deprived of what we both so obviously want.

He takes my face in his hands, giving me a hard look; gone is my passionate, would-be lover. "I told you to quit the job, Lia." As his words sink in, it's the equivalent of ice water in the face. I stiffen and pull out of his arms. I'm suddenly furious with the bastard in front of me.

"Fuck you!" I whisper-shout as I poke my finger into his chest for emphasis. "Some of us regular people actually have to work for a living. I may go to an expensive college, but I don't come from or have money, Lucian. If I quit this job just to sleep with you, then I wouldn't have a place to live, food to eat, or books and supplies for school. Is that what you really expect from a woman? Are you so good in bed that I would give up everything I have, everything I am, just for a roll in the sack with you?" My chest is heaving, and I am fighting the urge to slap his arrogant face as he studies me intently.

When his lips curve up into a grin, I give into the urge to slap him, and my hand is flying toward his face before I know what is happening. A mere inch before it makes contact, his hand snaps up and halts my

progress. I'm horrified over this uncharacteristic show
of violence on my part. This is not me, and I'm stunned
by the strong feelings that this man—this stranger—
brings out. "You're full of fire, aren't you, Lia? It
appears I owe you an apology. You are correct; I had
not thought out the consequences of my demands on
your life. In my defense, I've been too caught up in my
desire to have you. Normally, I would have thought
things through more thoroughly. It won't happen
again."

I am surprised by the disappointment I feel. So,
that's it? He's giving up his pursuit of me. Did he think
that I was working as an escort for *Date Night* just for
fun? Of course, someone like him probably never had
to ponder the money challenges a poor college student
has. I suddenly just want away from him. I need to
clear my head of all things Lucian Quinn. I can't
breathe when he is near. Without meeting his eyes, I
mumble, "I'm sorry I tried to hit you. I just...lost it for
a minute."

Lucian laughs; the sound is almost musical. I look
into his smiling face, and my mouth drops as he says,
"Sexual frustration will bring out the animal in most
people, baby." He strokes my hair gently before using
its weight to pull my head back. I find that even the
small prickle against my scalp is enough to send
tendrils of desire racing through my sensitive body.
"Have dinner with me tomorrow night. I'll book it
through *Date Night,* so you'll be paid."

I raise a brow at his question. "It's okay to pay for a
date with me, but not sex?" I cringe when the question
is out. It sounds as if I'm whining about the lack of sex
tonight, and I'm not...am I? Oh, hell, who am I
kidding; we both know I am.

I stiffen as Aidan steps into view. He takes in the
close embrace between Lucian and myself and another
of those odd looks crosses his face. Am I really so
beneath his boss that my very presence confuses him?

Clearing his throat, he says, "Luc, you need to give your speech while everyone is still here and mostly sober."

Lucian runs a finger across my bottom lip, tugging it lightly before stepping away. "We can talk tomorrow night." Before I can answer, his larger hand engulfs mine and leads me past Aidan and back into the party. I try to pull away as he walks straight to the podium at the front of the room, but he keeps me firmly at his side and only drops my hand when he reaches the microphone. I take the opportunity to step behind his large frame and out of the spotlight. Curious looks are thrown my way, but I ignore them and focus on the man in front of me. He speaks with the ease of someone familiar with being the center of attention. Again, he is charming and polite, but I sense the public doesn't see much of the real Lucian Quinn. Maybe it takes someone such as myself who has spent years putting on a public face to recognize a kindred spirit. Even as he woos the crowd, I see the hand at his side digging into his thigh. It gives me no pleasure to know I'm right. Being haunted by my own demons for most of my life has given me nothing but sympathy for those who suffer, as well. Maybe I've made this whole thing up in my mind, and Lucian is simply a person who hates public speaking...but somehow, I don't think that's the case. Before I can ponder this further, he finishes to a round of applause and immediately turns as if seeking me. I hold my hand out for his, helpless to do anything else, and it's immediately taken. Some part of my body is once again joined with his, and it's far too natural of a feeling for strangers. *Who are you, Lucian Quinn, and what are you doing to me?*

With his speech over, Lucian keeps a firm grip on my hand and silently makes his way toward the door. It appears our evening is almost over, and I find myself hesitant to end my time with him. He nods a goodbye to a few people near the doorway, but all too soon, we are on the sidewalk, and he is leading me toward the car idling at the curb. I recognize the sleek, black Mercedes from our previous evening together. "Lucian, my car is here." I feel compelled to object even though I know it will be pointless. The driver is before us, opening the back door, and I am bundled inside before I can issue another objection.

We sit in silence for several moments, and I'm startled when his hand suddenly makes contact with my knee. Without turning in my direction, he says, almost absently, "I enjoyed tonight with you there far more than I would normally have."

I am filled with pleasure at his words. "I...thank you. Your speech was brilliant," I add shyly.

He sighs and admits what I had already suspected. "I hate those fucking things. I've done it a million times, and a million times I've detested every moment of it." I want to offer him comfort, something I suspect few people are allowed to do. Instead of saying the words, I lay my hand on top of the one that rests on my knee and squeeze lightly. We remain this way until we reach my apartment. As I start to pull away, he tightens his grip and pulls me forward for a hard kiss on the lips. My mouth tingles as he says, "I'll pick you up for dinner tomorrow night at seven." I nod in agreement, and as I'm pulling away, I hear him whisper, "Think of me tonight, sweet Lia, and know I'm thinking of you."

I stumble getting out and am grateful for the driver's assistance. As we reach the door, I turn and smile at him. "You've walked me to my door twice, and I don't even know your name to thank you."

He seems surprised by the question, but returns my smile and says, "Just call me Sam, young lady."

I laugh, telling him, "Call me Lia. 'Young lady' seems far too grand for a college student. Thanks for walking me, Sam."

"It's my pleasure, Lia. I'll see you tomorrow night, I believe." Without agreeing, I open my door and step inside. Rose is still in the same position in front of the television but is snoring softly in her sleep. I walk over and turn the television off, grabbing the blanket from the back of the sofa and draping it across her. As my stomach rumbles, I realize I haven't eaten all evening. I quickly fix a bowl of Captain Crunch cereal and carry it to my bedroom. Before I can question the wisdom of the action, I grab my phone and text Lucian.

"I'm starving. Isn't it customary to feed your dates?"

I am having a serious case of texting-regret when my phone chimes.

"Ah, I'm sorry. baby. The only thing I wanted to eat tonight was...you. Rest assured, we'll both get what we want soon."

My face flames, and I drop the phone as if burned. His words rush straight to my sex, and I know without a doubt that my fingers will soon be between my slick folds, relieving the ache he has caused there. As if reading my mind, another text sounds.

"Are you touching yourself while thinking of me?"

Oh, sweet Heaven, I should never have started this. I want nothing more than to do what he is saying.

"No, of course not. I'm eating a bowl of cereal in my flannel pajamas."

I giggle as I imagine the disgusted look on his face. He has probably never heard of flannel, much less dated a woman who would dream of wearing it. In reality, I'm wearing a tank top and panties, which are, of course, cotton.

"Touch your breast, Lia. Run your finger around the nipple and imagine it's my hand making it pucker.

As I hesitate, my phone chimes,

"NOW."

I feel strangely excited and naughty as I slip my hand under my top and caress my breast. My nipple hardens and I moan as I twist it. I'm lost in the moment when another text sounds.

"It feels good, doesn't it, baby?"

When my phone signals an incoming call, I know without looking who it is. I want to ignore the call, but I can't. I need to hear his voice. "Hello." I cringe at how breathless I sound.

With no preliminaries he asks, "Are you wet for me, Lia?" I sputter in horror. I can't believe he just asked me something so personal. "Put your hand between your legs and tell me how you feel, baby."

With a sense of bravado that I'm far from feeling, I joke, "I'm wearing flannel, remember?" Even as I tell the lie, I'm helpless to stop my hand and its downward descent. The cotton of my panties is wet as I reach my target.

As if my silence convicts me, Lucian whispers hoarsely, "That's right, baby. Feel what I do to you even when I'm not there." His voice is all the encouragement I need as I push the cotton aside and trail a finger over my slit. I gasp as I caress my sensitive clit. Lucian moans low in his throat as if my

sounds are torturing him. "Push one finger deep
inside." I moan in pleasure as my tight passage
spasms. With his voice in my ear, it's entirely too easy
to imagine its Lucian's cock inside me as my finger
strokes deep. "Oh, baby, I bet you feel so fucking good.
Add another finger, Lia, and pump them in and out of
your wetness." I obey his command, and my sex
twinges at the extra width. I'm so slick that soon both
fingers are gliding effortlessly in and out of me.

"Lucian!" I cry, as my body climbs closer to release.
I'm frantically riding my hand while cradling the
phone against my shoulder.

"Do you need to come, Lia?" he growls.

"Yes, God, yes," I shout. I can only imagine how loud
my voice is in his ear as I've lost all inhibitions. I hope
Rose is sleeping soundly; otherwise, there is no way
she will miss the noise I'm making. I normally try to
keep quiet when I'm masturbating, but I've never been
this excited before.

"Pinch your clit, baby. Imagine my big hand
tweaking it while I fuck you hard. Feel me pounding
into you." That's all it takes; I explode into a rainbow
of dizzying colors. I feel lightheaded with pleasure as
my body contracts for what seems like hours. I've
dropped my phone, but it's close enough to my ear to
hear Lucian swearing harshly. As I float back down to
earth, the realization of what I've done is enough to
make me want to end the call and hope I never see
him again. I hear him calling my name, though, and
know any escape would just be temporary.

"I'm...er...back." Damn, that sounds so pathetic. "I
mean...um, I should let you go now."

Lucian chuckles, but it sounds pained. I wonder if
he's touching himself, but I'm not brave enough to ask.
"You have no idea how much I want to fuck you right
now. It's taking everything I've got not to come to you."
It's taking everything I've got not to tell him I'll be
waiting. I need some time to process, though. This

man turns me into someone I've never been, and I have no idea how to handle it; I know it would take very little to be consumed by all he is. I'm terrified...I'm exhilarated and completely at his mercy.

In a last-ditch effort of self-preservation, I say, "Lucian...I don't even know you. What are we doing?"

All is quiet for a moment before he says, "I don't know, Lia...but I can't stop." I accept his answer, because it reflects my own thoughts perfectly. It seems we are both powerless to understand or explain this attraction between us and unable to stop freefalling into the unknown. Before I can reply, he adds, "I'll see you tomorrow tonight." With those words, he is gone, and I'm oddly lonely without the sound of his voice in my ear.

My bowl of cereal is beyond saving, and I tiptoe to the kitchen to pour it out. I'm grateful Rose still seems to be sleeping deeply on the couch. I might hear her and Jake often, but I don't relish the thought of her hearing me having phone sex. My body still tingles from its earlier excitement as I run quickly through my bedtime routine. I'm exhausted when I finally roll over onto my stomach to go to sleep. Once again, Lucian fills my waking and sleeping hours.

Lucian

I palm my rock-hard cock and roughly run my hand up the rigid length. I can't remember the last time I had phone sex probably my teenage years. The text from Lia tonight was unexpected and what followed after, completely unplanned. She lacks the polish of the women I've spent the last several years with. She is attractive with a body few men would look past.

What draws me the most, though, are her eyes. They show an innocence that is foreign to most women her age, but at the same time, I sense there is almost a weariness there. What events have transpired in her life to put that look there? She is correct; I haven't done my homework where she is concerned, which is unusual. I did assume she could afford to leave her job. I've already placed a call for a full background check. Nothing I find there will stop my pursuit, but it possibly will give me a better understanding of her.

My naked body moves restlessly on the bed as my pace increases. The tattoo on my chest ripples as I remember Lia's moans of pleasure. She was so lost in the moment; I doubt she was aware of chanting my name while she brought herself to completion. It was both torture and unbelievably erotic. If not for scaring her to death, I would have been at her apartment and inside her within twenty minutes. Patience is not something I am familiar with; whether right or wrong; people with money rarely have to wait for anything they want.

I moan Lia's name as streams of cum shoot from my cock and onto my stomach. My body quivers in release. My cock is still semi-hard. It wanted the real thing, not a hand and a memory. If nothing is resolved at dinner tomorrow night, I'll resolve it for her soon; waiting is no longer an option. I get off the bed to clean up and hear a text chime as I walk back into my bedroom. The pang of disappointment I feel at seeing Aidan's name is disconcerting.

"So, who was the girl tonight?"

Fuck, just what I didn't need, Aidan nosing around Lia. The fact he is curious enough to text me this late is a bad sign.

"None of your damn business."

A few moments pass without a reply, but I am not worried about pissing him off with my harsh statement. Aidan and I have been friends for too long to be easily offended by the other.

"Interesting, brother."

I am getting tired of this conversation and don't want to encourage him to continue his cryptic messages.

"Is there a point here?"

He fires back almost immediately.

"No point. Just a ghost walking over my grave tonight. I'll see you tomorrow."

With those words, he is gone, and I don't bother to reply. We both know what he is referring to. I can only hope to God this isn't my main source of attraction to Lia. I, more than anyone, know you can't go back. The only option is going forward, and that is what I'm ready to do. Why her and why now, I have no idea, but I have no desire to stop...I can't stop.

CHAPTER FIVE

Lia

This entire day has been shit. I overslept this morning and am late to my first class. I detest having to walk in after everyone is already sitting...staring at me. I'm always one of the first to arrive. I like to find a seat so there is no danger of being in the spotlight. Heck, half the students have probably never realized I'm in their class. I also discover that the books I need for my new math class are twice as expensive as I expected. Textbooks are like buying bars of gold that will be useless in a few years. How can they possibly justify what they charge? And, Lucian wants me to quit my job? I laugh a laugh completely devoid of humor. I need to do the opposite: work even more in the coming months to offset my expenses.

I received an email earlier from *Date Night* with a job request; this time he used his real name. I want to be pissed off about him booking the date through my job, but pride goeth before the fall, and after today's discovery, I need the money more than ever. I'm in a quandary, though, because he has seen both my dresses. This problem has never arisen. Even with my repeat customers, there are months between the bookings, and I feel safe in assuming they don't

remember what I wore previously. Both of my dates
with Lucian were recent, and I feel sure he remembers
every detail. I have no money to purchase something
new, so I'm left with groveling to Rose. We are the
same size, although she is taller than I am. She also
has a blue silk dress I think would be perfect. I'll offer
to do the dishes for a week. That is something she
would give almost anything for since she hates that
particular chore.

I arrive at home in time to see Jake with his tongue
in her mouth and his hand on her ass. Crap, can't they
ever take it in the bedroom? Rose looks up, not
seeming the least bit embarrassed; I'm pretty sure she
wouldn't care if I watched the whole thing from start
to finish. Jake, however, has the grace to blush, which
looks adorable on a macho guy like him. "Hey, chick,"
she says. "Do you want to go for some Mexican food
with us? Jake's parents sent him a gift card to the
place down the street." My stomach rumbles at the
mention of food, and I'm disappointed to turn down a
free meal at one of my favorite places.

"I wish I could, but I'm working." I decide to hit her
up for the dress while Jake is here. She is less likely to
turn me down while her doting boyfriend has her in a
pre-sex state of bliss. "Could I possibly borrow a dress
for tonight?" Shit, I don't want to admit to her that I
am seeing the same guy; that is unusual enough to get
her attention. "I...haven't had a chance to do laundry,
and I spilled stuff on my other dresses." To my relief,
she gives me no more than a passing glance before
returning her attention to Jake. "Sure, take what you
like." She is wrapping herself around her man when
she adds absently, "You know the routine." Obediently,
I walk over to the pad of paper in the kitchen and
write down Lucian's name, but only put a question
mark beside the location since he is picking me up.
There is no way I am sharing that information with
Rose. It's our rule that I always have my own car. I

can't assure her he isn't a serial killer without telling her the whole story, and that isn't going to happen tonight. I run to her room, grab her blue dress, and decide to push my luck and borrow her matching heels, as well; they are better than anything I own. It would probably be safer to wear old jeans and a ratty t-shirt, but I want to look like someone a man like Lucian Quinn would have dinner with tonight.

I quickly shower, apply some of my honeysuckle lotion, and wear the one matching black bra and panty set I own. The teal-blue dress fits like a glove and hits me just above the knee. The V-neck makes the most of my breasts and I twirl, happy with the results. My blonde hair hangs in soft waves down my back. My makeup is minimal, but I do add some eyeliner to give my eyes a smoky appearance. I'm almost ready when I experience a moment of panic. If Lucian comes to my door, there will be questions, and a lot of them. With ten minutes until he is due to arrive, I grab my purse and run out of the apartment. His car is just pulling to the curb when I breathlessly walk down the walkway. Surprisingly, Sam stays in the car and Lucian steps out of the back. He is wearing another suit, which screams expensive. His thick, dark hair beckons me to run my fingers through it. The man must spend some serious time in the gym because there doesn't appear to be a spare ounce of flesh anywhere on him. He is stunning. He looks surprised when he sees me standing there gawking at him. "Lia, I was coming in to get you."

"My, um, roommate and her boyfriend were…busy on the couch. I thought I would just meet you outside." My face colors at his look of surprise. My big mouth and me. Couldn't I have volunteered a little less information?

He recovers quickly, giving me the smirk I've become accustomed to. "Not much of a voyeur, huh? Pity."

With my best serious look, I say, "Oh, you like to watch? If we're quiet, we can slip back in. They should be to the good part by now." Where did that come from? The things he brings out in me are unexpected, to say the least.

He pulls me into his arms, laughing softly against my hair. "I'd much rather taste you than watch them." With those words, his lips descend onto mine, and I'm drowning in all things Lucian Quinn. The kiss is brief, but when it ends, I'm hanging onto his waist for support. He loosens my hands and helps me into the car. Once again, I'm seated entirely too close to his large frame for comfort. His hand on my bare leg keeps me firmly in place. "I like the dress," he murmurs. "You are beautiful, as always."

"Thanks, I borrowed it from Rose. I pretty much exhausted my options this week. I'm not usually this social." Cringing, I wonder why I feel the need again to divulge this much information.

Lucian sounds genuinely upset when he says, "I'm sorry, Lia, I should have thought of that. I guess I assumed you kept clothing on hand for your...job."

I cover his hand with mine saying, "Normally, I'm fine. I've never been out with the same person three times within a week, though." I've already admitted to being a poor, college student, so I don't see the need to lie to him. If anything, it should drive home the fact that I need my job. He is quiet after my admission. I ponder removing my hand from the top of his, but I enjoy the feel of his skin against my palm too much to deprive myself. It seems unlikely that Lucian will continue to pursue me for long, so I vow to enjoy the moment while it lasts. Too few things in my life have given me pleasure, and I find myself wanting to grab onto the feeling regardless of the cost.

A short while later, the car comes to a smooth halt in one of the outlying areas of Asheville that I recognize. The tree-lined sidewalk connects to an array of stores and restaurants. I'm surprised Lucian has picked such a busy area for dinner; I pictured somewhere quiet and elegant, such as Valentino's from last night. This area has more of a college-town air, far better suited to me than to him.

As if he knows what I'm thinking, he pulls me closer as we leave the car and says, "A friend of mine owns an Italian restaurant here. I have a place close so when I stay there, I tend to end up here."

I turn to him, surprised. "You live here?"

"Among other places," he adds. "I have an apartment at the office, one here, and a house near Biltmore Village. The apartment at the office serves a purpose when it's late and I'm too tired to go anywhere else. I bought the apartment here back when they first started development because I enjoy the area and the house...was my childhood home."

Curious, I ask, "Do your parents still live there?"

"No, they died when I was young. The house was left to me with a trust for maintenance. The apartment here is my preference and where I spend most of my spare time."

He steers me toward a brick building on the corner and holds the door open for me to precede him in. Without waiting to be seated, he leads me to a quiet booth in the corner. Other than the opening, it's completely private on the remaining sides. I slide into the middle and he follows suit, sitting in close proximity. A server appears almost immediately, and Lucian orders a bottle of wine. I barely have time to look around when I feel his hand on my thigh. I gape as my dress slowly inches up. "Luc...what?"

"Shhh, if I can't taste you now, I want to feel you." My core floods at his words and his intention. "Spread your legs for me baby," he whispers against my ear. With no thought of denying him, I inch my legs apart and gasp as the cool air hits the damp fabric of my panties. With no preliminaries, he is at my apex, pulling the lace at my leg aside. My breath stalls as he plunges his finger into my wetness. I turn my face into his neck and moan. He strokes my clit as he asks, "Are you this wet because you want my cock, Lia? Do you need to be fucked?" His finger stills as if awaiting my reply.

"Yes," I breathe.

"Yes, what, baby?"

"I need you," I whimper, "to...fuck me." Oh, God, I can't believe I've actually said that to him. At this point, though, I'd confess to anything if it meant his finger would start moving again. When it does, I want to weep with relief.

I am completely focused on the tension building inside me when the waiter suddenly appears at the end of the table. I jump in my seat, but Lucian is the picture of innocence. Unseen, he lazily removes his hand from my panties and takes the proffered wine glass. I almost die in horror when he runs the finger he has just removed from my sex against the rim of the glass before taking a drink. He licks his lip appreciatively. "That's perfect, Jeffrey, an exquisite vintage." The server beams his approval before filling both of our glasses. I shouldn't be this turned on by the fact that Lucian has just spread my juices on his glass and licked them off in front of our server...but I am.

Lucian orders for us both and I anxiously wait for the waiter to leave so Lucian's hand will return to me. Lucian, however, keeps his hands on the table, and if not for the flush still staining his cheekbones, I would think I had imagined the whole thing. "What are your plans after graduation?" he asks, surprising me. It's suddenly clear that I'm to be left frustrated again tonight. My palm itches as I fight the urge to smack his arrogant face. It will be a cold day in Hell before he sees how much he is getting to me. I may be uncomfortably aroused, but I'm not battling a hard cock, as he no doubt is; sometimes it pays to be a woman.

I take a sip of my wine, finding it cool and refreshing. I have little experience with anything other than a bottle of Arbor Mist, but I don't doubt this is expensive. As a general rule of thumb, if the waiter needs your approval to fill a glass, it probably has a hefty price tag. I match his neutral tone as I say, "I would like an entry-level position as a business analyst. I hope to find a company that supports continuing education so I may continue my schooling in the evening and obtain a Master's Degree."

Looking genuinely interested, Lucian asks, "Why a business analyst?"

"I would love to help a company remain competitive by proposing ways to improve their structure, efficiency, and profits. To have my recommendations be key in their continued development and growth. I don't want to just work and collect a paycheck. I want to look at past problems and see what failed and why. I want to understand every facet of the business and make it stronger; find answers others have never considered. I want my ideas to make a difference... to be the difference." Turning in my seat to face him, I ask, "You've done that, right, Luc? With your own company?" Lucian smiles, seemingly captivated by my passion.

Nodding, he says, "I have, Lia, and I still do every day, even though I pay a lot of people to do it for me. Analyzing a company from the bare-bones up is damned hard but the only true way to see its capabilities. When I started out, different scenarios for my company raced through my mind every waking moment. You are correct; it's intoxicating to conceive and chart a course that works. There are so many factors to consider. At the end of the day, it's about change, and sometimes change is the hardest thing to gather support for, even when you have a track record for success."

He twirls the stem of his glass as if deep in thought. "Starting out, although scary as hell, was a high unlike any I've ever known. I had little sleep those first few years, but man, what a fucking rush. Living on the edge will do that for you. Knowing I could succeed or lose everything just by making a decision was like betting everything on one roll of the dice." Looking up and giving me a wry smile, he adds, "As I've said, though, now I have people working overtime to outthink me, so it's unlikely Quinn could tank from just a bad judgment call on my part. I think you'd enjoy spending a day with me there, though. Maybe some field experience to prepare you for the corporate world."

I'm thrilled by his offer; I would love nothing better than to shadow him at work one day. I Googled his company while I was supposed to be studying in the library today, and Quinn Software is at the top of its game. Lucian was mentioned as the wonder boy who invented a new kind of programming script that was quickly adapted and is now widely used as the gold standard.

The article mentioned that at twenty-nine years of age, he is one of the youngest CEOs of a Fortune 500 company. When he speaks, people listen. I am most surprised by his age. To look at him, he looks younger, but his worldly-polished image portrayed to the world makes him seem older. Just talking as we are now, he seems light-years ahead of my twenty-three years of age. It's the power that emanates from everything he does. He is a man used to getting what he wants without asking twice. Why he has centered his attention on me when I have turned him down is intriguing. I want all that his eyes and his hands have promised me; I am lost in this beautiful man. I want more than anything to solve the puzzle of who Lucian

Quinn is, because I know he is so much more than I've seen thus far. I realize I've been staring at him as he waves a hand in front of my face. "Er...sorry about that. I was just thinking about..."

Before I can finish my sentence, he says, "You were thinking about me...thinking about us...together."

It's useless to deny; I'm sure it's written all over my face. "Yes." I decide to be honest regardless of how pathetic it probably sounds. "I don't understand why I'm here. We have nothing in common. You and I are not from the same world. You should be out with someone like Cruella." I see his lips twitch at my nickname for Monique.

"Monique scares the shit out of me, so please don't wish something like that on me." His hand covers mine where it lays on the seat between us. "I'm attracted to you, Lia, as you know. I know the budding analyst in you wants to break down all the reasons why, but sometimes it's as simple as that. Most types of relationships are built around some type of attraction. I'll work things out so we can spend more time together, if that is okay with you?" I agree, thrilled he seems to have gotten past his hang-up over my job with *Date Night*. Our food arrives before I can comment, and we spend the next hour enjoying the most delicious manicotti I've ever had.

I try to hide my disappointment when, instead of taking me to his nearby apartment, he does nothing more than hold my hand as Sam drives us to mine. He kisses me lightly on the lips. "I'll call you tomorrow, and we'll make plans."

"Okay," I answer as Sam opens my door. Again, I'm delivered to my apartment and bid goodnight. Rose and Jake are still out, and I trudge to my room, frustrated and confused; I had fully expected to be in Lucian's bed tonight. I resist the urge to text him, not wanting to come across like a teenager who texts after each date. He said he would call; I just have to accept

that Lucian does things on his own timeline. As I
ponder relieving the ache he started earlier, my phone
signals a text.

**"Good night, Lia. Don't even think of touching
yourself. That's my job now."**

I jerk, looking around the room as if expecting to see
him. I want to ignore his text, but the devil in me
cannot resist.

**"Then you need to handle the job before
someone else does."**

I giggle imagining his reaction.

**"Just for that, I'll fuck you hard the first
time."**

Oh, my, I've stirred the hornet's nest now. How
unfair that he expects me not to touch myself after a
statement like that; I want nothing more than to push
a finger in my sex and imagine it's his cock.
Emboldened, I ask,

"When is the last time you touched yourself?"

His answer comes almost immediately,

"Last night...Sleep well."

The image of Lucian touching himself while
thinking of me is so hot. I want this man with a
ferocity that is foreign to me. I know my dreams will
once again be filled with him. Sleep has deserted me
since meeting Lucian, and I'm counting the hours until
our next encounter.

Chapter Six

Lia

"When I find him, he's dead!" I've chanted nothing but my intentions to kill Lucian for the last hour. I'm so furious with him; I'm shaking. Normally, Fridays are my favorite day of the week. I only have two classes, which leaves me with the afternoon to catch up on schoolwork and run errands. In addition, I allow myself to splurge on a Starbucks frappe while I enjoy their Wi-Fi. I have received no notification from *Date Night,* so either Lucian doesn't plan to see me tonight, or he isn't using *Date Night* to do it.

I stop at the mailboxes in the lobby of my apartment building and thumb through the envelopes on the way up. When I find one from my bank, I cringe. Just what I don't want to see today, my bank statement; proof in writing each month that I'm barely holding my head above water. I know better than to ignore it. I run so close some months that one little mathematical mistake on my part could equal disaster. A returned check and the fees associated with it would put me into the red. My pay from *Date Night* this week has been better than usual thanks to Lucian, and even though I feel guilty about taking his money, it's a relief to be caught up on my bills at the moment. I'm surprised when instead of a statement, it appears to be a receipt. Surprise turns to shock when the receipt shows a deposit into my account for ten-thousand dollars.

Opening the door to my apartment, I'm met by a pissed-off Rose. "Bitch, why didn't you tell me about your new job?!"

"Wha—What?" I ask, still freaked out over the bank's mistake.

"I had to hear about it from our machine? You had to have known about it for a while if you've already quit *Date Night*." I want nothing more than for her to go away so I can call my bank before this mess gets any worse. No doubt someone is wondering where their money is about now.

"I have no idea what you're talking about. I need to make a call. My checking account has been screwed up."

Rose gives me a hurt look and walks over to the answering machine we keep for our regular phone. Rose's parents insist we have it in case there is an emergency and both our cell phones are dead. A little paranoid on their part, but they pay the bill, so we don't complain. It is also my contact number for school and work. "Lia, it's Carrie at *Date Night*. I received your email about your new job at Quinn Software. I'm so sorry to lose you, but congratulations, and give me a call if you ever need a job again."

Suddenly, everything becomes blindingly clear. I would bet my last dollar that my bank account balance is no mistake; Lucian promised to take care of things and he has. I am his new woman—whore—and he's paying for the privilege. Rose looks at me in confusion as I literally growl in anger. I run back out the door and to my car. As I start the engine, I realize I have no idea where to find him. I could call or text, but I am spoiling for a fight, and I want it to be in person. I quickly Google his company and find the website for Quinn Software. Bingo, there on the contact page is the address I need.

My anger abates little as I drive entirely too fast to the downtown Asheville area. A parking space in front of the building is empty so I pull in. Quinn Software is an older building that has been carefully restored. I'm surprised; I would have expected all glass and steel. I

step into a sleek, modern lobby with shining marble
floors. I resist the urge to stomp my feet on the
company name etched in the marble floor. I only make
it a few steps before I'm forced to stop at the reception
desk. Shit, I should have known I wouldn't be able to
reach Lucian without going through his people first;
the element of surprise will certainly be lost now.

A perky redhead I estimate to be around thirty asks
politely, "May I help you?"

"I need to see Lucian Quinn." Her eyes widen in
surprise as they pass over me. Apparently, Lucian
doesn't receive too many visitors dressed in old t-shirts
and cut-off jean shorts. She probably thinks I'm a
homeless person looking for money. If she hands me a
dollar, I'm going to choke her.

Showing a great deal of restraint, she simply asks,
"Do you have an appointment with Mr. Quinn?"

"No," I snap, "I don't." I can see the refusal hovering
on her lips, so I quickly add, "Could you please just tell
him Lia is here."

"Miss Adams, I thought that was you." I whirl
around to find Lucian's driver, Sam, standing behind
me with a genuine smile on his lips. The perky
redhead looks surprised that Sam seems to recognize
me. I resist the desire to stick my tongue out at her.

"Hey, Sam, it's good to see you again. I, er...need to
see Lucian. Is he here?"

Sam nods before saying, "He is. Does he know you
are dropping by?" By this point, the receptionist is
shamelessly listening to our conversation. I take Sam's
arm and pull him away from the desk so we can have a
little privacy. I release a breath and decide the truth is
the only way to go here.

"No, he doesn't. Honestly, I'm completely pissed off
at your boss, and I came here to tell him all about it. I
didn't really think things through, though."

Instead of looking worried, Sam looks amused. "So,
the boss is in trouble with you. That sure didn't take

long. He's a good kid, so take it easy while you point out the error of his ways."

I laugh despite myself; hearing Lucian referred to as a "kid" is somehow hilarious. Nodding my head toward the still-staring receptionist, I say, "It doesn't look like I'll get to him, anyway."

"That's too bad," Sam says thoughtfully. "I was just going to chat with my friend Cindy...Lucian's secretary. I would be happy to have some company on the trip up if you have some free time."

It takes a moment for his meaning to sink in. Sam is offering me a way of reaching Lucian's office without actually coming out and saying it. He probably doesn't want to be fired for helping me past the lobby. I look at my watch then back at him. "Sure, I've got some free time. I would love to meet your friend." Sam puts a hand in the small of my back and leads me past the receptionist to a bank of elevators. He slides a key card into a slot, and we are on our way up to the tenth floor. This floor looks similar to the lobby with more marble bearing the company name; no expense has been spared. Sam leads me by another smiling but curious receptionist before coming to a middle-aged woman whom I suspect guards the double doors behind her desk.

"Sam," she smiles, "you're early, and he isn't ready yet. He's still going through some contracts." She looks at me then back at Sam with a raised brow. Sam makes what I feel is a timely excuse to go to the bathroom and takes off in the other direction without further explanation.

This is it. If I have to explain myself again, I'll have lost the element of surprise and possibly be turned away. I square my shoulders and bolt toward the doors behind Cindy and wrench one open before she can stop me. I hear an exclamation behind me and quickly shut and lock the door. The handle twists futilely as I lean against the frame. In my haste to beat Lucian's secretary into his office, I have completely forgotten about the man himself. Looking up, I find him sitting behind a massive desk, staring at me in bewilderment. He is so gorgeous with his thick hair rumpled and his suit clinging lovingly to his shoulders; I have to remind myself that I'm mad at him. He stands, saying, "Lia...?"

I march toward his desk, all of my former anger returning. "How dare you make decisions for me! You lied to my employer and put money in my bank account. You knew I would have never agreed to that, Lucian! I'm not some prostitute you can pay. What's the difference between you paying *Date Night* to go out with me, and you paying my bills for sex?" He moves to stand in front of me, and I see his eyes glitter with anger and what looks like frustration.

"Lia, I told you I would take care of everything. What did you think that meant?"

Throwing my hands in the air, I say, "I thought that meant you were okay with my job. I had no idea you would get me fired and then replace the money with your own. I never intended that, Lucian."

He sighs, taking my shoulders in his hands. "I thought we both decided we wanted whatever this is between us to move forward?"

"We did, but I can't be your whore." I fight the urge to cry; I've become attached to him in such a short time, and now it's going to end before it even starts.

Suddenly, the door behind us bursts open and Aidan, followed by a flustered Cindy, flies into the room. "What the hell are you doing?" Lucian snaps at them.

Aidan smirks while Cindy stammers to explain. "I'm sorry, Luc. This woman ran into your office and locked the door. I was afraid there was some danger to you, so I called Aidan to come up with his key."

Without thinking of the consequences, I blurt out, "Lucian was just about to give me a job. It seems I've

been awarded employment with Quinn Software."
Both Cindy and Aidan are now looking at Lucian,
waiting for his reply.

Lucian squirms before saying, "Actually, I was
telling Lia we don't have any openings right now."

"How about the new housekeeper?" Cindy asks,
appearing confused. "Did you not want me to run that
ad for you?" I give Lucian an evil smile and he knows
what's coming next.

"Why, no, Cindy, I believe we've already worked the
salary out. I'm Lucian's new housekeeper." Cindy looks
at her boss uncertainly. He runs a hand through his
hair before giving her a nod.

"So be it. Cindy will give you all the information."
The look on his face makes me think I've jumped
straight from the frying pan into the fire. I've just
demanded a position that will ensure I spend hours
per week in Lucian's house. What in the hell was I
thinking?

As I turn to follow Cindy out, Aidan steps into my
path, extending a hand. "Welcome aboard, Lia." With a
sexy grin he adds, "It looks like I'll be visiting Luc
more in the future." I hear what sounds like a growl
from Lucian before I hurry out of the office. Dear Lord,
what have I done?

Just as Cindy turns to shut the door behind her, I
hear Lucian say, "I'll need Lia to start tomorrow." I
close my eyes briefly, suddenly feeling uneasy. This is
what happens when you try to cage a lion; I've gone
from wanting to have sex with him to washing his
underwear.

I can tell Cindy is curious as to how I know Lucian,
but she is too polite to ask. Instead, she writes his
address down for me, and when I ask about the hours,
she assures me the previous housekeeper kept a
flexible schedule and Lucian was okay with it.
Apparently, he doesn't care when his apartment is
cleaned, just as long as it is. I note the address must

be the apartment near the restaurant we dined at last night; I recall him mentioning he spends most of his time there.

Thanking Cindy, I head for the elevator in a slightly different frame of mind than the one I entered in. I can't help but wonder if I just walked neatly into some kind of trap, but I can't imagine Lucian would have known I would demand a job. In hindsight, the smart thing would have been to return his money, beg for my job back at *Date Night*, and walk away. I barely know the man, so why does the thought of never seeing him again cause panic? It's a question that scares me to answer, and I forcibly shove it out of my mind. I want to see where this takes me...I must.

Lucian

I find my gaze helplessly glued to the curve of Lia's sweet ass as she leaves my office with Cindy. The jean shorts she is wearing have my cock stirring to attention. I look over and see Aidan's face turned in the same damn direction. *Mine!* I want to shout. *Keep your fucking eyes off what is mine.* I clear my throat instead as the door closes. I don't ask him to leave because I know he will go straight for Lia, who I hear talking to Cindy. Instead, I control my impatience as he settles in his usual chair in front of my desk. "So," he begins, "what's going on with Lia?"

I return to the chair behind my desk and start shuffling papers. I would love to avoid his question, but we both know he has me cornered. If I ignore him, he'll go after Lia just to gauge my reaction; the bastard knows me entirely too well.

"She's just someone I am seeing." I'm mentally calculating how long it will take Lia to leave the building so I can toss Aidan's nosey ass out of my office.

"What happened with the woman from *Date Night* I set you up with? I haven't heard you mention that, but Lia seems to have suddenly appeared soon after." It's useless to keep up the charade; he'll just keep digging until I confirm what he has already figured out.

"Yes, Lia is the woman from *Date Night*. We...connected and have been seeing each other. As you heard, she is going to be working for me."

Aidan doesn't look surprised, but he does look curious. Why is everyone suddenly so damned interested in my love life? There have been other women over the years, so why is Lia such a novelty? "This girl is a complete one-eighty from your usual women. She's attractive, I'll grant you that, but there seems to be more going on. I saw the way you looked at her. How is that possible when you barely know her?"

I resist the urge to stand and strangle my best friend. He sees entirely too much, and I want to get rid of him before he asks any more questions; I don't want him scrutinizing Lia or my relationship with her. "You're starting to sound like my father. I don't sit around and nag you about all of the women you run through. Have I even mentioned your date with Monique?"

Aidan grins, effectively sidetracked. "Monique has skills. I don't know why you try so hard to avoid her because she is a hellhound in bed. She drained me and was begging for more." I relax my guard as he continues to provide details of his night with Monique. A part of me wants to tell him he can do better, but after accusing him of sounding like my father, I decide to keep the advice to myself. Aidan has only ever loved one woman in his life, and she'll never return that love. He receives a call and leaves, reverting back to all business in the blink of an eye. Cindy buzzes to remind me of a lunch meeting and I follow Sam out to the car.

Lia will be at my apartment tomorrow, but I find it hard to wait. All our obstacles are out of the way now, and I am out of patience. I have been forced to masturbate like a schoolboy since meeting her, and the relief I find at my own hand does not last. I've been hard since seeing her in those skimpy shorts and form-fitting t-shirt. While she was in my office, furious with me, I wanted nothing more than to lay her out on my desk and bury my face in her pussy. I want to feel her convulse around my tongue as it darts deep into her folds. Fucking her is secondary to the need; I have to taste her.

Looking down, I curse as my cock digs into my zipper. Have I been reduced to getting myself off before I leave my office now? The decision is made; I can't wait until tomorrow. Tonight, Lia will get a preview of what's to come. Tonight...I'll know her taste, and tonight...she'll scream.

Lia

I spend the afternoon holed up in my room, studying for a sociology test I have the next morning. Rose is going to dinner at Jake's parents' house tonight, so she is frantically getting ready. They are just so normal it's hard to understand. There is little doubt she will marry Jake after they graduate, and they will have two kids, live in the suburbs, and drive a mini-van. There is nothing wrong with that. I love to think my life will be that stable at some point. Rose grew up with two loving parents, as did Jake. They will always have a support system to fall back on, whereas I only have myself. I am not bitter; what would be the point? I learned a long time ago that hoping and wishing only bring disappointment. I am in charge of my future, and it's up to me as to where my story goes. I think of Lucian and feel I've made the right decision. I cannot let him take care of me, but I can work for him. What is the difference, really, between working for him versus working for *Date Night* but being paid by him? I would rather see him than continue to date strangers. I hear Rose yell from the other room, and I walk out to see what outfit she has decided on.

She turns around, showing me the pink cardigan set paired with a black pencil skirt. I smile knowing she is a parent's dream come true; smart, beautiful, and so obviously well-bred. Jake's parents will be eating out of the palm of her hand before the dessert course rolls around. "You look beautiful," I say and mean it. I give her an impulsive hug of reassurance.

She beams at me, pleased by my compliment. "I left you the other coupon Jake had for a free pizza. You'll just need money for the tip. Save me a piece, though, because I will probably be too nervous to eat anything tonight."

My stomach growls at her words, and we both laugh. She grabs her sweater and walks out to meet Jake. I know he would come to the door for her, but she is too keyed up to wait. I decide to go ahead and order the pizza, knowing the place is probably crazy-busy tonight. I'm thrilled to find a repeat of *Pretty Woman* on television. I am dreaming of all things Richard Gere when a knock at the door startles me from the couch. Picking up my wallet, I run to open the door for the delivery guy.

My mouth hits the floor as, instead of the teenager with an ill-fitting uniform I'm expecting, there stands Lucian Quinn holding a pizza box with a grin that makes me want to knock the box away and climb him.

"Where—what?" I'm making little sense as I continue to stutter.

"I ran into the delivery man in the lobby. Apparently, he thought I lived here and asked if I knew which apartment was yours. I nicely offered to bring it up for him."

"But...I had a coupon," I say, waving the paper Rose left.

Lucian chuckles, saying, "Save it for next time then. It's only fair I pay since I plan to eat half of it." When I continue to stand there, he pushes gently past me and closes the door behind him. As he walks toward the table to put the box down, I gasp. He is wearing snug-fitting jeans and a black t-shirt. I've never seen him so casual before, and it looks good...so damn good on him. "Do you have plates and something to drink?" Finally, the shock of seeing him wears off, and I run to the kitchen for our stash of paper plates. No doubt he is used to fine china, but that isn't on the menu tonight.

"We have Dr. Pepper and Coke. Do you like either of these?" I yell over my shoulder. I almost jump out of my skin when arms come around me from behind, and I'm pulled firmly into a very hard body.

I moan as his tongue licks the rim of my ear. "I'll have the Coke." The contrast of the cold air in the refrigerator on my front and Lucian's warm body at my back causes me to shiver. His hands climb to my breasts, feeling the hard nipples pushing against the fabric of my t-shirt. I am braless, and he moans at the discovery. "You have no fucking clue how many times I've thought about this body today." He drops one hand to my belly, just touching my waistband. "These shorts are etched in my brain." I throw my head back and whimper as his hand dips lower, touching me through the denim. His mouth is back at my ear as he says, "I'm going to fuck you tonight. Nothing is going to stop me this time." I spread my legs further apart, ready for him to take me right there. One touch from him and

I'm on fire. His hand pulls me against his cock briefly before he loosens his hold.

"Luc," I protest, trying to follow the heat of his body with mine.

He leans closer again for a moment and grabs two, a Coke and Dr. Pepper from the refrigerator. "Bring the plates, baby, I'm starved." I stand there looking dazed and confused until he gives me a stinging slap on the ass.

"Hey!" I protest, rubbing my hand over the tender flesh.

"Chop, chop, baby." He laughs and takes the box to the coffee table in the living room. For tonight, at least, it appears Lucian can do casual very well. I drop the plates on the table and sit on the place he pats next to him. He opens the lid of the box, and we both inhale appreciatively. He puts two pieces of the supreme pizza on each plate, and I smile as he picks off the mushrooms before putting a piece in his mouth.

We both turn toward the television, as Julia Roberts seems to shout her trademark line from *Pretty Woman*, "Well, color me happy, a sofa for two."

I burst out laughing as Lucian smirks, saying simply, "Indeed." Lucian seems different tonight, more relaxed and carefree. I would never have imagined him sitting in my small apartment, cross-legged while eating pizza and watching *Pretty Woman.*

Before taking another bite of pizza, I ask him teasingly, "So, what happened to your last housekeeper? Did she flee in terror?"

He tweaks my nose playfully before answering. "Hardly. Apparently, I wasn't dirty enough for her." Dr. Pepper comes flying from my mouth, spraying everything in the vicinity. Lucian starts mopping me up with one hand while patting my back with the other. Shaking his head, he says, "Maybe I should have phrased that a little better. I meant she was used to taking caring of families, and I don't require that much care. She didn't feel the work was challenging enough. I rather thought she enjoyed that aspect since she seemed to nap a lot during the day."

"Thank you for clearing that up," I say as I look down at the stain on my shirt. As I ponder getting up to change, he finishes his piece of pizza and suddenly stands, holding out a hand. As I hesitantly take his proffered hand, he pulls me to my feet.

He looks around before asking, "Where's your bedroom?" I point toward my door and allow him to pull me in that direction. Either he's going to change my shirt for me or this was it. The door shutting behind me sounds like a gunshot in the small room. I open my mouth to ask him what we're doing when suddenly he is on me. My back hits the door as his mouth fuses with mine. The laughing man of a few moments ago is gone and in his place is a man brimming with intensity. His hands seem to be everywhere on my body at once. I grab his waist and hold on for dear life. He licks, teases, and sucks every inch of my mouth before moving on to my neck. I feel him sucking the tender flesh there and know I will wear the evidence of his passion tomorrow. My tank top is gone before I can register a protest, and when his dark head drops to take a nipple in his mouth, I'm past caring.

"Luc." I moan as his teeth nip at my tender peak. He rolls the other nipple between his fingers, and I feel moisture flowing from my core. As if he knows where I need him, he drops one hand to my stomach and slides it under the waistband of my shorts. I cringe as I remember the cotton underwear I'm wearing; at least they're pink instead of white. When his fingers part my slick folds, I feel Heaven knocking at the door.

"So fucking wet for me," he groans as his finger slips easily inside me. My back arches and I quiver as desire races through my body. I never felt this way with Jackson, and the intensity of the feelings he is awakening in me are frightening. I gasp as another big finger invades my tight passage, feeling a twinge of discomfort. Before I can pull away, he rubs my clit and like a tidal wave crashing against the shore, my body comes apart. I have never achieved this type of climax at my own hand, and my legs are threatening to fold beneath my limp body. "That was just to take the edge off, baby," he murmurs before swinging me into his arms and walking the few steps to my bed. My shorts and panties are pulled off in one swift movement with his following after.

I have limited experience with a naked man, but to me, Lucian is beautiful. I want to study him like I would a work of art. Stepping forward, I put my small hand on his chest, marveling over the ripple of muscles there. I trace my fingertip down the tattoo on his chest and then notice something that hasn't been visible before. A scar runs the length of his neck, right below his Adam's apple. As I touch the skin there, he jerks away. Looking up in surprise, I ask, "I...does it hurt?"

His eyes cloud and he turns his head away. "No, not anymore." Before I can question him further, he pushes me backwards, and I sprawl in an inelegant heap across my bed. He studies my body for so long I start to fidget. How can a man like Lucian not find me lacking? My breasts and my hips seem unusually large on my otherwise-slender frame. Maybe Lucian is an ass man. The thought is so absurd I have to fight the urge to giggle. Probably not a good idea when a man has his cock at eye level; there is certainly nothing to laugh about there. Rose had mentioned more than once in the crude college way that Jake was hung like a horse. I don't think he could possibly even give Lucian a run for his money. My poor sex quivers in equal parts excitement and terror. He is huge, and I have no idea how something that large will fit inside such a small space. "Like what you see?" My face flames as Lucian looks at his cock, then back at me. I nod shyly; why bother to hide it? "Spread your legs."

"What?" Oh, my God, he didn't just say that.

"Spread your legs. You're tiny and I want to make sure you are ready for me." When I don't immediately obey, he drops to his knees in front of me and nudges his body between my thighs. I watch in fascination as his hand is once again between my legs, a finger sliding back inside my body. Unable to hold back, I moan as he swirls the tip around. "Your pussy is tight; how long has it been since you've been fucked?"

"A...while," I manage to whisper. He is now working two fingers in and out of me, and I'm mortified to hear the wet sound as my juices coat his fingers. When he adds a third finger, the pinch of pain has me gasping before my body stretches to accept the added width. His three fingers are now gliding into my sex as my body starts to clench. An amazing second orgasm is waiting in the wings, and with a few firm strokes to my clit, I see stars.

A protest forms on my lips as he pulls out, but I hear the sound of something tearing and then he is back. Still riding my orgasm, I feel his large hands move me up the bed and then he is over me, his arms bracing on each side of my head. Pleasure tingles along my nerve endings as I feel a nudge at my entrance. I realize with a start that it's Lucian's cock. Momentary panic hits me and my eyes fly to his.

"I'll take care of you, baby. Just trust me. Keep your eyes on mine so I know where you are." Without another word, he slides in slowly, and I catch my breath. He is big, so much bigger than I had imagined. "Wrap your legs around me." As I focus on obeying his request, I inhale sharply as this new position pushes his cock into the hilt. We both freeze as I struggle to adjust to his size. He drops his forehead to mine and nuzzles against me. "Are you okay, baby?" I have no idea how to answer that question. The pinch of pain is gone, leaving in its place an uncomfortable, but not unpleasant, fullness. Experimentally, I push my hips against his and marvel at the sensations it produces. The strain of holding back is evident in the trembling of his big body against mine. "I can't wait any longer," he whispers before pulling almost completely out and slamming back home. My hips rise instinctively to meet his, pushing past the twinge of pain as his huge cock batters inside me. "Fuck...Lia," he shouts as he pulls back on his heels, pushing his hands under my ass and bringing my bottom off the bed.

All reason has left me; I am aware only of the needs of my body and the driving force to reach completion. I feel every inch of his cock as it powers in and out of my pussy. If someone yelled fire right now, I'd gladly go up in flames; I'm too caught up in all things Lucian. I hear someone moaning loudly and realize in surprise that it's me. "Please, Luc...oh, God, please!" I say, begging for release. I feel his hand against my clit, rubbing roughly, and that's all it takes. I shatter again and again as he continues to fuck me. My spasms against his cock finally push him over the edge, and I feel him jerk, grunting as if in pain.

"Lia...baby, fuck!" He pulls out and rolls next to me. The ragged sounds of our breathing fill the room. I'm completely blown away by what just happened. My sexual encounter with Jackson doesn't even rate on the scale of sex with Lucian. To me, it's the difference between being with a boy versus a man. Through the haze of my afterglow, I wonder what comes next. Sex without love seems complicated. Will he leave now? I want to curl into his arms, but I am unsure of his reaction to that. I didn't have to make decisions last time since Jackson left after discovering my scar. I'm grateful my back has been to Lucian the entire time, and I vow to keep it that way. I don't want to see the same distaste in his eyes I saw in Jackson's. Lucian makes the decision for me as he stands and stumbles toward what I assume is the bathroom. I giggle as he opens the closet door instead. He looks toward me, a smile forming on his lips as I point toward the other door. I hear the sound of running water and a few moments later, he is back. He looks at me uncertainly, and I decide to throw caution to the wind.

"Stay, please," I say, hoping I don't sound as clingy as I feel. He looks torn for a moment before walking back to the bed and settling in beside me. I wrap my body around his with my head on his chest. I purr like a kitten as his hand settles on my back, stroking up and down. "That was amazing," I admit. "Was it...good for you?" Oh, crap, why did I ask him that? My lack of self-confidence couldn't be more obvious.

His hand stills for a moment before resuming its path over my hip. "Yes, it was. I hope I wasn't too rough with you."

"No, I...liked it." Talk about the understatement of the year; I want nothing more than for him to take me again, right this second.

"How long since you've been with a man?" I wonder what his obsession is with that. Was it so obvious that I lack experience? Shit, of course it was to someone like him.

"It was last year," I admit, hoping it's the end of the conversation.

"And before that?" he probes. I stiffen, knowing he is not going to let it go. Maybe he should have worried about my level of experience before he slept with me.

"He was my first and only." *There, are you happy now*? I feel the urge to ask. It would serve him right if I started questioning his sexual conquests.

He sounds surprised as he asks, "Why? You're a beautiful woman, Lia; I'm sure there have been a lot of opportunities."

"Not any I was interested in. Between work and school, I really haven't had the time or inclination for a social life. Jackson was friends with my roommate's boyfriend, so he was just there. It was a mistake, and I moved on." Humiliation will do that for you in a hurry.

I assume we are finished discussing my pitiful love life when he asks, "Did he hurt you?"

Stiffening, my mind automatically goes to my stepfather before I realize he is talking about Jackson. "Not physically," I answer honestly. Jackson's scars had been of a different variety.

His warmth wraps around me as I snuggle deeper into him. I have no idea if I will see him again after this, so I want to revel in the moment. All too soon, drowsiness takes over, and I find myself dozing, lulled into sleep by the sound of his heartbeat against my ear. "Sleep, baby," I hear faintly and then I am drifting away.

How long I had been asleep, I have no idea. The room is dark, but someone near is choking. The gurgling sounds fill my ears as I frantically push the webs of sleep away and grope for an answer in the darkness. Someone thrashes next to me as I jump from the bed, rushing to turn on a lamp to light the darkness.

Lucian is on his back, his body twisting as if in agony. His hands are holding his neck and gasping sounds escape from his throat. Oh, dear God, he is choking, but on what? Rushing toward him, I put my hands over his on his neck. "Luc," I whisper, not wanting to startle him further. He continues to wither as if in great pain, so I shake him lightly. "Lucian. Wake up, you're scaring the hell out of me!" Just as I decide to call 911 in case he is having some sort of seizure, he bolts upright in bed, looking around wildly. I stroke his arm, trying to soothe him. 'It's okay, it's me...Lia." His other hand rubs against his throat, but the gurgling sound has stopped. I'm weak with relief that he appears to be unhurt. As suddenly as he jumped up, he sinks back down to the bed, forcing me to move aside as he lowers his head in his hands, taking deep breaths. Sitting beside him, I hesitate before starting to rub his back in slow, soothing circles.

"I'm sorry," he says hoarsely. "That...hasn't happened in a long time. I didn't hurt you, did I?"

I continue to rub his back, trying to digest his words. That this has happened to him before is obvious. I wonder if this has anything to do with the scar on his neck, but I'm not brave enough to ask. "No, I was just worried about you. Would you like a glass of water?" He looks so young and vulnerable sitting here with his shoulders slumped forward that I feel something in my heart twinge. I don't think this is some random bad dream for him. Someone hurt this man badly, and I find myself wanting to protect him, which is absurd. Just because I live with past traumas doesn't mean everyone does. He pulls away mentally before he does physically. I see the shutters going down and the walls going up; I'm an expert at this behavior, so it's easy for me to recognize.

"I'm fine, Lia; it was just a dream." He makes a point of looking at the clock, which shows it's just after midnight. He gives me a quick kiss before standing. "I really need to go, though. I have some emails to return before morning." Instinctively, I grab my shirt from the floor, keeping my back turned away from him until I am covered. At this point, I don't think either of us could handle any more upset tonight, and I'm in no shape to answer questions. I want him to stay, but I know he won't; he needs space and this I understand too well to try to stop him.

He quickly dresses, and I'm pleasantly surprised when he takes my hand, pulling me behind him from the bedroom and into the living room area. There is no sign of Rose, so I assume she is either staying the night with Jake or has stopped somewhere on the way home. Lucian surprises me further when he drops my hand and quickly walks to the table to pick up our leftover pizza and drink cans. He makes short work of throwing them in the trash. "Maybe I should be the one hiring you as a housekeeper." This surprises a laugh out of him, and I smile in return.

His hand again takes mine, and I am pulled into his arms. His kiss this time feels more as if he is giving me comfort, rather than the fire of earlier. I think he is embarrassed by what happened and wants to make sure I'm not upset, which is sweet but unnecessary. I wrap my arms around his waist and hold him tight for a moment, giving him the reassurance I feel he needs. "Goodnight, baby," he sighs against my neck. Pulling back, he raises a questioning brow. "I'll see you in the morning?"

"Yep, I don't have a class till after lunch. I can come for a few hours in the morning so you can show me around, and then I'll be back in the afternoon."

"What time shall I have Sam pick you up?" I'm helpless to suppress a giggle at his question. He looks for the world like someone who missed out on the joke and is running through the conversation in his head. I decide to put him out of his misery.

"I don't think the cleaning lady typically gets chauffeured to and from work unless she is Cinderella. I have a car, and I'm driving myself. Besides, I need my car for my afternoon classes."

Stubborn, Lucian insists. "Sam can drop you and pick you back up." Shaking my head, I open the door and push him bodily through it.

"Don't even think of sending your car. I'll ignore it and drive myself anyway. Sam doesn't want to deal with that." I see he wants to argue but instead turns on his heels, looking like a spoiled child for a moment as he mutters under his breath and stalks off. Declaring victory in our battle will have to wait until morning; I'm not confident he won't ignore me and send the damn car anyway.

CHAPTER SEVEN

Lia

"What's going on with you? I thought you were going to stroke out when you ran out of here yesterday."

In a pathetic attempt to change the subject, I ask, "So, how was dinner with Jake's parents? Since you did the walk of shame this morning, not even an hour ago, I'm assuming it went well?"

As I suspect, she is not that easily deterred. "It was fine, but let's get back to you. Did you really leave your job at *Date Night*? How did you get another job so soon? I had no idea you were even looking? What is the position? What will..."

"Whoa...take a breath, for God's sake." I set aside my bowl of cereal and prepare to give her enough information to satisfy her curiosity. Shit, there is no way I can tell her the truth; she just wouldn't understand. How could she; I don't even know what I'm doing. "Er...well, I didn't really apply for another job. You know the date I had with the guy I sent you the picture of?"

She thinks about it for a moment before smiling. "Oh, yeah, the hot one. I couldn't say a lot in front of Jake, but seriously, what a freaking hot piece of a wet dream." My laugh comes out more like a snort. Rose has a way with words, and ogling men is her favorite pastime; she is like June Cleaver with a dirty mind.

In this instance, she is right on the money. Clearing my throat, I continue, "Anyway, he owns Quinn Software, and he sort of offered me a job." About the only things true within that sentence are Quinn and job; Rose doesn't really need to know the rest at this point.

"Shut up! You lucky bitch, I can't believe that." Wiggling her eyebrows she asks, "Does Mr. Wet Dream provide any extra benefits?" I feel my cheeks bloom, and I hope she assumes it's just embarrassment and not guilt.

"Don't get excited. I'm just his new housekeeper." Unless I want to dress up every day to clean Lucian's house, I have to confess to my new position. She would think it odd if I wore shorts to an office job.

"Yikes," she visibly cringes. "Why in the world would he offer you that kind of job? You probably make more money with *Date Night* than sweeping some hottie's floor."

Feeling the need to defend Lucian, I say, "He pays really well and is willing to let me keep a flexible schedule." The memory of Lucian's cock pounding inside my pussy has me jerking like I'm having some sort of attack. Rose gives me a curious look before shrugging her shoulders.

"If someone is going to be grabbing your ass, it might as well be a babe." Using her best stern tone, she adds, "I expect you to be able to answer a burning question tonight: boxers or briefs." I catch myself at the last minute before blurting out the answer I have already discovered. Looking at my watch, I grab my purse and rush toward the door. Mr. Wet Dream is waiting, and suddenly I need to see him. Skipping the elevator, I jog down the stairs and am relieved to see

Sam is nowhere in sight; maybe there's hope for Lucian after all.

The area around Lucian's home is busy and congested. I am absurdly grateful for the parking pass his secretary Cindy has given me. because without it, I would have been walking from a mile away. Instead, I pull in beside a sleek, black Range Rover. Obviously, it belongs to Lucian since it's one of four spaces with his apartment number. On the other side of the Rover, there is some sort of black sports car. The man certainly likes that color. There is no sign of the Mercedes Sam drives.

There is an elevator right off the parking garage, and I use the card Cindy has given me to access the penthouse. Somehow, referring to Lucian's home as an apartment is probably a gross understatement. When the elevator stops, I step out into a hallway with a double set of doors directly in front. A quick glance shows no other doorways, so I am reasonably sure this is the right place. A sudden case of nerves immobilizes me, and I shift uncertainly from one foot to another, trying to force myself to ring the buzzer.

When the door opens, I jump back, blinking in surprise. Holy moly, Lucian—in nothing but dress pants and a sexy grin—stands before me. I can't take my eyes off his muscular chest and those flat nipples I licked just hours before. He clears his throat and an apology is on the tip of my tongue before I am quickly pulled in the doorway. "I was just pouring a cup of coffee; would you like one?" I manage to squeak some kind of agreement out as I follow him through a massive foyer and into a bright and airy kitchen. The space is made up of granite, stainless steel, and gleaming hardwood floors.

I jump as he brushes his front against my back, trailing his lips against my ear. "Are you hungry?"

"No," I croak out. Heat floods my core at the feel of his body against mine. What is happening to me? This man is all but a stranger to me, but when he's near, I can think of nothing but how I want him inside me. Before I can stop myself, I push my ass back against his crotch, moaning when I feel the hard ridge of his arousal against me.

"Lia," he breathes against my neck. His hand circles around my body, finding the snap of my shorts. In a move that speaks of years of experience, he has my shorts and panties down around my ankles and lifts me to kick them away. I shriek when my ass makes contact with the cold granite.

"Luc...What?"

"Shhh, lay back, baby." When I hesitate, he gently puts his hand behind my head and lowers me until I am sprawled out on the icy surface. When I try to sit back up, he holds me down with one hand while pulling my hips forward with the other. I stop squirming as he puts first one, then my other leg over his shoulder and is poised with his head between my legs.

"Oh, my," I say in amazement as his dark head descends toward my sex. My body wages a war between panic and fascination as his warm breath whispers across my wet seam. No one has ever gone down on me before, and I both want and fear it. "Luc..."

As if sensing my inner conflict, the hand on my stomach strokes me reassuringly, and I watch his head close the distance. At the first touch of his tongue against me, my hips jerk. He moves a hand to anchor me and then he is on me. He penetrates my seam, licking my full length. I moan, grabbing the edge of the counter as white-hot desire claws through me. At first, his tongue swirls and sips, causing my need to build gradually. When my hips shift, begging for him, he starts nipping and sucking my clit, working it relentlessly. By this time, my hands are buried in his thick hair, holding his tongue in place. The words and moans coming from my mouth would make a hooker proud. "That's it, baby, let go..." he encourages as I ride his hand.

I am beyond desperate to be fucked at this point. My pride has taken a backseat to my need. If there was a vibrator in the vicinity, I would use it in front of Lucian without a second thought. He is fucking me with his fingers and his tongue, but still it isn't enough; I want...need more. "Luc...please," I shout, needing to end this ache inside me.

"What do you want, Lia?" he grunts as he circles my opening, denying me the full penetration I crave. I follow his hand with my hips, trying to take what I need. When he smacks one cheek sharply, I yell out, stunned. "Answer the question, and I'll give you what you want."

Furious and frustrated, I snap, "I want you to fuck me, okay? Is that clear enough for you?" I shove my foot against his chest, and he has the nerve to laugh before pulling me to my feet. He positions me with my hands on the counter and my feet apart. "What are..."

"Please tell me you're on birth control. I don't want anything between us this time."

My mind is so addled it takes me a moment to process his question. "Yes!" I shout in excitement, "I'm still on the pill." A blush steals over my cheeks as I imagine how that must have sounded. I had started taking the pill at Rose's urging before I slept with Jackson. Even though it was only the once, I had continued taking them since the local health department provided them for free. I loved the fact that I barely had a period anymore on them. "Um...yeah, I am," I add more calmly.

"Thank fuck," he whispers against my ear. As he braces his hands on my hips, I feel the head of his cock brush my entrance. My hips jerk forward as he goes balls-deep in one hard thrust. He growls my name as I moan helplessly. This is what I've been wanting since the moment he opened the door. His big cock is deep, so deep in this position that he is bumping against my cervix. The discomfort just adds to the flood of sensations racing through me. With each thrust, my nipples brush against the cold granite, bringing me closer to orgasm. Lucian's mouth burns a trail of fire down my neck as he nips and laves me. My hips meet his, eager to take every inch he has to offer. Soon I am close, and I know from his frantic movements that he is, as well. His big hand comes around, finding my slippery clit, and I clench around his cock as my orgasm explodes. He pounds hard before his cock starts twitching within me. Without his support, I would be face down on the floor. I am spent and wasted. There is no denying I've been fucked by Lucian Quinn; his stamp is all over me both inside and out.

He continues to move leisurely in me for a few moments as we both get our breathing under control. I whimper as he pulls out, my body sore and sensitive. A feeling of warmth washes over me as I feel his lips against my spine before he helps me turn. I am too tired to protest when he picks me up in his arms and moves through the apartment. We pass through what I assume is his bedroom and into a large bathroom. He lowers me down gently onto my feet and starts the water in the shower. I stand apprehensively, wondering if we are showering together. When he steps into the steamy, glass enclosure and extends a hand to me, I have my answer. Without thinking, I throw my shirt quickly off and follow him.

Now that the sexual fog was somewhat abated, my usual shyness is returning in full force. Stupid, I know, since the man had his head between my legs just moments ago, but things always feel different in the light of day, so to speak. As I reach for the soap, he takes it instead, creating a rich lather before starting to wash my shoulders. Neither of us speaks as he washes first my front and then his with quick efficiency. If I was expecting an encore shower session, I was out of luck; he might as well have been washing a Buick. Just the thought of that brings a smile to my face and then a giggle escapes. Lucian holds the washcloth suspended as he looks at me as if I've lost my mind. "What?" he asks, looking adorably confused.

Somehow, that just makes me laugh harder until I am leaning against the wall of the shower stall holding my sides; the whole situation is so absurd it's hilarious. How in the world has someone such as myself ended in up Lucian's Quinn's shower being washed by him, after having what can only be called dirty sex on his kitchen counter? It really is too much to take in. I barely know the man, and he's washing my hoo-ha, as Rose calls it, after just having licked it thoroughly. The sensible Lia Adams has left the building and in her place is a...tramp? Me, a tramp? That's unreal. Most people have colon cleanings more than I have sex. Why him, though? We are worlds apart in every way, but I feel so damn comfortable with him. He is familiar, and when I'm dying to have him inside me, I just want to be with him. He begins to look worried as he continues to study me. "Sorry, I just lost it there for a minute. I...I'm just not used to someone washing me." He smirks before grabbing my arm and pulling me forward.

"Let's finish the job then." I can only blame what happens next on my complete absorption in all things Lucian. As he twirls me around to face the wall, I laugh until I hear his harsh inhalation. Oh, fuck. Oh,

my God, how could I have forgotten my back? As I
attempt to jerk around, he holds me immobile. "What
the fuck is this?" he asks too quietly. I shrink as far
away from him as I can. I feel the need to apologize as
if I have deceived him somehow.

"It's just a scar," I say instead, dropping my head in
shame. Like Jackson, he won't want me anymore. I am
marked...ugly. "Please, let me go, Luc." I hate that my
voice wobbles as I beg him to release me. When
instead I feel his hand softly gliding over my marred
flesh, I jolt as if I can still feel the hot brand of the
iron; no one has touched me there since that day.

"Lia...baby, how did you get this?" Before I can
answer, he adds quietly, "It almost looks like an iron."
Whereas just a moment ago, I was laughing, I now feel
tears start to flow, blending in with the water from the
shower. I want to disappear, to escape the
embarrassment beating down on me. How could I have
forgotten? How could I have let him see my back? His
grip on me has loosened as he stands looking at my
back, and I take advantage of it, wrenching myself free
and stumbling from the shower. I have to get away; I
need to cover myself from his prying eyes. Not
bothering with a towel, I try to pull my shirt on over
my wet skin.

Lucian jumps out of the shower, taking in my
struggle to dress in one glance. Without saying
anything, he takes the shirt from my hand and wraps
me instead in a fluffy bath towel. He puts another
towel around his waist and then just stands, looking at
me.

Picking imaginary lint from the towel, I say, "It is
an iron; at least, it was." He curses low under his
breath but doesn't move.

"Who?" he asks. Lying seems pointless; he doesn't
know me or my family, and I'm unlikely to see him
again after this.

"My stepfather." When his face goes molten and he throws his fist at the wall, I jump, stunned.

"Fucking hell!" he snarls. My teeth are chattering as I start to shake. His eyes widen as he takes in my reaction; he looks instantly contrite. He slowly approaches me, pulling me gently against his chest. "I'm sorry. Shit, I didn't mean to scare you. That's probably the last thing you need to see." He works for a moment to get his breathing under control as he slowly strokes my back. "It just makes me sick to think of some bastard laying his hand on you, or any woman, for that matter. When did this happen? The scar doesn't look recent, but it's burned so deeply into your skin."

"It...was five years ago. Before I left home." In the warmth of his arms, I find myself clinging to his strength. "I'm sorry. I should have warned you."

Lucian pulls back, holding me at arm's length. "Lia, you don't have anything to be sorry about, and I'm an asshole if I made you think that. Honey, I know I don't have any right to ask you this, but did he...were you, fuck, did he rape you?"

"No," I whisper. "After a while, he didn't want me that way." I drop my head back to his chest, soaking up the comfort he offers.

"Thank fuck," he sighs, holding me closer for another moment. We stand that way for another few minutes. I sense he wants to question me further, but he doesn't, and I'm grateful; I don't want more of my past ugliness spilled onto him. We both start dressing, and he helps me into my shirt. His cellphone seems to be alternating between texts and ringing, and I know he needs to go. He quickly leads me through the apartment and quietly answers my questions. The place is mostly clean, and I can't imagine having more than an hour of work to do here. As I walk him to the door, he rubs my arm, saying, "You know this isn't necessary. I don't need you to be my housekeeper. I would much prefer hiring someone and having you concentrate on your schoolwork. Hell, if I could keep my damn hands off you, the office would be a much better place for you to learn something beneficial."

My first smile since the revelation in the bathroom stretches across my face. Despite my scar, he still wants me. I release a breath I hadn't been aware of holding. "I don't mind, Luc. I've never been given anything for free, and I don't intend to start now. I would love to witness the inner workings of your company, but not if it would be a distraction for you." Giving him a teasing grin, I add, "Since you don't seem to be a slob, this should be an easy job with a flexible schedule for school." He still looked undecided, so I push him gently toward the door. "Go to work and make some millions or whatever brilliant thing you do there. I've got countertops to clean."

He throws his head back, laughing at my reference to his counters and our earlier activities. "All right, point taken. I had better go before Sam stops calling and comes up here to drag me out." We both look uncertain for a moment. Should I kiss him goodbye? Thankfully, he takes the decision from my hands and drops a quick kiss on my lips. Thank God; if it had been the forehead, self-doubt would have reared its ugly head again to choke me. "Lock the door behind me," he orders, and then he is gone.

After I lock the door, I turn to survey his home. Floor-to-ceiling windows make up the living and dining room areas. Two cream-colored leather sofas provide comfortable, but modern, seating areas in front of a large fireplace. The adjacent dining room has seating for eight around a long, mahogany table. Rich hardwood floors flow into the kitchen I briefly glimpsed this morning. I figure this was a good place to start my new duties. As with the rest of the apartment, it appears mostly clean. I empty the coffee maker, cleaning it before resetting it for Lucian. I find some granite cleaner under the cabinet and wipe down all the surfaces. I know I am blushing as I remember what we had been doing on the kitchen island just a short time ago.

Lucian has a restaurant-grade stainless steel stove I take a moment to familiarize myself with. I don't know if cooking is part of my job description, but I think it would be nice to have a meal for him this evening. I can always leave it in the refrigerator if he doesn't arrive home before I leave.

After finishing in the kitchen, I head to the laundry room. I wash the items in the basket, but assume from the dry-cleaning bags in his closet that he must have his suits professionally cleaned. That is a huge relief since I have no desire to ruin something so obviously expensive.

His bedroom is large but relaxing. The walls are painted a tan color with the darker brown bedding that's a perfect complement. The hardwoods are here, as well, with rugs on each side of the bed. There is nothing worse than putting your feet on cold floors first thing in the morning, and apparently Lucian feels the same. I quickly make his bed, stopping only to appreciate the soft sheets; the thread count is probably off the charts on these babies. The bed smells of Lucian, and I have to fight the urge to lie down and snuggle into the sheets.

The bathroom is next on my agenda, and I pause for a moment there. Discomfort floods through me at the memory of Lucian touching my scar. I was moved that he was so angry on my behalf, embarrassed he knows what had happened to me at the hands of my stepfather, and curious as to his strong reaction; his anger had been palpable when he struck the wall. Running my hands over the area, I feel a small indention. Had it been my pain that he'd felt or had it brought back memories of his past?

I know next to nothing about Lucian even though we have been intimate. With the standard third-date rule, do you ever really know anyone before you sleep with them? I have a longer relationship with the guidance counselor at St. Claire's than I have with Lucian. Surely, such a successful person is a Google dream. I vow to find out more about the man who I am not only sleeping with, but also working for. I don't want to be one of those people they interview after their boyfriend shoots up his workplace, and she's just standing there like a deer in the headlights. My motto is 'knowledge is power, and it's time to gain some; I need to know more about Lucian before whatever is between us goes further.

Lucian

"Good morning, Sam." I greet my driver and friend as I slide in the back of the Mercedes. Asheville is hardly Los Angeles, and I could easily drive myself to the office each day, but I am too much of a multitasker to concentrate on one thing. I like starting my day from the comfort of the backseat; normally, I return calls, answer emails, and study the stock market. I also enjoy having Sam around. He knows my schedule better than I do, and I have begun to rely on his reminders. Cindy generally leaves this part of the day to him. I suspect Cindy and Sam discuss more than work and my schedule each day, but to each his own.

Today, I find myself unable to concentrate on my normal routine. I can't get the image of Lia's scarred back out of my mind. I had downplayed what I saw there. The outline of a fucking iron was as plain as day. The scar was deep, red and puckered. If it happened five years ago, how horrific must it have been then? Scars might never go away, but they generally fade with time. That the burn had been excruciatingly painful was obvious. I barely know this girl, but I want to fucking kill on her behalf. How dare someone do that to her!

Things had blurred for a moment, and I had been in another time, another place, and with another woman. Was I destined to relive every painful moment of my past again? Some invisible force had been pulling me toward her since the moment we met.

Sam drops me at the front of Quinn Software, and I make my way up to my office, greeting employees as I pass. I'm grateful to find Cindy isn't at her desk; the need for relief is gnawing at my guts, and it would be torture to be waylaid. I shut and lock my door behind me before walking swiftly to my desk. In moments, the side drawer is unlocked, and I am opening the small case that contains my Heaven and Hell. With unsteady hands, I lay out everything I need; the process helps to center me. I work it as I would any job. Shoddy work is foreign to me, even in this. Soon, I'm ready and as I snort the first white line, it's there. The clearing of my senses, the instant clarity, and as always, playing around the edge, is the rage at my inability to leave the crutch behind. This has been my answer to dealing with a life that has, at times, resembled a horror movie. I don't know any other way. There are times when I have been almost free of it, but I'm always brought back by a woman, only the face has changed this time.

I'm fully functional on cocaine, possibly even better; I have never considered myself an addict, even though most would disagree. It would be more socially acceptable if I were in therapy taking an array of prescription medications to deal with all that is fucked-up in my head. Antianxiety medication is as common as Tylenol in this stress-overloaded world, but it has never been my answer. At first, it was simply availability. Cocaine was easy to acquire, and I had friends who used it regularly. When my world imploded, I was encouraged to snort a few lines to help me deal. I have survived on cocaine; hell, I have thrived professionally on it. Personally, the weakness eats at me. It's my best friend at times and the worst fucking enemy I have ever faced.

These days, Sam makes sure my supply is replenished when needed. He has a nephew who keeps me well-supplied for a price. I don't ask questions anymore. I give him the money, and he takes care of the rest. The only thing I have stipulated is that he never tells Cindy. I don't want her involved, and if I am honest, I hate to disappoint her. Aidan, on the other hand, knows most of my secrets, and the coke is no exception. It's not a big deal to us; we've seen and done worse.

When Cindy knocks at my door a few moments later, I wipe my nose and walk over to unlock it. My public face is firmly in place. Cindy would never suspect the only difference between me and the bum on the corner is a higher-priced monkey on my back.

CHAPTER EIGHT

Lia

My last class finishes earlier than normal, and I am stopping by the apartment to change clothes before going back to Lucian's to finish up for the day. To my surprise, his cabinets have been well-stocked as if he actually has meals at his apartment instead of eating out every evening. My plan is to fix a simple dinner of shrimp pasta. Pasta in all forms is something I am well-acquainted with; it is easy, quick, and cheap.

I drop my book bag and walk to my bedroom when a knock sounds at the door. More than likely, it's someone looking for Marissa next door. I have my suspicions as to why she is so popular, but who am I to judge? Several times a week, we have mostly men knocking at our door, looking for her apartment. At first, I wouldn't answer the door when I didn't recognize the person through the peep-hole. After a while, though, it just seemed easier to point them in the right direction to prevent it happening each time they visited. For safety, we always keep the chain firmly in place and speak through the small opening.

Another stranger looks back at me through the small glass, and I shake my head as I crack the door open. "Marissa is next door in 5B."

Before I can shut the door, I hear the person ask, "Miss Adams?" Wow, I so wasn't expecting that; it's a rare day I have visitors.

Uneasy, I reply, "Can I help you with something?"

"Are you Lia Adams?" Well, crap, I don't know whether to answer or not. Curiosity finally gets the better of me.

"Yes, who are you?" I instinctively take the envelope he thrusts through the opening.

"You've been served." I stare after his retreating back, wondering what's going on. The white envelope weighs heavily in my hand as I pull it slowly through the doorway. The university has never hand-delivered mail before. If they suddenly feel the need, then it can't be good news. The only writing on the front is my name in printed form.

I shut the door behind me and carry the envelope like a bomb to our small kitchen table. I drop it in front of me, staring for a moment. Shit, this is so silly. *Just open the damn thing and get it over with.* What could it possibly be? Maybe I have some seriously-overdue book from the library or something. Impatiently, I rip open the flap and unfold the single enclosed paper. As I skim the official-looking document, I feel my heart stop for one brief moment. No, surely I have read it wrong. Taking my time, I read back through the jumble of words once again before dropping weakly into the nearby chair.

PLANTIFF: MARIA ADAMS DAWSON VS DEFENDANT: JIM NELSON DAWSON. YOU ARE HEREBY SUMMONED to appear. The words on the paper leap out at me as my head swims. I haven't seen or spoken to my mother or stepfather since leaving home four years ago. Dear God, what is going on with them? Why is my mother going to court against her husband, and why am I being dragged into it?

There is only one person who might possibly be able to find out. Debra, my friend and previous boss, has a connection through her boyfriend. Martin's brother Eli works with Jim at a tire factory, or he had the last time I heard. Almost in a panic, I punch in Debra's number and pray she will answer.

"Lia? Where the hell have you been, honey?" This is Debra's usual greeting, and I smile despite my apprehension. I love this woman like the mother I never had, and I know she loves me, as well. Her only complaint is I don't see her as often as either of us would like.

"Hey, Deb. It's so good to hear your voice, you have no idea." She knows me well and immediately picks up on the strain in my voice.

"What's wrong, honey? Do you need me? I can be there in just a few minutes." Closing my eyes, I feel a tear slip out. She gives me everything and never asks for anything in return. I don't see or talk to her as often as I used to, but I know that with one phone call, she would drop what she is doing and come to me.

"Have you heard anything from Martin about my mother?" I can tell by her silence that she is shocked by my question.

"No, he hasn't mentioned anything. Why?"

"Something is going on with her and Jim. I was served papers today requiring I show up in court at the end of the month." Picking the paper up, I read her the rest of the summons. The whole thing still feels unreal to me. The one time I hear from them, and it's something like this.

"Son of a bitch," she spits out the curse, her voice vibrating with anger. "I don't know what those two fuckups are involved in now, but I'm going to find out. Just sit tight, honey, and try not to worry about it. I'll call Martin and see if he can get some answers. You know I will be with you every step of the way. Those monsters can't hurt you, Lia; I would never let that happen again." She gives me more words of comfort laced with insults for my mother and stepfather before ending the call. I'm sure the line was barely free before she was calling Martin. If anyone can find out what is going on, it's Debra.

I would love nothing better than to crawl in my bed and have the nervous breakdown I feel beating at my door, but I don't want to slack on my first day of work. Lucian would understand if I said I wasn't feeling well, but getting out of here right now can only help the panic I've been feeling since receiving the damned summons. Quickly, I gather my things and run to my Honda as if afraid more bad news will befall me. Luckily, that's not the case, and I navigate through the heavy afternoon traffic to arrive back at Lucian's around three. The same vehicles are parked in the garage with no sign of Sam and the Mercedes.

The last load of laundry has been put away, and I'm arranging ingredients for dinner when my phone rings. I see Debra's name on the caller ID and answer quickly. I barely get out a greeting before she starts talking. "Lia, you aren't going to believe this. Are you sitting down, honey?" She sounds worried, which in turn freaks me out; Debra is normally unflappable, so it must be bad.

"Go ahead, Deb." I slip onto a barstool at the counter and brace myself.

"That asshole beat the hell out of your mother, and she has either wised up or is just trying to stick it to him. She filed charges against him for abuse, and I think they are summoning you as a witness for her. She must have told them you had seen him beat her. She probably also told them he had done the same to you."

"Oh, my God!" Not only am I going to have to face him in the courtroom, but now everyone would know what he had done to me; everyone would see the scar, the damage. I feel sick to my stomach. Bile rises in my throat, and I literally gag on it. I hear Debra yelling my name in the background as the phone clatters to the floor. My hands cover my face as my body trembles in fear. I am so caught up in my terror I never hear the door open or the footsteps until someone touches my shoulders, causing a scream to escape from my throat.

"Lia, baby, what's wrong?" I struggle against the hold until I recognize Lucian's face, full of concern, looking at me. Without thinking, I launch myself from the chair and into his arms. After a moment's hesitation, he pulls me against him, murmuring, "Shhh...baby." Still holding me, he reaches down to pick up my phone lying near his feet. I pay little attention as he speaks briefly to Debra. I know she must be shocked to hear a man on my phone, and I absently vow to call her back later to explain.

Lucian pulls back a little to look me over, probably searching for signs of injury. Seeming satisfied that there is no blood, he gives me another moment before asking, "What's happened to get you so upset?" Mutely, I reach for the summons and hand it to him. He skims it before looking at me in question.

"Its...it's from my mother and stepfather. He...hurt her, and she is pressing charges." Choking on a sob, I add, "They are going to make me testify against him, about what he did to her and me." Lucian bites off a curse before pulling me back into his arms. After seeing my scar that morning, there is no way he can miss the fear I feel.

"I'll give this to my lawyer tomorrow and find out what in the hell is going on, okay? I won't let that bastard hurt you. Please believe that." Sinking further into his strong arms, I let his words wash over me. I relax for the first time since reading the summons, feeling some of my fear lessen. This beautiful man is offering me protection; when has that ever happened to me before? Even my own mother doesn't give a damn whether I live or die. I have no idea how she even knew my address to have me served. "Now," he says against the crown of my head, "I'm starving; how about we go out for dinner?" I think about the clothes I'm wearing and fight the urge to ask him if there is a Burger King nearby.

His arms drop as I step back. Putting on a smile that is still forced, I say, "I was planning to fix dinner to impress my new boss. I already have everything laid out if you'll give me half an hour." He looks over the items I have on the counter before opening a wood panel that conceals a large wine cooler. He studies several different bottles before selecting one.

I fully expect him to go relax in the living room, so I'm pleasantly surprised when he says instead, "I'm going to go change clothes, I'll be back to help in just a moment." I shake myself from my staring-at-Lucian daze and pull a skillet and sauce pan out of the cabinet for the shrimp, pasta, and cream sauce. Thankfully, Rose has shown me how to make homemade Alfredo since there are no jarred sauces in Lucian's cabinets. I have just pulled a red and green bell pepper from the refrigerator when he returns in jeans and a worn-looking Bon Jovi shirt. My mouth waters, and my body hums; Rose is right, he is a walking wet dream, and I am like an animal in heat around him. As he turns to get wine glasses, I ogle his taut ass, my hands tingling with the urge to cup his cheeks. His dark hair curls against his neckline, and I remember how it feels to have my fingers buried in its silky softness. When he is facing forward again, my eyes drop to the outline of his big cock nestled against one leg. Oh, sweet mother, my panties are wet and getting wetter. When his fingers snap in front of my eyes, I lift my eyes from his crotch. His sexy grin assures me he knows exactly what was on my mind. What is happening to me? I have never been a cock-gawker. The man has been home less than an hour, and I am staring at his package; somehow, I don't think that is part of my job description.

He chuckles behind me as I spin around, trying to hide my embarrassment and get a grip on my libido. He puts a wine glass down next to my hand, and I mutter a sheepish, "Thanks," before turning back to the stove.

"What can I do to help? Do these peppers need chopping?" Now, that I wasn't expecting: Lucian offering to help with dinner. Personally, I am all for throwing the whole meal in the trash and begging him to fuck me against the stainless steel appliances, but nowhere in the word 'housekeeper' does it spell slut, so I keep those thoughts to myself.

"Er...yes, that would be great. I'm making shrimp pasta, so I'm going to sauté those in olive oil before mixing them with the shrimp." I continue explaining the entire meal to him before I realize I am rambling. He listens to me attentively, although I'm sure he couldn't give a crap as to how long shrimp cook before they are ready.

We have just settled at the bar on our stools, and I'm taking my first bite when he asks as casually as you would mention the weather, "Do you have a vibrator?" My fork clatters back into my plate as I look at him in disbelief. He takes a moment to chew and swallow before looking at me. "What? It's a simple question." I have no idea how the man can continue calmly eating while asking me such a personal question. My first inclination is to tell him to shove it... unless he is open to equal sharing.

"If I answer your question, will you answer one for me?"

With no hesitation, he says, "Within reason, yes." I have no idea if my question is considered reasonable, but if he doesn't answer it, I won't answer any other questions he might have.

Picking up my fork, I spear a piece of penne pasta before answering. "Yes, I do." He shows no surprise at my answer, and I quickly ask my own. "Have you slept with Monique?"

"Yes," he answers as he pops a shrimp in his mouth. I'm not sure what surprises me more, that he has slept with Cruella or that he admitted it. Really, I already knew the answer before I asked; Monique is too possessive of him without there being more involvement, even though he seems to feel nothing for her in return. "How long were you with the guy you slept with?"

Ugh, why did I agree to this little question-and-answer session, and why does he care about my sexual history? It's obviously nowhere near as busy as his. I debate shutting it down, but dammit, I want to know more about him, and I have a feeling this is the easiest way to go about it. He already knows I don't have much experience, so it's not like I am revealing shocking facts. Somehow, it is still embarrassing to admit. "It just happened one time." It appears I now have his undivided attention. You would think I have just admitted to having two vaginas. Clearing my throat, I add, "It's my turn again. How many times have you slept with Monique?" Shit, why do I keep harping on that? Wasn't knowing he slept with her enough? Do I need details? Yes, it appears I do.

He raises his glass, taking a drink of the wine before answering. "Just the once and before you ask, it was one time too many. Monique is very...aggressive, which is fine in bed, but I quickly grew tired of her palming my cock every time our paths cross. I started to get the feeling she'd bite the fucking thing off if necessary to get what she wanted." He surprises me by trailing a finger over my lips. "Please feel free to palm, lick, or suck me anytime you want, anywhere you want, sweet Lia." I don't need a lot of sexual experience to suspect I could come right where I sit, with no clitoral stimulation. Sexy, casual Lucian is deadly, and I want to puddle at his feet in a needy heap. "I believe it's my turn now," he says as he removes his hand to continue eating. "Why was it just the once? You're a beautiful, sexy, responsive woman. Did he not take care of you?"

Closing my eyes briefly, I wonder why I've let this continue. This is going to be a humiliating admission. "I...it was my first time, so it was uncomfortable and over pretty quickly. He thought something was wrong with me...when he saw my back." It was Lucian's turn to drop his fork. He appears angry as he stares at me.

"Are you fucking kidding me? Did that bastard say something to you?"

Tracing my fingers over the granite of the countertop, I say, "He acted like I was some kind of freak. He...left and then told his friends I had something. Jake, my roommate's boyfriend, was so angry; he knew what had happened to me from Rose." Lucian's chair scrapes back, and he is at my side. I continue to look down, mortified that someone as perfect as Lucian would know of my shame.

"Lia, look at me." Reluctantly, I obey, seeing the fire simmering in his eyes. "You don't have anything to feel bad about. Everyone has scars; some are visible and some aren't. This punk didn't deserve to be your first. He had no interest in pleasing and putting you first. Don't waste a fucking thought on him; he isn't worth it." I can't stop myself from climbing into his big arms. He is warm, strong, and smells panty-meltingly divine. I want to take my tongue and lick every inch of his body. Before I can put that plan into action, he pulls back, looking down at me.

"Hey, don't you owe me another question?" I tease. He nods in agreement, and the scar on his neckline catches my attention. I run my finger across it, feeling his body stiffen. "How did this happen? Were you in an accident?" He freezes before pulling abruptly away.

"I have some work to do tonight. I'm going out of town tomorrow for a few days. You have your key, so you can come and go as your schedule allows. There shouldn't be much to do here while I'm away, so don't worry if you have schoolwork to do. He points at the dishes, adding, "I'll clean this up later. Let me walk you down to your car." He hasn't looked at me through his entire speech, and I am reeling. I don't think it was a coincidence that he is all but throwing me out the door after I questioned him about the mark on his neck.

"I can clean the kitchen before I leave. It won't take long," I offer.

"Just leave it," he snaps before taking a deep breath. "Can you just do as I ask?"

"Okay," I answer, walking out of the kitchen to find my handbag still sitting in the foyer. He follows quietly, opening the door for me. The ride in the elevator to the parking garage is silent, and I fidget with the strap of my bag. If not for my job with him, I fear I would never see him again; of course, there is no guarantee I will. As I unlock my car door, I mumble, "I'll see you when you get home." I cringe knowing it came out more like a question than a statement. He leans over and kisses my forehead, and I fight the urge to cry; he is putting distance between us. Even a quick peck on the lips would have been preferable to the platonic kiss he has given me.

"Be careful," he says as I shut my door. I give him a half-hearted wave and back out of the space. When I pull onto the road, he is still standing where I left him, looking down toward the ground with his hands in his pockets. He looks like a little boy at that moment, and I wonder what has happened in his past to make him shut down so quickly. With so many issues of my own, I find it hard to believe that I have developed some sort of dysfunctional relationship with a man who is also chasing demons. Damn, couldn't I have found a Jake? Someone who treats me well, doesn't have baggage, and does all the normal, uncomplicated boyfriend things? There is one thing I know for sure: if I do hear from Lucian again and continue down this unknown road, things will never be normal because we are both fucked-up. Even knowing that, I will be waiting, praying I hear from him again.

Rose texts me just as I'm parking my car near our apartment; she is around the corner at Starbucks and wants me to meet her there. My fingers have already tapped out an excuse when I think better of it. Tonight, I need a friend, and I think it's time to tell her what's been going on with Lucian. She has more experience with men than I do, and I could use the advice. I let her know I'm on my way and in moments, I enter the campus Starbucks and see her waving from the back. "I know it's doing nothing but putting extra fat on our asses, but we are having a frappe tonight instead of the usual low-calorie shit."

"Amen," I say as I grab the frappe and drink enough to cause a brain freeze. "Boy, I needed that," I sigh gratefully.

"A drink and a smoke would probably be better, but you gotta work with what you have." I study Rose, noting my normally-unflappable friend looks disheveled. She is even chewing her nails which is a no-no for someone who pays a small fortune for regular manicures. Have I been wrong about Jake being the perfect boyfriend?

"So...what's got you committing death by frozen drink? Is everything okay with Jake?" When she actually blushes, I'm dying to know what has happened.

Even though it kills me, I give her a few minutes to fidget before she finally blurts out, "Jake wants to try anal sex!" Wow, I wasn't expecting that at all. First, I'm rather surprised Rose is so appalled, since she seems pretty free where their sex life is concerned. Second, I never pictured Jake being that adventurous. It's not really the conversation so much as the position of the players that throws me; I can totally picture Rose trying to pressure Jake into it.

"Hmmm, okay...and you aren't into it?" She looks at me, surprised by my reaction. She seems to expect me to fall to the ground, shrieking in horror. While I've never had anal sex, nor have any desire to, it's just a minor blip on my radar. When you were raised in a living hell, consenting sex between couples is minor and not a big deal. Jake, at least, cares for her enough to talk to her about it first instead of trying to force her; at least, I think so. "Did he try to make you do it or just let you know he was interested?"

I am relieved to hear her say, "Duh, Jake would never do something like that. He just...wants to give it a try. I guess some of those shithead jocks he hangs out with have all been bragging about how great it is. Now he seems to believe he is missing out on something."

Taking her hand, I say honestly, "If you don't want to try then just tell him. Jake cares about you and even though it might be something he wants, he will understand if you don't."

She gives me a curious look, asking, "Would you do it?" Before I can plead ignorance, she spells it out, "If a guy wanted to have anal sex with you, would you do it?"

I'm blushing; I can feel the heat rushing up my cheeks. "I...don't know...maybe. It depends on the person and I guess whether I really trusted them."

"You bitch!" I almost jump out of my chair. People near us stare as she yells, "You had sex again and didn't tell me!"

Slinking lower in my seat, I hiss, "Why don't you say it louder, I don't think the people on the sidewalk heard you!"

"Fuck-sticks," she says in a lower voice. "I knew something was going on with you. It's the God, isn't it? You've been all over the place since you went out with him." In true Rose-style, she jumps quickly to the hard stuff. "How is he? Does he fuck as good as he looks? Does he have a big cock? Is he into kink? Oh, shit, did you do anal with him? Is that why you are on Jake's side?"

Wishing the floor would swallow me up, seems to be getting me nowhere. I close my eyes, but when I open them again, she is still sitting there looking like a rabid dog. There is no way she is letting me off the hook until I answer her questions. So, I take them from the top, saying, "Good, yes, oh yes, maybe, and no." It takes her a moment to match my answers with her questions, and I see the moment she does.

"Oh, yummy, he is hung. You lucky thing. Jake has a big one, too, but it's not huge. So, like, do you two do normal-couple stuff or just have sex?"

"I've known the man less than two weeks, so there is no couple involved. We have gone out to dinner, if that counts."

Her smile widens as she says, "So, let me get this straight: my mostly-virginal friend is having a fuckionship?"

"A what?" I sputter out.

"A fuckionship. You know, a relationship that is only about fucking. There ain't no shame in it, babe; I'd roll over and spread my legs for a man like that, too, and I haven't even seen him in person. Wait...is he one of those guys who is good from far, but far from good? Photographs like Chris Hemsworth, but looks like a troll in person?"

She is so serious, it sends me off in a fit of giggles. "No..." I gasp out. "He is beautiful. His chest, sweet mother, I could lick it for hours. And Rose...he has a tattoo."

Rose drops her head on the table dramatically. "Now you're just being mean. Hey, do you think he would be interested in a threesome?"

Shaking my head, I laugh. "Really? You don't want to do anal with your boyfriend, but you want to have a threesome with someone you've never met?"

"Don't judge me, tramp...Wait, I know, it's crooked isn't it? There is no way he is gorgeous, hung and rich. Does it have a wart on it? Hairy?"

Rolling my eyes at her, I say, "Give it up. Other than a scar across his throat, the man is perfect. I have no idea what he sees in me. I'm probably his 'good from far, but far from good.'"

"A scar? Maybe he cut himself shaving. Jake has come close to bleeding out a few times when he was too cheap to replace his razor."

I ponder just letting it go, but I want to talk to her about how Lucian reacted when I asked him about the scar. "It's not something he could have gotten from shaving. It goes almost from ear to ear. It doesn't look recent, but it must have been a really bad cut. I...asked him about it earlier, and he just froze. It got really tense and then he ended the evening quickly. There is a story there, but I understand enough not to push it. He was really great about my back and about the court papers."

Rose is in the middle of nodding when her eyes widen. "Whoa, what about court papers; what the hell are you talking about?" Had it really just been hours since I was served papers by my absent mother? I haven't even had a chance to tell my best friend.

"When I came home to change clothes today, some guy knocked on the door and served me papers. I called Debra in a panic and found out my stepfather beat my mother up, and she is pressing charges against him this time. I would have been impressed with that if she wasn't dragging me into it. I have to go to court to testify about what a monster he is. I'm not sure how that is possible without admitting she is, as well."

Rose puts her hand over mine, gently stopping my fingers from digging into my palm. "Honey, I'm so sorry. That fucking blows. I can't believe that bitch is doing this to you. Even a dog takes care of their puppies better than that wacko took care of you. I'm so going to go to court with you and kick her ass!" This is one of those moments when I realize how lucky I am to have Rose in my life. She is crude and irreverent, but she would defend and protect me until the end. After a lifetime of being loved by no one, it is still hard for me to accept that someone could care for me. I am so used to handling everything on my own.

"Luc said he would have his lawyer find out what was going on. He promised he wouldn't let anything happen to me." I wait for Rose to jump on this statement, but she simply smiles.

"Well, Lucian...or Luc sounds okay in my book. When can I meet him?" She holds up her hand as if she is taking the witness stand and says, "I pledge to ogle him discreetly. He will never notice when I stare at his ass and his crotch. This will be a total covert mission. I'm just doing this for you."

"Yeah, right," I smirk. "He's going out of town for a few days, so I'm not sure when he will be back. Besides, it's not really normal between us. I don't see him doing a double-date."

"The man is only twenty-nine, Lia; it's not like he is a senior citizen or something. He has to have fun sometime."

I don't know why I'm surprised that she knows his age, but I have to ask. "How do you know how old he is?"

She raises a brow as if to say 'come on'. "I googled him, of course. The man is seriously loaded, and there are like a bazillion hits on him. He's not much for the dog-and-pony show, though. I guess Asheville isn't exactly the hub of socializing, but you would think there would be more pictures of him in a tux with some stick-figure woman on his arm. But there really aren't. There is mostly stuff about his charities and what a walking brainiac he is. If he is a man-whore, he does it out of the spotlight."

Thinking of Lucian with other women makes me want to throw something. Not a good sign when you're just in a 'fuckionship', as Rose calls it. For all I know, he may have rushed me out the door tonight because he had other plans. I know next to nothing about him... well, other than the fact that he fucked Monique. Some part of me understands how she must feel seeing me with him. Wouldn't I turn into a Class – A bitch if that happened to me? He treats her as if she means less than nothing to him. I have to accept the fact that I could be her in the possibly-near future.

CHAPTER NINE

Lia

Lucian has been gone for a week, and I have heard nothing from him. I continue to go to his apartment each day, disappointed when there is no sign he has returned. I have been tempted to make up an excuse to text him but manage to talk myself out of it. Since there is really nothing to clean, I have rearranged his entire CD and DVD collection into alphabetical order. I am just putting the last DVD in place when I hear keys in the door. My body starts tingling, knowing he is near. I reach the foyer just as Lucian walks in. The welcoming smile slides from my lips as I take him in; he looks like walking death. He staggers on his feet as he crosses the threshold, and I rush forward to grab his arm. He seems startled to see me standing there. "Lia...baby, not feeling so good." Before I can reply, Sam steps out from behind him carrying a suitcase and briefcase.

"Hey, Lia. Our man here has the flu. He spent yesterday in the bed at his hotel before losing his mind and flying home today. I pretty much carried him through the airport and to the car." By this time, Lucian has put an arm around my shoulders and is leaning heavily against me. Sam sets the luggage down and takes his other arm. "Let's see if we can get him in the bedroom."

Between both of us, we were able to easily guide him down the hall. Sam braces him against the wall while I turn the bed down. I stand there uncertainly, wondering if I should undress him. Luckily, Lucian seems to recover enough to sit on the bed and take his shoes and shirt off. I quickly find a freshly-laundered pair of lounge pants and t-shirt and put them on the bed beside him.

"Sam, I'm going to run to the store and pick up some supplies for him. Can you stay until I get back?"

Lucian squints up at me, saying, "No, Sam will take you. Don't want you going out alone anymore, not safe." What is he talking about? I thought we had settled the subject of Sam driving me everywhere.

Sam pulls out his keys, obviously agreeing with his boss. "Lia, Lucian has already told me I need to watch out for you. We'll wait until he's in the bed and then go. It won't take long."

"But I don't need to be watched, Sam; I'm an adult." I can tell Sam is uncomfortable being caught in the middle. I also know he will do what Lucian wants; after all, he signs his paychecks.

"Lia," Lucian rasps out, "Worried about your stepdad, please just let Sam do his job. Too tired to argue about it, baby." Well, shit, it seems pretty childish to continue arguing over something so minor with someone so sick. We can take up this discussion again when he is feeling better. Sam looks relieved when I nod my head in agreement.

"Okay. Is there anything in particular you need? I'm going to pick up some ginger ale and Tylenol."

"Sounds good, money in my wallet." Lucian is already snuggling under the covers. I have enough money to buy what he needs; I certainly don't plan on going through his pants pockets. Sam follows me out and grins as I open the front passenger-side door instead of getting in the back.

Soon, we are pulling up to a Walgreens. He insists on going in with me and following me around as I fill the cart with drinks and every flu medication I can find. When I toss two boxes of Kleenex in the cart, Sam shakes his head and adds another. "Trust me, that boy is going to need that and more. He damn near blew the windows of the car out with his sneezes on the way home. I should probably go ahead and warn you, too: he is cranky as hell when he's sick, which thank God isn't often."

Rolling my eyes, I mutter, "Wonderful, that's just what I need to hear." I wonder if Sam thinks it's strange that someone who Lucian hasn't known for long is preparing to take care of him while he was sick. Maybe this isn't unusual in their world. I am probably one of many who have walked in and out of Lucian's life. I am dying to ask Sam, but I figure it's wrong to put him in an awkward position. He insists on paying for the purchases, saying he has an expense account.

When we arrive back at the apartment, Sam carries the bags in while I check on Lucian; he's moving restlessly but is sleeping. I return to the kitchen as Sam finishes unloading the bags. "I'm going to fix him something to drink and try to get some medicine in him when he wakes. Sam, I'll be fine here if you want to leave. It's getting late, and you're probably ready to end your day."

"Are you sure, Lia? I'd be happy to stay if you aren't comfortable handling all this."

Giving him a smile of reassurance, I say, "I'm fine. If I have any problems, I'll call you." I follow Sam out and lock the door behind him. Returning to the kitchen, I fix a glass of ginger ale and a dose of Nyquil Flu and Cold. I am just picking the drink up when I hear a crash, followed by yelling from the bedroom. Heart beating fast, I run in that direction, skidding to a stop as I see Lucian face down on the floor. "Luc! What happened?"

As I drop to my knees and put my hand on his back, I hear, "fuckingfellovermyfuckingshoes." The words are so jumbled I have a hard time figuring out what he's saying. The multiple 'fucks' and something about shoes, I get. Looking down, I saw his shoes from earlier lying between his feet. Shit, he had tripped. Taking his shoulder, I pull on him, trying to help him up; it's like pushing a brick wall with a feather.

"Luc, you've got to work with me here unless you want to sleep on the floor. I can't pick you up on my own." I hear another f-bomb roll out of his mouth before he struggles into a sitting position. I help him lean back on the side of the bed while he regains his strength. His hair is damp and sweaty, and his face is pale. Putting my palm against his forehead, I gasp in surprise at the heat there. I gently smooth his hair back with my hand, whispering, "You're burning up. We need to get some medicine into you. Can you stand?" In response, a shiver racks his body, making his teeth chatter.

Leaning his head against me, he says, "Cold, baby." My heart melts. He looks so much like a sick child cuddling against me for warmth. I want nothing more than to put my arms around him and make it all better. I wonder if there is someone who has more of a right than I do to be taking care of Lucian. Surely, Sam would have mentioned that. I harbor no illusions that just because I had slept with him, I am the only woman in his life. Someone who looks like him couldn't possibly lack for company...ever. I am here, though, and I want...no, I need to be the one to help him.

"Okay, on the count of three, you do your best to stand, and I'll help. One..."

"Have to pee." The bathroom door looks a mile away. Damn, I should have made Sam take him before he left. I can do this. I can do this.

"All right, on the count of three, we go toward the bathroom then." When I hit three, I take a deep breath and stand, pulling on his arm. He doesn't appear to be trying to help at all. It's no secret to any woman that men turn into big babies when they are sick. Jake got the flu last year, and Rose almost strangled him before it was over. A woman can work twelve hours with PMS and a heavy flow and not complain; men can stub their toe and be bedbound for a month. Maybe he needs some reverse motivation. "Luc, you stay right here, and I'll go get a bowl."

He opens one eye, peering up at me. "Bowl?"

Trying to appear nonchalant, I say, "Yep, since you're too weak to make it to the bathroom, I'll just help you pee in a bowl right here. We have to do what we have to do, right?" Oh, please, don't let him agree. I will indeed do it, but I so don't want to…at all. I almost laugh when he starts scowling. Bingo, the male pride has taken a direct hit. He struggles to his feet, weaving slightly. I take his arm, putting it around my shoulders, steering him toward the bathroom door. It's a slow process, but we make it without either of us falling or peeing on ourselves. He falls back against the wall while I lift the toilet lid, praying he only has to pee. Things will get interesting if it's anything else. Looking at his pale face, I give him a bright smile, saying, "You've got this, right? I'll be right outside the door. Just yell when you're finished, and I'll help you back in the bed." As I get to the door, I look back to see him struggling to pull his pants down. Don't those pants have a pee hole? If they do, he seems oblivious. I pause, watching him start to stagger. He's about two seconds from falling into the damn toilet when I straighten my spine and walk back to him. Without saying a word, I reach for his pants and lower them to his knees. I feel like a total pervert when I admire his cock. Even soft, he's big and beautiful. I quickly avert my gaze as he takes it in his hand and what sounds like two gallons of water splashing fills the room. When the sound stops, I pull his pants back up and help him to the sink, washing his hands for him.

He's trembling all over when we finally make it back to his bed. I tuck him under the covers and end up in a less-than-graceful belly flop onto his chest when he didn't release his hold on me. I try to push away, but he only holds tighter. "Stay; you feel so warm."

"Luc," I squeak out, "you need to let me go. I'll get your medicine and a drink and be right back." For a moment, I think he's going to refuse, but his arms drop limply away, and I pull back before he changes his mind. Running back to the kitchen, I pick up the abandoned glass and Nyquil, hurrying with it to the bedroom. I sit beside him, putting a pillow under his head so he can drink the liquid medication, followed by a few sips of ginger ale. He's still shivering, so I find another blanket in the closet, tucking it in around his shoulders.

He grabs my hand as I'm pulling away. "Sleep with me, Lia; so fucking cold." The school required flu shots so I have had mine, but I'm not sure it will help if I am in such close contact with him. The sound of his teeth chattering makes up my mind. I quickly pull my shoes off and crawl in the other side of the bed. Lucian immediately seeks my warmth, pulling my back firmly to his front, sighing against my neck. The feel of his breath on the sensitive area along with his firm body is enough to make my panties go damp. Lucian might be physically sick, but it appears I am mentally sick if I'm lusting after someone as ill as he is. A yawn escapes my mouth as I settle against him. It's a little after nine, early for bedtime, but it looks like I'm going to sleep; I don't want to disturb Lucian with the noise of the television.

Sometime later, I wake to the sounds of Lucian choking; I know instinctively he's dreaming as he did the last time we were together. "Luc," I say quietly, trying not to startle him. "Luc, wake up. You're dreaming." When he doesn't respond, I put my hand on his head, starting to gently run my fingers through the thick, damp strands. "Shhhh, it's okay. You're safe; no one is going to hurt you, Luc." He continues to struggle for a few minutes more before my voice and the comfort of my hand seem to reach him. As the horrible sounds stop emitting from his throat, I slowly settle my body back against his. Instead of turning away, I bring my arms around him until I am stroking his back soothingly. His head still feels hot against my neck as he turns into my body, seeking the comfort of my arms. "I've got you, baby; go back to sleep." The endearment slips out in the dark, feeling foreign but somehow right on my tongue. His arms lift, pulling me into him. Soon, the soft sounds of his snores vibrate in my ear, but still he holds me as if holding onto a lifeline. I have spent my whole life searching for shelter from the storms that chase me, so I give him what he needs without reservation, holding him tightly the rest of the night.

Lucian

The room is spinning, and I have an overwhelming desire to puke. Fuck, have I passed out drunk? The room finally comes back into focus, and my stomach quiets as the spinning slows to a ripple. I try to move, but there is a weight on my chest and my legs are wrapped around something...or someone. Tentatively, I look down to see blonde hair. Lia? Shit, the way I feel, I'm not even sure. My hand slides under the cover, coming to rest on the curve of an ass my body recognizes. Yeah, Lia. Even though I feel like I have been beat to shit with a steel bat, my body stirs as it always does when she's anywhere in the vicinity. When her body shifts, pushing her tits into my stomach and her pussy against my cock, I groan, waking her. "Luc," she croaks, her voice heavy and husky. The sun coming in through the blinds slants across her beautiful face, filled with concern. "How are you feeling? Do you need me to get you something?"

A harsh laugh escapes my lips. How I feel is like shit, what I need is to fuck her until I either pass out or die; either way, I'll go happy. "Yeah, baby, I need that sweet pussy all over my lips. Just fucking sit on my face and give it to me hard." When she jerks back as if she has been slapped, I know I've actually given voice to my dirty thoughts. Fucking hell, the jig is up. Any illusions she's been harboring about me being a nice, but horny, guy are over. I'm a dirty motherfucker who thinks about doing equally-dirty things to her pussy most of the damn day and night. After she does a bang-up imitation of an owl for another minute, peals of laughter fill the room.

"Well, I see you are feeling better this morning. You've been so sick that, trust me when I say, even if I sat on your face, you'd probably fall asleep before the first lick."

The fuck? Why wasn't she running in horror? Most of the rich bitches I've slept with want their sex straight up; no kink. Even the cock-gobbler Monique is a fan of plain missionary. The women Aidan and I shared...now, they're a different story. If you are willing to let two men fuck you at once, you don't have many hang-ups, but then again, that's not something that appeals to most women. I'd half-expected Lia to freak out when I had fucked her from behind in my kitchen, especially being as inexperienced as she was, but she seemed to love it.

She's right about one thing now, though: I'm as weak as a newborn kitten. But I'm not ready to give up. "You could fuck me," I suggest, curious as to her reaction.

Sitting back on her heels, she nods as if actually considering it. "Yes, I could...but I'm not going to. You've been in the bed for two days, Luc, and another day before you flew home. Other than fluids, you haven't had anything to eat in days, so I know you're weak. How about I fix you some toast for breakfast?" Toast seems to be code for no pussy.

Suddenly, it all comes back to me. Sickness had hit me like a sledgehammer. I'd woken up in a strange room, too weak to move. How I had even made it to the airport and onto my plane is a mystery. I remember Sam coming on board and half-carrying me to the car. Then I recall only bits and pieces of Lia stroking my forehead with a washcloth or helping me drink. I also vaguely remember holding her to me while I tossed and turned. Shit, she has been taking care of me for days, I assume. The look of tender amusement she is giving me now makes me shift uncomfortably. How have things gotten this far out of hand? She is now officially my longest relationship in eight years. Even if I don't want to admit it, I know why I was drawn to her; hell, even Aidan knows why. I'd never intended for things to go beyond sex with her. Goddammit, though, she has something none of the other women I've dated in years had; she needs protection and that fucking slayed me. Her being my housekeeper is complete bullshit. I allowed her in my home because I want her here, and she needs a reason for it to be acceptable for me to take care of her.

How many women would have spent two days taking care of a virtual stranger? I remember enough to know that not only has she watched over me, she has cared for me. It's been a long time since I've allowed someone to be around me while I'm vulnerable. Well, I didn't exactly have much of a choice in the matter since I'd been so fucking sick, but I had let her stay and so had Sam, which certainly said something. Sam, Cindy, and Aidan are not only employees; they are family. We might fight amongst ourselves, but we are also fiercely protective of each other. Sam would never leave some random woman in my house while I'm too out of it to know what's going on. They all know I don't bring women here. I should probably fire his ass, but strangely enough, I'm glad. Sometimes there is no replacement for a woman's touch. At times, I've missed having someone around other than my small circle of friends.

I'm abruptly pulled from my thoughts by Lia's small hand pulling on my toe. "Hello? Are you sleeping with your eyes open or just trying to ignore me?"

Giving her a lazy grin, I let my eyes slide leisurely up and down her body, pausing to admire the way my t-shirt outlines her tits. What man isn't turned on by a woman wearing his clothes? "I could never ignore you, sweet Lia. I was just working out the details of you sitting on my..."

She sticks her hand up, yelling, "Stop! Don't finish that sentence. That is not on the menu for you this morning. The only thing I need to know from you is whether you would like scrambled eggs with your toast."

We both know what I want to say, but I decide to take mercy on her and myself, as well. Unless she is willing to do most of the work, I don't have it in me yet to fuck her, no matter how much I want to. "Yeah, baby, I'd like some eggs."

"Coming up. Just stay here, and I'll bring a tray when everything is ready." She jumps from the bed, and I bite my lip as the luscious curve of her ass peeks out from under my shirt when she bends to slip what appears to be a pair of my socks on her feet. If she doesn't leave the room soon, I will be begging her to ride my exhausted body.

Easing to the edge of the bed, I put my feet on the floor and stand on shaky legs. The room spins for a moment before righting itself. It takes much longer than usual, but I use the toilet, brush my teeth, and cringe at my reflection in the mirror. Even if I have to crawl, I am taking a shower after breakfast. Maybe I can play on Lia's sympathy and talk her into taking one with me. There are worse things in the world than having a beautiful woman wash your cock. If the twitching in that region is anything to go by, my cock completely agrees.

The kitchen seems miles away as I make my way slowly there. Lia is humming while scrambling enough eggs to feed an army. My stomach growls in response to the smell of food after days without it. I pull a stool out and slump in it. Damn, am I actually sweating just from that small amount of activity? I must look as washed out as I feel, because Lia turns, giving me a look filled with sympathy. "It's almost ready. Do you want butter on your toast?" When I nod, she slathers it on several pieces before reaching up to get glasses out of the cabinet. Her shirt once again rides up, and I grit my teeth. It's no myth; men are horny in the morning, and even sick, the urge to spread her out over this very counter I'm sitting at is strong. Instead, I push my throbbing cock down from where it seems to be trying to break out of the top of my lounge pants.

Lia puts a plate of perfectly-cooked eggs, toast, and bacon before me. She adds a tall glass of orange juice and a jar of strawberry jelly. In what is probably an embarrassing display of table manners, I attack the plate like a starving animal. When I've devoured everything in record time, she silently refills it. I grimace as I note her full plate. "Sorry about that; I guess I was hungrier than I thought." Now that the empty feeling has been sated, I resume my breakfast at a more-leisurely pace. "What day is it?" Man, when was the last time I had to ask that? I wonder if she should be in class this morning instead of cooking for me.

"It's Sunday. Sam brought you home on Friday evening while I was here cleaning up. Other than me waking you for medicine, fluids, and um...the bathroom, you slept right through until this morning."

It's unsettling to think of losing so much time. My last solid memories are of meetings with some of my development team in our New York office. I haven't had the flu in years, and it completely kicked my ass. Sam had it last year and, truthfully, I'd wondered why it had taken him an entire week to recover. Hell, I understood now.

I look across the counter at Lia, taking in her beautifully mussed appearance. Her long blonde hair is in a lopsided ponytail on the top of her head...in a bread tie? Her face, devoid of makeup, is flawless. Her blue eyes sparkle, framed by thick lashes, and my shirt collar hangs off one side, exposing the creamy flesh of her shoulder. Most women I know would never be seen in front of a man in less-than-perfect condition, but Lia doesn't act self-conscious at all; actually, she looks completely comfortable. After seeing me at my worst for the last few days, she probably figures it doesn't really fucking matter anymore, and I like that. Clearing my throat, I say, "Thank you for taking care of me. I...hope I didn't ruin any plans you might have had."

She takes a sip of her orange juice, seeming pleased by my words. "You're welcome. I'm glad I could help, and no, I didn't have any plans. I usually spend the weekend studying, doing laundry, and visiting Debra if I have time."

"No big parties? Isn't that the best part of college?" I tease.

She shakes her head, and somehow I already know she isn't a typical college student. "Nah, that's not really my thing. I have gone to a few parties with Rose when she refused to take no for an answer, but I don't enjoy that kind of thing. I'd rather curl up with a good book than watch a bunch of drunks making fools of themselves. I...didn't have many friends growing up, so crowds kind of bother me."

The pain that crosses her face is impossible to miss. I find myself wanting to comfort her, wanting to kill the fucker who put that look there. "Tell me about your life growing up, Lia. Were there good times for you?" She looks agitated, and it's on the tip of my tongue to tell her to forget my question when she starts talking.

"Good times? No, there were none of those. There were moments that weren't as bad as others. My real father was never in my life, and my mother spent her whole life reminding me of how I ruined everything for her. I don't know why she didn't just give me away; we would have both been better off."

Dreading the answer, I ask, "Did she beat you?"

Lia shrugs her slim shoulders saying, "She smacked me around, slapped my face when she was angry, threatened me, insulted me. Just depended on her mood."

"What about your stepfather? Did he hit you?" I already knew the bastard had scarred her back.

"He, um...threw things at me sometimes. Like beer cans, and he liked to slap my butt and insult me."

"And he never raped you?" Even though I have asked her this before, I need to clarify it. She is tiny and would have been so easy for someone to take advantage of, especially a drunk bastard like her stepfather.

"No...I told you I took care of that." She shuts her eyes, and I curse as a tear leaks out.

"How, baby? How did you stop him?" I ask softly.

She wipes her cheeks, turning her head away. "He was constantly insulting women who weren't stick-thin. He rode my mother about her weight. He had...started making comments to me about my body and touching me in small ways at every opportunity. I knew what was coming unless I did something. So, I started to eat...to gorge, until I gained so much weight I barely recognized myself anymore. Kids at school made fun of me, but it worked. He was completely repulsed. I could handle all of his cruel jokes and insults if it meant he wouldn't touch me in that way, and he didn't. Eating myself half to death saved me. He and my mother sat around laughing, calling me every version of fat they could think of, but he wasn't interested in...anything sexual with me. I saved myself."

I drop my head into my hands, not wanting her to see how her story moves me. What girl that age has to come up with ways to make sure the people who are supposed to protect her don't violate her instead? My lonely life growing up without my parents suddenly pales in comparison to what she has faced. "How about the burn? How did that happen?"

She shudders, and I feel like a bastard for making her talk about something so painful. "It was right before my mother kicked me out. They were fighting and I was doing the laundry. He was mad and drunk. I was using the iron when they came in and I set it down, trying to leave before they noticed me. He...somehow burnt his hand on it, and he was so mad. My mom ran out when he turned his attention to me." A tear slips down her face as she continues. "He told me not to worry about him touching me, but that I needed something to remember who I belonged to. Co—Cows are branded by their owner. Oh, God, I just remember the smell, the awful smell. Then the pain; my whole body was on fire."

"Fuck," I spit out, so angry on her behalf that I want to rip someone's head off. And now her cunt of a mother wants to put her daughter right back in the line of fire again? I've already got my lawyer looking into it; now I plan to have my investigator find out more about the fuckers who put a poor, innocent girl through Hell. I pick up her hand, stroking the soft skin. "How did you make it this far on your own, baby?"

She uses her other hand to wipe the moisture from her eyes before answering. "I applied to every college around during my last year of high school. I was offered a full scholarship to St. Claire's and was just trying to make it at home until school started. I hadn't really thought of all the other expenses outside of what was covered. When my mom kicked me out, I was lucky enough to meet Debra, who you spoke with on the phone, and get a job at a diner she owns. She and her boyfriend Martin helped me so much. I...worked there and lived in my car to save money for school."

My stomach flops, and I feel bile rising as I gape at her. "You lived in your car? I thought you said they helped you. How is that help?" I know my voice is rising when she flinches away. I lower it, fighting for control. "Honey, I'm sorry. I'm just trying to understand."

"Debra asked me to stay with her;" she says quietly, "but I...just didn't trust anyone at that point. I had the car I had bought from her, and at least it was mine. I spent a lot of time at the library and the break room at work, so I wasn't really living in the car. When school finally started, all my savings went so fast. Debra tried to loan me money, but again, I just couldn't take it. My roommate told me about *Date Night* where she was working, and well...you know the rest."

Indeed, I fucking do, and it makes me furious on her behalf all over again. I am stunned to know all she has gone through. It's amazing she has made it to her last year in college, all on her own, after living in a fucking car. "Have you seen or heard from your mother since you left, or your stepfather?" She shakes her head slowly.

"No, I don't know how they found me; I've been so careful to stay away from areas I know they frequent. St. Claire's is miles away from where they live, and I've never known them to have any business around here."

"Honey, thanks to the internet, finding someone is nothing anymore." She looks terrified at my words, and I scramble to reassure her. "I don't want you to worry about them, okay? I have my people on this. If you do have to go to court, you'll be well-protected, and you'll have someone there to watch out for your interests."

She squeezes my hand back, looking so fragile in that moment. "Thank you, Luc. I'm sorry to put this on you. This probably wasn't what you were expecting when you asked me out." She is right about that, but in a different way than she means. She is so much more than I was expecting, and I'm freaking reeling from it. Her story, though different, is eerily familiar to me. The need to protect her is overwhelming. The lines between her and my past are blurred further as I'm drawn to her, fucking lost in my desire for her.

When she stands to start cleaning up the kitchen, I silently collect our plates and help her load the dishwasher. When we are finished, I take her hand and tug her back toward the bedroom. "Come rest with me for a while." She settles next to me without protest, and I pull the comforter over us. I'm still too tired to touch her like I want, so instead, I settle for curving my body around hers, shuddering as she tucks her tight ass against my groin. I push up my shirt she is wearing and feather my fingers over her stomach. The sound of her soft breathing lulls me into sleep. When I wake in the evening, she is gone, leaving a note on the pillow saying she has gone home to get ready for school tomorrow. The smell of her scent on the pillow beside me makes me feel something I haven't admitted to feeling in a while: lonely.

CHAPTER TEN

Lia

As I sit through my last class of the morning, I accept the simple truth: I'm dying. There is no other explanation for it. My throat is on fire, my body aches, and my head is pounding. I'm barely able to keep myself upright in my chair. When I woke this morning, I was tired. I blamed it on worrying about Luc all night and not sleeping well. Now, I think it's something more. This isn't simple fatigue; I suspect it's the flu. Spending almost three days in constant close proximity with someone contagious was not my brightest moment. The flu shot isn't going to save me this time; I can only hope it shortens the duration as it promises to.

When the class ends, I close my eyes for a moment, trying to gather the strength to walk home. Oh, dear God, how far away am I? Squaring my shoulders, I stumble to my feet and sway for a moment before catching myself. I can do this...I have no choice. It's a painfully slow process, but I make my way through the hallway and outside. The fresh air on my face revives me only slightly but also sends a shiver through my body. I know I'm running a fever; I feel it burning through my body.

I have no idea how long it takes me, but I finally make it to my apartment. The stairs are sheer Hell, and I have to stop every few steps. Finally, a few from the top, I give into the urge to crawl. The door is another struggle, but soon the keys are in the lock and its opening. I have no idea if it even closes behind me; at this point, no one could do anything worse to me than what I'm already feeling. I face-plant onto my bed, and that is all I know. Dimly, I'm aware of something chiming over and over, but I'm too out of it to care. Surely, someone will answer the damn phone at some point.

Something cool touches my face and I gasp in shock. My eyes are blurry as I try to focus. Someone is bashing my skull and I moan, wanting to beg for mercy. "Baby, can you hear me?" Despite the fog surrounding me, I know that voice and turn instinctively toward it. "Lia, baby, wake up." He sounds upset and even in my state, I am worried about him.

As my eyes blink open, I see Lucian bending over me, concern etched deeply in his face. Behind him is...Sam? Where am I and what are they doing here? "Sick..." I mumble the obvious.

"Baby, I know you are. I'm going to take you home now. Just try to hold on to me, okay? Let me know if you need to stop." I groan as Lucian puts his hands under me, gently lifting me into his arms. I am surprised to see a shocked-looking Rose and Jake standing just outside my bedroom door as Lucian carries me past. He stops and says something to them I don't catch, and they nod before he walks on. At least their presence answers one question: we are at my apartment.

Lucian takes each step slowly as I lay weakly against him. When we reach the sidewalk, Sam runs ahead and opens the back door of the Mercedes. I have no idea how he does it, but Lucian manages to slide in the seat without releasing his hold on me. As my teeth start chattering, he pulls me closer, folding me against his chest and wrapping his suit jacket around me as best he can. "Where?" I say against his throat, but he seems to know what I'm asking.

"I'm taking you home with me. Fuck, you about gave me a heart attack. I've been calling and texting you for hours and you weren't answering. When you didn't show at the apartment either, I knew something was wrong. I was afraid..."

As out of it as I am, I know what he was worried about; he was afraid my stepfather had harmed me. "S'ok...I got sick during class. Don't know how I made it home."

"When I got to your apartment, your roommate was freaking out. You left the front door open, your keys were in the lock, and your purse was lying on the floor. She was getting ready to call the police, because she thought someone had either taken you or had you inside. Sam and I found you passed out on the bed, burning the fuck up. It's the first time I've ever been grateful someone had the flu, because the alternative would have been so much worse."

"I'm sorry," I whisper. His strong body is tense beneath my hands as I try to soothe him. I don't know why he's so upset, but I feel guilty for doing this to him. He doesn't answer; he just pulls me closer and rests his chin against the top of my head. I drift as the car moves quietly through the night. If I know nothing else, I know Lucian will take care of me.

When we reach his apartment, despite my weak protests, he again carries me. Sam opens the door before asking which room Lucian is taking me to. "My room," Lucian answers and Sam walks ahead, turning a bedside lamp on as Lucian deposits me gently on the edge. Sam leaves and returns with a glass of water and a bottle of medicine. Lucian coaxes a couple down my throat and I choke on the water before catching my breath. "Sam, you can go now. I think we still have enough supplies here."

"All right, Luc. Could you call me later and let me know how Miss Lia is doing?" When Lucian agrees, Sam walks out of the bedroom, and I slump backwards on the bed.

"Just kill me now," I groan; at this point, death would be a welcome respite. Just as I feel myself starting to drift off again, Lucian is pulling me back up into a sitting position as I feebly try to push him away.

"Come on, baby; let me get you into something more comfortable, and you can go to sleep."

Opening one eye, I peer up at him. "If you think you're getting sex, you are out of your mind." I sound like someone fresh off a two-week drunk. He looks down at me, seeming to be trying to contain the smile pulling at his lips.

"I'll try to control myself until you are upright. Now, just sit there and let me get you changed." Like a child, I let him lift my arms, pulling off my shirt and despite my weak protests, my bra follows next. He puts one of his soft t-shirts over my head before kneeling at my feet to remove my shoes and pants. Thankfully, he leaves my panties on, although at this point, I wouldn't have fought for them. He pulls back the covers and tucks me in on his side of the bed. I inhale appreciatively as his scent clings to the pillow. He asks if I need anything, but I wave him away, only wanting to sleep. I wonder for a moment why I'm here. Why would he want to take care of me? Maybe just returning the favor. My thoughts spin away as sleep once again claims me.

I moan as something cool strokes across my cheeks. "Feels so good," I groan. When a straw slips between my dry lips, I drink greedily; the feel of the cold liquid against my throat is Heaven. When the straw is pulled away, I reach out, trying to bring it back.

"Not too much, baby; it might make you sick." Oh, that voice. Shivers run down my spine as I blink my eyes open to see a casual Lucian sitting beside me, tousled hair and a five o'clock shadow darkening his handsome face. I want to climb him like a tree and eat him up. He looks down at me for a moment, giving me a sexy grin; he seems to know exactly what I'm thinking. He curls a strand of my blonde hair around his finger, asking, "How're you feeling?"

I lie there for a moment, taking stock of my body. The throbbing in my head is down to a dull thud, and my throat, although dry and scratchy, is no longer sore. I still feel like I've been run over by a car, but it's progress. "Better," I croak out around the cotton in my mouth. He gives me another sip of what I recognize as ginger ale. "How long have I been in bed?" It's a strange feeling to lose awareness of day and time, and I'm desperate to fill in the blanks.

"I picked you up Monday afternoon, and now it's Wednesday morning, so not too long."

"Oh, shit," I try to jump from the bed. "I've got a class this morning, a test...I've got to go." Lucian puts a hand on my chest, effectively holding me down. Just that small amount of effort has winded me, and I lie back against the pillow exhausted.

"Not today, Lia. You're still too weak to go anywhere. We'll see tomorrow after another day in bed and some food."

Giving him my best innocent look, I say, "Maybe you could just take me home then? I can rest there, and I'll be closer to school in the morning."

He tweaks my nose playfully saying, "Good try, but no. You'll just crawl to your class if you are close enough. I'm afraid you're here today."

My bottom lip rolls out and to my horror, I'm pouting. "Don't you have to go to work? I can be at home alone just as well as I can here."

"I do have to go in for a meeting this morning," he admits, "but then I'll work from home the rest of the day as I did yesterday." Surprised, I turn to stare at him.

"You stayed home with me yesterday?" Is it my imagination or does he look uncomfortable at the question?

"Well, I could hardly bring you home with me and then leave you, could I?" Suddenly, images of how I had taken care of him run through my mind. Oh, dear God, surely he hasn't taken me to the bathroom. I can't remember anyone ever doing such personal things for me.

"So...was I really out of it? I mean, did you have any trouble...taking care of me?" He gives me an uncomfortable look...is he blushing? Oh, no, it must be worse than I thought if he is embarrassed about something. Even though I'm curious, I don't want to know. I'd rather believe I woke up from my flu-induced daze to take care of my own business each time it was needed.

He avoids my questions and stands. "I'm going to fix you some breakfast in bed and then catch a shower. I'll be back soon." When I hear him in the kitchen, I exit the bed as quickly as possible in my weakened state and use the bathroom. I finger-brush my teeth and consider a shower before deciding to wait until Lucian is gone.

He has nothing but a comb in his bathroom cabinet, and I do my best to pull it through my hair, wincing as it catches on tangles. Looking around the bathroom, I search for something to put my hair up with; hiding the mess is the only answer. I find a roll of dental floss and pull out enough to make a three-ply string. It's not easy, and my arms are shaking from the effort, but soon I have something that resembles a ponytail on the top of my head. It will have to do until I can find something better.

When I walk back in the bedroom, he is standing beside the bed holding a tray. For a moment, I have an overwhelming urge to cry. People just don't do things like this for me. It's surreal, but so sweet I am choked up. Luckily, he blames my glassy eyes on the flu and actually clucks his tongue at me for getting out of bed. Turning away, I crawl back under the covers, pulling them up so he can deposit the tray on my lap. Holding up a phone, he says, "I picked up a charger for your phone yesterday and let it charge overnight. I'll leave it here in case you need it." I thank him, touched by how much trouble he had gone through for me. "You might want to call your friend Rose today; she has been blowing the damn thing up. I don't think she believes me when I say you're okay."

"Crap, I'll do that first thing. She isn't used to me having...help." We both decide to let it go at that, knowing full well what I mean. "So," I say brightly, "the food looks great." He has made toast, juice, and eggs; it's the same thing I fed him a few days before.

While I pick up the fork and eat a bit of the eggs, he studies my face and hair. When he touches my ponytail, I try to pull away. "Is that...dental floss?" At my nod, he starts laughing. "Boy, you make use of whatever you have, don't you? First, a bread tie and now dental floss. Am I going to come home one day to find my underwear in your hair?"

Childishly, I stick my tongue out, which only serves to amuse him further. I watch him as I sip my juice. You would never know he had been sick just a few days prior. "You look like you feel better," I remark.

"Pretty much back to normal," he agrees. "It's been years since I've been sick enough to stay in bed for more than a day." His eyes seem to drift away after that statement, and I wonder what has put that faraway look on his face. When my eyes slip down to the scar on his neck, I wonder if that is the memory he is thinking of. Surely, an injury like that had required a hospital stay. Without thinking, I stroke the top of the hand resting next to mine, and he jumps noticeably. He had been far away, and he is distant now, looking but not really seeing me. "I've got to get ready if I'm going to make my meeting," he says lightly as he stands. Before I can reply, he takes some clothing from his closet and shuts the bathroom door behind him. It makes me angry to think of someone hurting him physically. In such a short amount of time, I have become protective of this beautiful but complex man. If I never saw him again after today, I would still be forever grateful that for once in my life, someone had made me feel protected and cared for.

When he walks from the bathroom a short time later, fully dressed in a form-fitting suit and tie, my mouth drops open, and I literally drool all over the bed covers. I've never felt sexual desire like I do when he is near. I shift my legs together, trying to ease the throbbing of my clit. My body knows its master, and every part of me is begging for his attention. At that moment, he could fuck me in any way he wanted to, and I'd beg for more. As he moves closer, my eyes roll back in my head; he smells even better than he looks. I'm so horny; I fight a battle to keep from leaping into his arms and wrapping my legs around his waist. As he leans over to remove the tray from my lap, his eyes lock on mine and he knows. His pupils dilate and his nostrils flare as if smelling my arousal. I grip his silk tie as he remains frozen over me, the tray all but forgotten between us. When I lick my suddenly dry lips, he groans as if in pain. "So...I guess you have to go to work now?"

"I guess so," he agrees, making no move to pull away. He runs his thumb along my bottom lip, and I part my mouth, licking the tip. He stares as if mesmerized before slipping his finger inside, saying hoarsely, "Suck it." I have no idea what comes over me, but I suck his thumb deeper, swirling my tongue around the tip before nipping it. He jerks back in surprise and an apology hovers on my lips. He takes his injured thumb and sucks it into his mouth, never breaking eye contact with me. "You're fucking killing me here." Unable to resist, my eyes lower to his crotch and the impressive tent there; he isn't lying, I am getting to him. He clears his throat, and I look up to find him smirking knowingly at me. "That's right, baby; when I get back, you'll suck that, too, so get some rest." With those words, he removes the tray from my lap and leaves the room. A few moments later, I hear the front door slam, and I slump back onto the pillows, using a shaking hand to fan myself.

Suddenly, I'm dying to touch myself. The need to touch my clit and put a finger inside my aching sex is almost overwhelming. The thought of masturbating in Lucian's bed is dirty...but erotic. Just imagining his reaction if he found out is enough to have my hand lowering, stroking myself through the damp material of my panties. I let out a moan that echoes through the empty apartment. The sound of an incoming text from my phone brings my wandering hand to a halt. Using my free hand, I grab my phone, looking at the screen.

LUCIAN: You better not touch yourself while I'm gone.

Wildly, I look around the room, almost expecting to see him standing there, but he isn't. He couldn't possibly know what I'm doing. This is just some kind of twisted foreplay.

LIA: I'm sleeping, sicko.

I chuckle at my clever reply.

LUCIAN: Liar. You're touching that sweet pussy. Do you want to be fucked with my tongue, baby?

OH. MY. GOD. No one has ever talked dirty to me the way he does, and it drives me out of my mind. The things he makes me crave should embarrass me, but they don't. The fact that he lets me see how much he wants me gives me confidence I've never had. We are both scarred, and maybe that is what draws us to each other like a moth to the flame.

Lia: Yes, I need you...

My answer, though short and simple, is completely honest; I need all he will give me. We are miles apart in every way, but he was there when I needed him, he took care of me, and now I desperately need the physical connection to him.

Lucian: Me too, baby. I'll be home around noon. Be laying on the chaise in the living room. I want you completely naked with your legs

spread and your ass at the end. You better be wet and swollen, or I'll know you touched yourself.

I'm panting as I read his text. How can he say stuff like that and expect me not to touch myself? I need an orgasm the way an addict needs his next fix. Can you die of sexual frustration, because I feel like I'm close.

Lia: I'll try my best to wait.

I hope he knows I'm being honest and not trying to taunt him. I'm in such agony that agreeing to wait seems impossible. I'm also shocked at how easily I'm discussing something this personal with him.

Lucian: If you're a good girl, I'll eat you for lunch. If you're a bad girl, I'll jack off on your tits and leave you to suffer all night.

The breath leaves my body in a painful whoosh. Instead of being intimidated, I'm gushing between my thighs. How will I ever make it?

Lia: Stop talking to me! I'm going to shower, you evil man.

He doesn't reply to my text. He is probably laughing his ass off over getting me so worked up, then telling me to wait three hours for relief. Insults fly from my mouth as I stomp to the shower. I can't handle it cold, but even warm, it's a much-needed distraction. My nipples are hard as stone as I run the soap over them lightly. I make quick work of the rest of my body; my skin is too sensitive to handle the texture of the washcloth.

When I have toweled off and dried my hair, I pull another of Lucian's shirts from his closet and settle back against the headboard in his bed. I need to rest before Lucian comes home; I have a feeling I'll need it. Turning on the television, I flip channels until I find Cartoon Network. There is nothing remotely stimulating about children's television, so I should be safe. A PG-rated love scene right now would send me over the edge in five seconds flat.

Lucian

A raging hard-on digging into my zipper has become way too familiar lately. I had intended to keep things smooth and easy with Lia for a while, but that's fucked now. I hadn't counted on wanting her this much. I spend too much time thinking of ways to get inside that tight little body of hers. Part of me wants to fuck her out of my system and part of me wants to fuck her further into my life. The one thing both parts were in agreement on was the fucking.

If not for the damn meeting this morning I had cancelled the previous morning, I would be balls-deep in her right now, pinning her to the bed. She is an innocent, but the fire burns bright within her. She is a man's dream come true. A woman who knows almost nothing about sex, but has the desire and instincts of a whore. She'd never be one, though; she would just make the lucky bastard in her life want to drop to his knees in gratitude.

One thing that surprises me is how much I enjoy just talking to her, being with her. The shit she finds around my house to put her hair up in is fucking hysterical. Watching this beautiful butterfly come out of her cocoon fascinates me. I am enthralled by her and scared out of my ever-loving mind.

I had waited around for her Monday morning since she usually came by the apartment before her first class. When she didn't show up, I assumed her schedule changed and went on to work. I texted her a couple times during the day...and nothing. I told myself she had probably forgotten her phone, but I was uneasy and not getting a damn thing done at work. At four, I had given up the battle and had Sam bring the car around. When I reached my apartment, Lia wasn't there, nor had she been there. I'd texted and called her a dozen times before having Sam take me to her apartment. Her roommate had been standing outside of their door freaking out. She didn't know who the hell I was but seemed relieved to have someone take charge. If she found it odd that I walked straight to Lia's room without asking, she didn't mention it.

The fear that Lia's stepfather had harmed her was riding me heavily; I wanted to lose my shit just as bad as her roommate did. My heart almost stopped when I saw her small body, face down on her bed, eerily still. I stood locked in place for a moment, looking for visible signs of injury. When she shifted slightly on the bed, everyone in the room seemed to release a breath. It took me two seconds to reach her and roll her gently over. Heat emanated from her body in waves; she was fucking burning up. Without asking, Sam brought me a cool cloth, telling me to wipe her face with it. This seemed to bring her around slightly and as I started talking, her head followed my voice. "Baby, can you hear me?"

Sam dropped his hand on my shoulder, saying, "Luc, I'm thinking she caught the flu from you. That is pretty much how you were when I got you home from the airport. She needs something for the fever and a few days in bed. Do you want me to go to the store and pick up some stuff while you get her settled?"

"I'm not leaving her here. She's coming home with me so I can take care of her." Sam looked surprised but learned long ago to adjust quickly. Her roommate's mouth has dropped open at my statement, and she looks nervous.

"I...um...who are you? I mean...you're the God, obviously, but I'm not sure if Lia should leave with you while she's sick."

I brushed off her concern, saying, "Lia should leave with me precisely because she's sick. She'll call you when she's feeling better." I pull out my wallet and hand her one of my business cards. "If you need anything, just call my office, and they'll get a message to me." Before she can object further, I lift Lia in my arms and carry her down to my car.

Over the next couple of days, I do stuff for a woman I've never done before; I change her clothes, sponge off her face, sit her on the toilet and hold her in place so she doesn't fall off onto the floor. I coax medicine down her throat, and hold her in my arms when she's burning with fever but freezing to death. Then I do it all over again...and again. There is one bonus, though: she is fucking adorable on Nyquil. I don't think she even remembers how she would talk ninety miles a minute and suddenly pass out in mid-sentence. I swear, one moment, she was asking me a question and before I could get the answer out, she was snoring with her mouth hanging open. One of the funniest things I've ever witnessed.

The office is in some kind of uproar, though. After being out sick a few days myself, then staying home to be with Lia, Cindy is convinced I have some kind of terminal illness I'm not telling them about. Aidan is also calling every hour, 'just checking in.' Yeah, when the hell has he called that much in a twenty-four hour period? Sam is the only one who actually believes me since he has been witness to most of it. It doesn't say much for me as a person if those closest to me can't freaking grasp that I could care about someone enough to doctor them back to health. Maybe care isn't the right word; returning the favor might be more accurate. It is definitely less terrifying.

Well, fuck, Aidan is standing on the sidewalk smoking when Sam drops me at the curb. Being interrogated before I even walk in the door is not something I'm looking forward to. "Hey, man." He grins, taking in my impatient stance.

"Aidan," I say in return. Looking at my watch, I add, "We've got a meeting in twenty minutes. Are you ready?"

He almost looks offended as he says, "Of course, aren't I always? We should be wrapping up around lunch; where do you want Cindy to make reservations?"

"Wherever you want. I'm leaving as soon as we are finished." Aidan takes another drag off the cigarette as he seems to consider my answer.

"The girl still sick then?" I know him well. His manner looks casual and relaxed, but he's anything but.

"She's better. I'm going to work from home again this afternoon just in case."

I jerk in shock when he growls, "What about Cassie? You replace her with a new-and-improved model?" As the shock wears off, I want to take my friend and pummel his ass right where he stands. How dare he ask me that; how fucking dare the bastard.

"That's none of your goddamn business. Lia has nothing to do with that."

Aidan, ever the chameleon, smiles, slapping me on the back. "Sure, I didn't mean anything by it. Just seems this girl is different for you. Strangely familiar, you know?" He stubs his cigarette out under his toe,

saying, "I'm just going to get a cup of coffee before
coming up." He walks off looking agitated. No matter
how many years we have been friends, Cassie is
always between us. For Aidan, she'll always be the one
who got away. I wonder if he would still carry that
fantasy in his head and his heart if he had been the
one involved with her beyond friendship. I barely
survived her love, and God knows I hadn't been as
emotionally invested as Aidan. Maybe if I had, things
would have ended differently. Who the hell knows; it's
too damn painful to even think about, and it's been
done to death already.

I make it to my office after collecting some messages
from Cindy. She, too, asks about Lia, but seems
genuinely concerned. I'm sure Sam has given her all
the details by now. She is probably just thrilled to see
I've been with the same woman for more than a week.
The urge to snort a line is strong as I shut the door
behind me, but I refrain; I need to stop using it as a
crutch to deal with everything that is fucked-up in my
life. Maybe that resolve comes from imagining what
Lia would think if she knew. Of course, with her
screwed-up background, it would take a lot to surprise
her.

Cindy buzzes my phone to let me know everyone is
in the conference room. I wonder fleetingly what I'll
find when I get home. Shifting my hard cock to a more-
comfortable position, I walk toward the door. Time to
take care of business so I can get out of here and see
what's waiting for me at home.

CHAPTER ELEVEN

Lia

"Well, I don't believe it. Look who finally learned how to use a phone." Uh oh, do I detect a tone of sarcasm in Rose's voice when she answers on the first ring. "Do you have any idea how close I've been to calling the cops to come rescue your ass? Jake had almost convinced me you were in a ditch somewhere, dead and dismembered. I kept holding out hope you were just being held hostage as a sex slave." I start laughing, liking her idea better than she could ever know.

"I'm sorry. I should have called you sooner. Truthfully, I have been out of it until today. I woke up this morning feeling like shit but thinking maybe I was going to live after all. I've never had anything come on so fast and hit me so hard." Rose makes sympathetic clucks in the background.

"Well, now," she says, "tell me all about Mr. Tie Me Up, Tie Me Down and Fuck Me Raw. I hate to admit this, but while he was kidnapping you, I was ogling his ass the entire time. I'm almost sure he caught me staring at his dick when he was talking to me. I want you to know, though, I put up a token protest before allowing him to leave with you. Give me points for that, because what I really wanted to do was rip you from his arms and wrap myself around him like a freaking ivy vine. Is it cheating to hump another guy's leg? Because I'd totally do it."

That's it for me; hysterical laughter pours out, and I fear I will pee Lucian's 1000-thread-count sheets before I am able to get myself under control. "Oh, my God, Rose; that is so messed up!"

"What? You get to have possession of what's hanging between his legs, and I'll take the leg itself. Do you think he's interested in that three-way?"

"No," I answer hastily, not knowing if that's true or not. I am discovering he has some kinky tendencies, but there is no way I would ever consent to sharing Lucian with my friend. I sigh, "He is beautiful, isn't he? I've never thought of a man that way, but he is. The best part is it's even better under his clothes."

"Oh, shut up," Rose groans. "That's just bragging."

We talk for a few more minutes, and I agree to let her know if I'm going to be home that evening. I have a feeling she and Jake having been enjoying some privacy, and there is no way I'm walking in the apartment without them knowing; I have no desire to see Jake in action.

Oh, no, he's early! I was in the bathroom trying to fix my hair when I heard the front door. I am so turned-on I can't imagine Lucian depriving me of sex for disobeying him. I haven't touched myself again, but I'm not on the chaise like he asked. The startled look on his face is comical as I slide sideways through the living room, running to the chaise and literally falling down on it. I quickly spread my legs and look no doubt absurd. I have been excited but embarrassed all morning imagining myself here, naked. Lucian coming home early has made the decision for me. Without thinking about it, I run to do as he asked.

My stomach twists as the room remains quiet. Surely, he won't walk off and leave me like this. There is probably nothing remotely sexy about the way my chest is heaving from the run through the apartment. I look up to see him standing in the same spot, his expression intense as he takes me in. Lying in this position, completely exposed to him, is unnerving, and I find myself wanting to break the silence. "You're early...I was just on my way to...do what you wanted." When he still doesn't say anything, I add, "I had ten minutes left!" A grins pulls at the corners of his mouth, and I find myself relaxing slightly. If I were an uninhibited person, I would be completely happy bringing myself to orgasm while just looking at him. He is just...delicious.

He strolls over to me as if he has all the time in the world. He moves like a sleek jungle cat, and I am his prey. When he reaches me, he trails a finger down my chest and over the tip of my breast. The nipple hardens immediately, begging for his attention, and my breath catches. "You have to be prepared for last-minute...changes, Lia. Were you a good girl while I was gone?" When I nod my head, he trails his finger lower, over my belly button and to my mound. He pauses there, looking back at me. "You do know I can tell if you're lying. Your pussy will be swollen and weeping for me if you haven't been satisfied. Now, spread those beautiful legs and let me see."

Oh, my! My legs part automatically as he runs a finger idly over my slit. "Luc," I groan.

"You only ever call me that when you're wet," he muses. "I wonder why that is." Before I can formulate a reply, he moves between my legs. I should be self-conscious, but each moment that passes just makes me want what he can give me even more. As he drops to his knees, I raise my hips, seeking his touch. His hand touches my inner thigh before going straight to where I need him. "You're soaking wet; have you been thinking of me? Thinking of what I'm going to do to you?"

"Yes," I whisper, wanting to beg him to take me now. One touch to my clit, one finger inside me will set me off.

He parts me and traces the lines of my inner lips. He reaches to take one of my hands, rubbing my finger where his were. "Feel how swollen you are. Moisture is seeping out of your pussy and pooling here." He lowers my finger against the pucker of my ass, and I jump. "Don't like being touched there, baby?"

"No," I answer automatically. Even though Rose and I have discussed it, I'm still not sure how I feel about it. He uses my finger to caress my tight hole for another moment before releasing it. Without thinking, I move to touch my clit, but his hand stops me before I can make contact. I growl in frustration, pulling against his hold.

"Oh, no, baby, this is mine. You've waited this long; I know you don't want to go another day without being fucked, do you?" Losing what's left of my pride, I frantically say no, and he grins down at me. "Good girl." He stands and pulls off his suit jacket, dropping it to the floor. He then pulls his dress shirt from the waistband of his slacks, unbuttoning it so slowly I want to scream. Finally, he shrugs it off and reaches down to pull his undershirt off behind it. His tattoo ripples as his big shoulders flex. My mouth has gone dry, and I am waiting with bated breath as his hands drop to his belt. When his gaze locks on my breast, I look down to find myself flicking my nipple. He would never believe I hadn't been aware of the action until now. His eyes smolder, but he doesn't comment. He pulls his belt from his trousers and drops it lightly across my stomach. Alarmed, I look at him for an indication as to what it's for. He never said anything about hitting me. I…no, he wouldn't.

"Luc…please…don't." He looks at the belt, then back at me, and his eyes soften.

He runs a soothing hand over my head, saying, "Baby, I'd never hurt you." I relax slightly, seeing the sincerity in his eyes. As he straightens to remove the rest of his clothing, I am fixated on his belt. Why hasn't he moved it if he's telling the truth. My hand has long released my nipple as I focus on the leather strap lying across my stomach. "Lia…" I look up to see his huge cock jutting out, moisture glistening at the tip. All thoughts leave me and need takes over. "I had planned for you to suck my cock, but I think we both need to take the edge off now." His hand encircles his girth, pumping lightly before saying, "Put your hands above your head and cross them at the wrists."

"Wh—what?" What reason could he possibly have for that? I am aching to touch him.

"Do it!" he snaps, and I rush to comply. He picks the belt up and I turn to stone. He rests a hand on my shoulder as if reassuring me before putting the belt around my wrists and pulling it snug. "Since you can't keep your hands off what is mine, they'll stay tied while I fuck you." My chest pushes out in this position, and I feel like a sacrificial lamb. He walks to the end of the chaise and again drops to his knees. He raises my legs until my ankles are at his shoulders. With no word of warning, he pulls back and slams into me.

"Ahhh," I scream, clenching against his sudden intrusion. "Luc, ahhh!" My tits bounce wildly as he sets a relentless pace. I feel wild and wanton with my hands tied, unable to brace myself, completely at the mercy of his driving body.

"Fuck!" he shouts, powering forward again and again. As sparks shoot through my body, I know I'm on the verge of coming. He holds my hips firmly in his hands, pulling me to meet his thrusts. By this point,

I'm yelling loud enough to be heard in the next city, but my only focus is the movement of his cock, gliding against my clit with every stroke. There is nothing I wouldn't do in this moment to find my release. My hips jerk, trying to take him further inside me. I am right there when he pulls out. *What the?* He flips me as if I weigh nothing. I am now on my knees with my ass in the air and my tied hands under my head. I remember how deep he was in the rear-entry position on the kitchen counter, and I tingle in anticipation. He caresses the cheeks of my ass, making me squirm before pushing the huge head of his cock against the slick lips of my pussy. I wiggle my hips, trying to push him inside. Instead of entering me, he glides through my moisture, before slipping back against my ass. I still, afraid for the first time of what he's going to do. Before I can brace myself, he suddenly slams back into my pussy, pushing my body up further onto the chaise. I'm back on the brink of coming when I feel something pushing against the puckered hole he has just left. His cock is buried inside my sex as my desire-muddled brain tries to decipher what is pushing slowly into the forbidden opening.

"Luc?" Surprise and fear have delayed my impending orgasm as I try to look over my shoulder at him. I feel his hand on my back, stroking me reassuringly.

"Shhh, don't think, baby, just feel. I'm not going to hurt you, you know that." His hand slips from my back and around to my clit. As he tweaks the bundle of nerves, he gently pushes what I now realize must be his finger into my ass. I freeze, trying to take in the sensations overtaking my body; it's too much to process. It feels as if Lucian has invaded every part of me. The twinge of discomfort from Lucian's finger in my ass only amplifies the feel of his cock buried inside me. He has stopped all movement except for his fingers moving against my clit. When I push back, his big body shudders and he pulls his cock out before slamming back in. The finger in my ass moves in tempo with his cock and within seconds, I'm blowing apart. My orgasm eclipses anything I've ever known. His pace increases and he swells impossibly large, setting off another wave of contractions inside me as I feel him shudder in release. "Fuck, baby, fuck!" he shouts as he sags against my back, his cock still twitching inside me.

I am wrecked, completely limp and boneless beneath him. Somehow, we have both ended up in a heap of tangled bodies on top of the narrow chaise; one wrong move by either of us and we'll be on the floor. If I'm ever able to move or think again, I'm buying a diary and detailing this experience. There is no way I'll ever have another sexual experience that will top what just happened. I recall Rose's description of him and start to giggle. "Geez, was she right," I say, my body shaking with amusement.

I feel Lucian move, his weight lifting from my back. "What are you talking about?" he asks against my ear, sounding curious.

"Mr. Tie Me Up, Tie Me Down, and Fuck Me Raw," I gasp out as another wave of laughter chokes me. Lucian flips me to my back, looking adorably mussed and inquisitive. "Rose named you that, and it's kinda true; you have to admit."

He looks like he's holding back his own laughter but settles instead for a heart-stopping grin. "It looks like your friend is a pretty good judge of character then. Although, I'd only classify this as a 'tie me down' moment. We'll have to work on the 'tie me up' soon. I also think I can do more with the 'fuck me raw' challenge." As spent as I am a jolt of heat sizzles through me at his words. I have been perfectly content with no sex life for years, but Lucian is changing that. He's showing me everything I have been missing, and it only makes me want more...with him.

We make our way slowly toward the bedroom and clean up. Bossy man that he is, he then demands I return to bed, despite my protests, while he works for a while. I want to put up more of a fight, but I am too damned tired, and we both know it. My head is barely on the pillow before I am out. When I wake, we share some Chinese food Lucian has ordered and then we argue about me leaving. I want nothing more than to stay with Lucian again, but I know I have to go back to school the next day. "I don't have any of my things here; it would be easier to go home."

"Sam and I can drop you on our way out in the morning. It's already late, and there is no need in either of us going back out." He turns back to the football game we have been watching as if the matter is settled.

"Does anyone ever disagree with you?" I ask as I snuggle back against his chest. We are lying on the couch in front of his big-screen television in the living room. The lights of the city below twinkle through the floor-to-ceiling windows, lulling me into a state of utter relaxation.

"Only you," he says against the top of my head as he shifts me closer. I drift away to the sound of his steady heartbeat against my ear and his heat surrounding me. In such a short time, I have become so comfortable with him. Here, in his arms, is more peace than I've ever known, and for a moment, I panic at the thought of losing it. What happens when this is over, and I'm just another Monique he's trying to avoid? For once, I understand completely the kind of sorrow the other woman must feel at seeing Lucian with someone else.

"No! God, no! What are you doing!" I blink, disoriented. I'm being tossed around and someone is yelling the same thing over and over. Moving my hands, I feel...Lucian. My body is partly on top of his, and he's trembling and jerking beneath me as if in agony. Even in my groggy state, I know he's having a nightmare. His voice has gone hoarse from yelling. I gently try to wake him, to soothe his distress.

"Luc...it's Lia. Baby, wake up, you're dreaming." I continue to murmur softly to him until he starts to quieten. He is still shaking, but his voice has lowered, and I think he's settling back into sleep. My body is relaxing when he starts to choke. His hands reach frantically for his throat and the sounds are so real I'm terrified that somehow, this time, something or someone is strangling him. "Luc...God, please wake up. Luc!" Suddenly, he rears up, and the momentum sends me flying through the air. I land in a sprawling heap against the coffee table, clipping my head on the way down. I lay there, trying to get my bearings, while Luc pants nearby on the couch.

"Lia..." Lucian sounds confused as he calls my name. I hear a click and then the light of the lamp creates a yellow glow in the room; we must have both fallen asleep on the couch.

"I'm here," I say as I struggle to my feet. I approach him warily, ensuring he is indeed awake now. I rub the knot forming on the back on my head as I reach him. "Are you okay?"

Looking bewildered, he asks, "What happened? Why were you on the floor?"

I sit next to him, rubbing my hand on his back. "You had a bad dream."

Turning to me he says, "Did I scare you? Is that why you were on the floor?"

"Um...no. I...fell off when you sat up." His eyes zero in on my other hand, still rubbing the place that made contact with the table. He reaches out to feel the area I'm touching and bites off a curse as he feels the bump.

"Fuck. Shit, baby, I'm sorry. I hurt you. I'm so sorry. Shit."

"Luc, it's fine. Really, it's not a big deal." He ignores what I'm saying, insisting on dragging me into the bathroom to look at the bump. He lets loose with another string of curses before sitting me gently on the side of his bed. He runs into the kitchen and returns with an ice pack. After a few moments, I remove the pack, handing it back to him. "I think that's good. Let's go back to bed." I yawn on cue and he gives me a soft smile, setting the ice down and tucking me into bed. When he leaves the room, I assume he's just going to throw the ice away. When he doesn't return, I realize he's not coming back. I get out of bed and walk quietly toward the living room. The lamp is still on, and I see Lucian's sleeping figure once again on the couch. On the table beside him is an empty glass with a bottle of scotch next to it. I ponder joining him, but I realize he is afraid to sleep with me again. Finding out he had indirectly hurt me tonight has shaken him. I back away; I loathe leaving him, but I'm giving him what he needs right now…space to breathe.

CHAPTER TWELVE

Lia

There has been little time to think in the last week with both Lucian and I battling the flu. When he and Sam dropped me at home this morning, it had suddenly hit me; my court date is coming up, and I had completely forgotten it. The happy bubble I have been existing in is effectively pierced.

It's obvious this morning that Lucian was still troubled by what had happened during the night. He checked the bump on my head again, and I assured him it didn't hurt. I wanted to ask him about the dream, but I didn't know how. The sound of him choking was bad enough, but his words last night had been even worse. He sounded so scared, so horrified; I knew these weren't just random dreams. How long had this been going on? I can't imagine waking up like that every night. I have had nightmares about my stepfather on and off, but nothing of that magnitude. He had given me a brief kiss and told me he would call when I stepped from the car earlier. I wanted to act like a teenager and demand to know when, but I just smiled instead and waved at him through the glass as the car pulled away. I felt a childish urge to cry and had no idea why.

It has been eight days since I've seen Lucian. He texted me a couple times to ask how I am doing, saying he has some things going on at work that are keeping him busy. Regardless of what he says, I know this is about the nightmare and his need to pull away from me because of it. I go about my life, and I continue to show up at his apartment on my usual schedule, but he is never there. Only the dirty clothes and unmade bed show me he is indeed coming home at some point. I try not to let it show, but the loss of his presence in my life is taking a toll on me. I miss him so damn much. I alternate between wanting to send him a nasty text and begging to see him again. Not stalking his office is one of the hardest things I'd ever done.

Rose has tried to question me about it, but she finally backed off when I snapped her head off one time too many. I also have my court appearance coming up at the end of the week, and I am a bundle of nerves at the thought of seeing my stepfather and my mother. I feel lonely and depressed as I walk down the hallway to Lucian's apartment. As I open the door and step over the threshold, I freeze. Even with no visual proof, I know he's here. The smell of coffee is heavy in the air and as I stand quietly, the sound of someone moving around in the kitchen can be heard.

I set my keys and purse on the entryway table and walk slowly in the direction of the sound. Lucian is standing at the island with his back to me. He's dressed casually in jeans and a polo shirt. His hair is damp, indicating a recent shower. I stand drinking him in, my eyes roaming over him hungrily. God, I have missed him so much. I see the moment he becomes aware of my presence; his body straightens, and his breath seems to catch. When he spins around, we both just look at each other. Finally, he gives me a lopsided grin, saying, "Hey, baby, I didn't hear you come in."

"Hi," I manage to croak out. He called me baby. Does that mean things are okay between us? Do I care? Shouldn't I be pissed off at him? I mean, I know we aren't in a formal relationship, but don't I deserve some kind of explanation for his disappearance? Shit, now I sound like all the other girls I knew who ended up complete basket cases over a man. When he walks over and pulls me into his arms, I am rigid, unsure of what we're doing.

I am completely floored when he puts his forehead against mine and simply stays there for a moment. "I'm sorry, baby." I know he's referring to the disappearing act he has pulled on me for the last week.

"Did I do something?" I cringe, knowing the question makes me sound like an unsophisticated child, but I really need to know if I have done something to make him pull away.

He pulls back to kiss the tip of my nose before pulling me fully into his arms. "No, Lia," he murmurs against the curve of my neck. "I just...lost it when I hurt you that night. It's been a long time since I've had those dreams, and that was one of the worst I can remember. I could have really hurt you, and it scared the hell out of me."

"Luc, it was nothing. I barely bumped my head. I should have known better than to startle someone who was clearly dreaming. If anything, it was my fault."

He leans down, kissing me lightly, his gaze roaming my face. "We just need to be more careful," he says lightly. "I...have some sleeping pills I can take at night that help if it continues to happen. Just get up and leave me the next time, baby. Please don't run the risk of touching me. Eventually, I'll wake myself up; I always do."

"What are the dreams about? You've obviously been having them off and on for a while. Are they...memories of something happening to you?"

He stares at some point past my shoulder for a moment, and just when I think he's going to ignore my question, he says, "It's something that happened a long time ago." He pulls back and motions toward his cup. "Coffee?" I know the subject is closed as far as he's concerned. I let it go because even with the secrets between us, I'm thrilled to see him and don't want to do anything to change that. I've only known Lucian a short while, and it's way too early in whatever kind of relationship we have to demand all his secrets.

I walk over to where he is pouring my cup of coffee and lean against his muscular back. I just need a few more minutes of physical contact after days of being deprived of his warmth. When he turns to pull me back into his arms, the look he gives me tells me he feels the same way. Whatever this thing is between us, one thing is clear: I'm not the only one who has suffered the last week. "I missed you," I admit against his chest.

His arms tighten around me, one hand tangling in my hair. "Me too, baby, too fucking much. Spend the day with me?"

I think fleetingly of my school and his work. I have just gotten caught up on everything I missed when I was out for a few days with the flu. I don't give a damn, though. If he is willing to play hooky today, then I'm more than happy to join him. "Really? What do you have in mind, handsome?" He chuckles against me, knowing I'm teasing him.

"I thought we could drive out to my house. I haven't been there in a few weeks, and I need to check on things. There's an indoor pool, so we can go for a swim, if you like. Just have a lazy day doing whatever we want."

Grinning, I say, "That sounds perfect, but I don't have a swimsuit with me. Could we drop by my apartment on the way?"

He pulls away, swatting my ass lightly. "Absolutely not. No clothes allowed in the pool. I'd just have to take them off to fuck you, so what sense would that make?"

He makes the statement so nonchalantly; I just shrug and say, "Good point. I'm ready when you are." In a few moments, we are in the parking garage, and he is leading me toward the Range Rover. I cover my mouth dramatically, saying, "Oh, wow! Lucian Quinn is going to drive today. Is Sam busy?"

He backs me up against the car, running a hand down between my legs to cup me through the material of my pants. "Maybe Sam doesn't want to see me touching your sweet pussy today."

I moan, shamelessly riding his hand. "Good point," I croak out, making him laugh. I want to object when he releases me but manage to swallow my protest; it's enough right now just to be with him again. For the first time in eight days, my world is bright, and it's all because of the man sitting beside me. When he reaches over to take my hand before setting them both on his thigh, I sigh in contentment.

Twenty minutes later, we are pulling through an impressive set of stone pillars, down a well-manicured driveway, and pulling to a stop in front of an equally impressive home. The bottom is made of stone and the top a shingle-type siding; it seems to sprawl out in every direction. Large picture windows gleam in the sunshine, and the circular drive in the front is lined on both sides with flowers. Even though the house must be worth a small fortune, I am surprised at how unassuming it seems.

Lucian walks around and opens my door, kissing me briefly on the lips before shutting it behind me.

"Welcome to Casa Quinn, baby."

"Why, thank you. It's really beautiful here." I look around, seeing no other houses in the distance. "I'm surprised you have this much privacy here. Most of the houses seemed pretty close together on the way in."

"My parents purchased several lots to build on. They loved the area but didn't want close neighbors. Come on, I want to say hello to Fae before she leaves." I assume Fae must be the caretaker; a house this size probably requires several people to keep it in such great condition.

I'm surprised when instead of using a key to enter his home Lucian rings the bell. The door is pulled open almost immediately and an attractive woman in blue scrubs stands there beaming at us. "Luc! Honey, I'm so happy to see you. Why in the heck do you insist on ringing the doorbell, though? You do know you own the place, right?" Before he can answer, she throws her arms around his neck and without hesitation, he returns the embrace. When she releases him, he turns to me, taking my hand to pull me closer.

"I want you to meet Lia. Lia, this is my Aunt Fae. She raised me after my parents died. She was my dad's sister." The woman studying me in something akin to shock looks far too young to be Lucian's aunt. Her long, dark hair is pulled up in a ponytail and even through her scrubs; her figure is fit and trim. Her face is unlined, and she could pass easily for his sister.

I extend a hand to her, saying, "It's great to meet you." Since Lucian has never mentioned her, I have no other pleasantries to add, and a moment of silence ensues.

Finally, the other woman takes my hand, giving me a genuine but curious smile. "It's a pleasure, sweetie. Sorry to zone out on you there, but my boy here hasn't brought a woman home since...well, you know, in a long time, so this is a bit of a surprise." A look passes between Lucian and his aunt so fast I'm not sure if I have imagined the whole thing. "Anyway, you two come on in. I have some coffee in the kitchen. I was just straightening up before I left for work." Lucian explains that his aunt works at the memorial hospital downtown as a nursing supervisor.

I follow Fae through a large foyer with Lucian trailing behind us. The house has an open floor plan with high ceilings and tan-colored walls. We make our way past a curving staircase and into a bright, airy kitchen. The cabinets are antique-distressed, and the granite is a matching light color. Fae walks straight to the coffee pot and fills her mug. A grin spreads across my face at the caption on the cup: 'Nurses do it for twelve hours straight.' Judging by the house, Lucian comes from money, so his aunt is a bit of a surprise. "How's the new groundskeeper working out?" Lucian asks.

Fae takes a sip of her coffee before answering. "He seems okay. I walked him through everything, but you might want to talk to him while you're here today. I saw his truck come in a few minutes ago, so he should be out at the barn."

"I'll go ahead and walk down there before he gets started." He turns and drops a kiss on my cheek. "I'll be right back. You going to be okay?" I nod my head when what I really want to do is follow him out of the kitchen. His aunt seems nice, but I have no desire to be stuck with a stranger until Luc returns.

When she offers me a mug and points to the pot, I gratefully accept it; at least I have something to do with my hands for a moment. "Let's walk out to the sunroom; it's nice out there this time of the morning." She leads to me into a sitting room with a comfortable sofa, matching armchairs, a fireplace, and coffee table. "So, how long have you known Luc?" I look up, noting that her interest in me hasn't faded.

"Um...about a month I guess." As we walk by the fireplace, I notice some pictures and stop in front of them. I squint down at one that shows two teenage boys and a girl. I recognize a younger Lucian immediately and the other boy looks familiar, as well.

Fae stops beside me and picks up the picture. "The three amigos. You never saw one without the other two close behind. They were nothing alike, but boy, did they bond." She points to Lucian, "my serious one," then to the boy on the other side of the girl, "and my golden one." When I point to the girl she has skipped over in the middle, she says quietly, "My dark one."

Pointing to Lucian, I ask, "I know that's Luc, but who are the other two?"

She smiles fondly. "The other boy is Aidan and the girl is Cassie."

"Ah, I knew I recognized him." I point to Aidan. "I've met him before. How about Cassie? Where is she now?"

Fae puts the picture back, walking to the sofa, and sitting down heavily. "She's...away. She doesn't live here." Her discomfort is obvious. I remember her calling Cassie 'her dark one' and wonder why. Out of nowhere, she says, "I'm so happy Luc brought you here. He hasn't let a woman close to him in so long."

I feel compelled to clarify my place in his life. I don't want her to think that things are serious between us when they're not. Heck, I don't even know what they are. "We haven't known each other that long, so we're just...seeing each other right now." I don't think she needs to know we are also having mind-blowing sex, so I keep that to myself.

She surprises me when she reaches over to pat my hand. "Honey, if Luc brought you here, then there is something more than casual between you. I'm not naïve. I know he has women in his life, but he never brings them here, and according to Aidan, he doesn't have them in his apartment either." I'm further astounded to see her blink back what are plainly tears as she adds, "He seems lighter, happier." Lucian walks into the room at that moment, settling on the couch beside me. I see him studying his aunt's face, possibly noticing the drying moisture there, but he says nothing. After a few moments, she stands. "I've got to get to work. You two should stay and enjoy the day. There is plenty of food for lunch."

Lucian drops an arm around my shoulders, smirking down at me. "I believe Lia wants to go for a swim, don't you?" I feel myself blushing as I dig my elbow into Lucian's side.

I want to groan as his aunt unknowingly adds fuel to his nasty thoughts. "Great idea. Luc can whip something up, and you two can just eat out there." His big body shakes beside me as he assures his aunt he had intended to eat out there all along. When I hear the door shut behind her, I jump up, putting my hands on my hips.

"You're just evil, you know that, right? By the look on your aunt's face, she knew exactly where your mind was...in the gutter!"

He holds his hands up, looking like the picture of innocence. "What? You did want to go for a swim, and there was some mention of eating something sweet out there. I was just agreeing with her." I huff in response, trying to look angry. In truth, now that the embarrassment of his aunt thinking I'm some sort of slut has passed, I'm just hot, bothered, and needy. His words have struck a direct line right to my clit, and it's throbbing for his attention.

"Oh, baby," he growls, seeing the look on my face. "Come here, I'm ready for my appetizer."

"No, oh, no!" I hold out a hand to stop him. "I'm so not getting naked on your aunt's couch."

He looks adorably confused as he asks, "What's the difference between the couch and the pool? I'm sure she uses both of them."

"The pool has chemicals and stuff to, you know...kill off the evidence." Lucian appears vastly amused by my statement.

"Baby, unless there's something I'm unaware of, I don't think we need to 'kill off evidence.'" He jumps to his feet, smacking my ass on his way by. "You want to be fucked in the pool, just tell me. No need to make up all these excuses." I sputter behind him indignantly.

Then, I surprise us both when I say, "Oh, hell, who am I kidding. I do want to be fucked in the pool." His mouth is hanging open as I walk by him, unbuttoning my pants. I have no idea where I'm going, but when he scoops me into his arms, I know he'll take care of the rest.

"That was seriously hot," he says as he cradles me against his chest. I smile proudly in return before looking around at where we've stopped.

"Oh, my," I stare in wonder. The room we have stepped into has huge sliding doors with a patio beyond them. Chaise lounges are arranged both inside and out. Lush greenery and a beautiful waterfall into the pool create a tropical paradise right out of a movie. "Oh, Luc, this is gorgeous."

He smiles at me shyly, seeming pleased by my comment. "My dad had this built for my mom. She had rheumatoid arthritis from a very young age, and the pool helped her with the discomfort. She used it almost every day. I know it seems like a waste to maintain it when it's not used that much anymore, but I just...can't stop."

Turning to him, I stroke his cheek. "Of course, you have to keep it." He takes my hand, nipping playfully at my fingers.

"I believe something was mentioned about feeding me lunch." I know what he wants, and even though I am far from the most seductive person, I want to give it to him. Without breaking eye contact, I slowly strip my clothes off until I am standing before him naked. He draws in a deep breath, his eyes blazing. When he makes to touch me, I evade his hand, determined to see my seduction through.

I lower myself to sit on the edge of the pool, leaning on my elbows. Looking back at him, I deliberately ease my legs apart...and wait. I hold my breath, praying he wouldn't be turned off by what he sees. I am tempted to look when I hear something hitting the floor but continue to stare ahead...waiting. And, oh, is it worth the wait. A splendidly nude Lucian walks down the cement steps looking like a Greek God. The tattoo on his muscular chest ripples, and even better, his big cock is stiff and standing at attention. I am staring...I am drooling. I am in danger of falling into the water and dying a happy woman.

"My face is up here, baby." As if he knows I am helpless to look away, he encircles the girth of his cock with his hand, stroking it up and down lightly. "See anything you like? I can't help but notice where your interest is...focused."

I literally choke on my own tongue, wheezing like someone with a bad case of asthma. "Uh...Hmm...Yeah...Okay." He looks like he's trying hard not to laugh as I mumble a bunch of unintelligible gibberish. So very cool, Lia. I'm blushing like a virgin faced with her first picture of a man's penis. So much for looking seductive; that all went out the window when naked Lucian made an appearance.

Thankfully, he submerges himself in water, covering his luscious anatomy enough for me to regain my composure. Well, until he surfaces between my dangling legs, latching on to them. I squeal, thinking he's going to pull me in. The water is only to his waist where I am sitting, but I'm not ready to try it out yet. Instead of pulling me in, his body pushes my legs further apart, opening my sex completely for his perusal. His hands wrap around my ass, sliding me closer to the edge, positioning me exactly as he wants me. When he is finished, there is no part of my pussy he can't easily see or reach.

Lucian runs a finger down the center of my slit, causing my body to jerk. "So perfectly pink, wet and swollen for me baby. Want my tongue or finger first?"

I 'm not sure if he's really expecting an answer to his question, but I supply one anyway. "Could I...have both?" Oh, dear God, that question came out sounding like I was asking him for an apple pie with my McDonald's combo.

I am really screwing this moment up. He slides the tip of his index finger inside me, saying, "Greedy, I like it. I'd love to give you both." And boy, does he ever. As his dark head descends toward my throbbing clit, sucking it into his mouth, I feel the finger go in fully. He licks, sucks, and finger/tongue fucks me to three orgasms sitting on the side of the pool. My fingers gripping his hair are all that's keeping me from collapsing backwards. The things he can do with his mouth are probably illegal in a handful of countries, and I love them all. When he finally lets me come up for air, I am boneless, ready to do nothing more than crawl into one of the lounge chairs behind me and go to sleep. Lucian, though, has other thoughts. "Time for a ride, baby. My dick has been punching a hole in this damn cement for thirty minutes; it needs something a little softer now." My lips barely had time to form an O before he is pulling me off the side and impaling me onto his cock.

"Luc!" I moan as he slides home. "Feels so good, so good." I feel the rough texture of the side of the pool dig into my back as he braces me against the pool. We both groan as I wrap my legs around his waist, pushing him deeper.

"Baby, fuck me, you feel good. So tight, sucking me dry." His dirty sex-talk is enough to bring me to the brink. As he uses his hold on my hips to slam me up and down on his length, I lick his neck, biting the tip of his ear. I have never done anything like that before, but the shudder that runs through his body shows me he likes it. I bite the vein standing out in his neck, and his hips go into overdrive. I scream, falling headlong into my release and setting off a chain reaction within him.

The concrete is now digging painfully into my back, and my ass has long since gone to sleep when I start wiggling against him. "You're getting heavy, babe," I sigh in his ear as I continue to stroke a hand down his back. He pulls back immediately, picking me up in his arms and walking back toward the steps to sit down with me on his lap. When I'm snuggled against his neck, I squeal as I notice his neck...and his shoulder. "Oh, crap, Luc, I can't believe I did that."

Looking more curious than anything, he asks, "What did you do?"

I drop my head on his shoulder, embarrassed at having done something so juvenile. "I...marked you. God, I'm so sorry. I had no idea I was doing it that hard."

He pinches my naked ass with a wolfish grin. "You gave me a hickey? Little bit eighties, but it's sexy as fuck. I think I'll return the favor." I jump up from his lap, trying to get away. Before I have taken more than a few steps, he is on me.

"Nooooo," I yell as I try to dodge him. Once again, he has me trapped against the pool and his mouth is lowering toward the vulnerable skin of my neck. "Luc," I giggle, "you wouldn't dare."

"Oh, baby, believe me, I'd dare." With that statement, his lips connect with my skin, and he is sucking on my neck. Who knew getting marked could be so damn sexy? My toes are curling and my nipples are hardening as he sucks my skin. By the time he pulls back, I am ready to ride his cock again. From the feel of his hot length pressing against my belly, he's of the same mind.

He releases my neck with a pop and pulls me from the pool. Without a word, he lies back on a lounger and pulls me astride him. "Take it deep, baby, and ride me." I line his cock up at my entrance and slowly lower myself on his massive width until he's fully seated inside me. His big body is tense, but he waits for me to adjust to his size and set the pace.

My body arches as my hips circle and buck. He puts his hands on my hips to guide me up and down, hitting the places we both need stroked. Again, within moments, I feel the pressure building inside me. When Lucian releases my hips to rub my clit, I float away. His mouth at my nipples, swirling and biting, sends me to nirvana. My body clenches and convulses around his length. His hips rise up off the lounger as he slams into me one, two, three more times before stiffening in his release. "Oh, Luc," I pant out... "That was so unbelievable."

I lay down against his chest, enjoying the heat of his body against mine. His hand rubs my lower back before moving upwards to stroke the rough skin of my scar. His hand pauses as he feels me stiffen against him. "Lia...you're beautiful and sexy as ever-loving fuck. This in no way takes away from that; it just makes me furious to think of how you got it."

I relax back against him, letting him continue touching me. "I have to go to court on Friday for the preliminary hearing for my mother." I hope I don't sound as nervous as I feel about it. I would rather Lucian believe I'm not terrified by the prospect of seeing my stepfather again.

I am floored when he says, "I know. My lawyer and I will be there with you, of course."

Pulling back, I look at him in astonishment. "Wh...what?"

"Of course, baby. I know you're scared; hell, anyone else in your position would be. I'd never let you go to something like that alone. Max is going to see if they will let you give video testimony so you don't have to be in the courtroom."

To my horror, I feel tears gathering and washing down my cheeks. It's like the floodgates have opened. Before I can stop the flow, I'm sobbing all over his chest. I can say nothing but, "Oh, Luc," as I embarrass myself all over him.

He seems stunned, then panicked at my loss of control. He sits up quickly, pulling me onto his lap. "Honey, what's wrong? What did I say?" He strokes my hair gently while I struggle for control.

"It's just...I'm not used to...people caring. Really, you will come?" I know I'm sitting there looking at him with my heart on my sleeve, but I'm powerless to stop. Debra and Martin would do anything for me, and I have Rose, but I've never had a man in my life, someone who seems to worry about me. I want to lay back and revel in the safety of his arms. I never want to leave them.

He wraps me tighter against him, kissing my ear. "I know you've been worried about it. I'd never leave you to face that alone. I talked to Max about it as soon as I found out. I'm sorry; I should have told you earlier."

I can't resist saying, "That's okay, you were too busy avoiding me for a week, remember?"

A faint blush lines his cheeks as he smiles at me. "Yeah, I remember. Sorry, baby. Just a lot of shit in my past I don't deal with too well sometimes. You make everything feel better, though. I want to move forward for the first time in so damn many years." His admission is both unexpected and touching. I am also more than a little curious as to what has happened in his past. I've seen pieces of a very complicated puzzle, but I'm not even close to solving the mystery. I decide to ask him one thing that has been bugging me. I'm curious as to his reaction.

"So, I saw some pictures that were on the mantle. One was of you, Aidan, and Cassie." Bingo, his harsh breath and taut body answer one question for me. Cassie might not be all of his past problems, but she is there somewhere. Both his and his aunt's reaction confirm that. I know I shouldn't, but I go one-step further. "Aidan works with you, but there hasn't been any mention of Cassie. I take it you all grew up together, so where is she now?" The hand that had been stroking my hair is now twisted in it, causing my scalp to sting. I don't think he is even aware of what he's doing. Not wanting to change the subject, I don't protest the pain.

"Lia...Cassie's been gone from here for years. She...lives elsewhere now. I just...please, can we not talk about her?" His skin beneath my hand has gone clammy, and his face is pale. I feel like an ass for pushing him on the subject. I wonder if Cassie is dead; maybe that's what he and his aunt mean by her not being here anymore. Whatever the reason, it causes both Lucian and Fae pain to talk about her, so I decide to let it go. Thankfully, when I make no further mention of Cassie, Lucian's grip on my hair loosens, and the pressure is gone.

Trying to lighten the mood, I sit back on my heels and lift my hair. "So, what does my neck really look like? You do realize people at school will notice this tramp stamp I have now." His chuckle is light, but shadows remain in his eyes. I stand, trying to wiggle my ass in some halfway-seductive manner and dive off the side of the pool into the deep end. When I surface, a smile plays over his lips, and the darkness is leaving him. I give him by best straight face and ask, "Do you guys have a pool boy who could come in and assist me? I fear the pool drain has captured one of my nipples." When he stands and prepares to jump in, I know...I've got him. He's mine for now. The past will have to wait.

CHAPTER THIRTEEN

Lia

It's the morning of my court appearance, and I'm a complete wreck. Lucian has done his best for the past week to keep my mind off this day, but now I must face it. Lucian's lawyer was unable to get an agreement from the judge to video my testimony; I will be making it in the courtroom, in front of my mother and my stepfather. Outwardly, I strive to appear calm and confident, even though inside I'm close to hyperventilating. I had never planned to see either of them again. I am, for all intents and purposes, alone in the world with no family. My mother hadn't spoken to her parents in years and to my knowledge, I'd never met them. Since I don't know who my father is, I have no idea about any relatives on his side. Hell, I wouldn't even know him if we passed on the street.

I had given my deposition earlier in the week, along with having my back photographed to use as evidence. The deposition seems useless now since I will be testifying in the court anyway.

Lucian walks in the bathroom where I'm staring into the mirror and moves to stand behind me. My eyes focus on his reflection. He is his usual beautiful, polished self in a grey suit with a lilac tie I picked out.

His dark hair is neatly styled and his jaw freshly-shaven; he looks every inch the wealthy, successful businessman. His hands settle on my shoulders as he pulls me back into his strong body. "Okay baby?"

"Yeah," I murmur, nestling closer. We both know it's a lie, but he can't make today go away for me. I know he sees the panic I'm trying so hard to bury.

His big arms wrap around me as he kisses the top of my head. "Kills me that I can't stop this. Fuck, believe me I tried. The judge is an asshole who doesn't see the big deal in dragging an abuse victim into the courtroom and having her face a monster."

Suddenly, calm descends on me as I turn to comfort him. In a way, this has been harder for Lucian to handle than me. He feels frustrated, helpless, and angry. I wonder again if it's even wise for him to accompany me today. Will he be able to stop himself from beating my stepfather to a pulp? He has told me that his lawyer advised him to keep it under control or he'd be removed from the courtroom. I know he'll try for my sake.

Since he walked back into my life after disappearing for days, things have been different between us...better. I have spent every night at his apartment. He continues to push my boundaries both in and out of bed, and I love it. To my knowledge, he hasn't had any more nightmares. He hasn't said anything, but I have seen him taking medication before bed the last few nights. He is sleeping deeper and looks groggy in the mornings. I know he is afraid of hurting me again, but I wish the medication wasn't necessary. Maybe, after this is all over, we should both check into therapy. If Lucian won't talk to me, possibly he will open up to someone else. I just hope that being involved with someone dealing with their own demons isn't pushing him to a place he can't handle.

I reach up to cup his cheek in my palm, rubbing the smooth skin there. He has become such a big part of my life that I can't imagine what I'll do when he's gone. I can't think about that now, though; I have to survive today before I can dwell on tomorrow. "I'm fine, Luc. He can't hurt me anymore. I'm glad you're going to be there; you make everything better."

He turns his head, kissing my palm. "I've got you, baby. We'll get this behind us today, then I'll bring you home and make love to you all night. Fucking bury that shit behind us where it belongs."

"Oh, Luc." A vice squeezes my heart at his words. I have no defense against him when he gives me sweet. He's possessive, dominant, and protective toward me, but sometimes so gentle and sweet it brings me to tears. In moments like this, I feel he would battle the world to take care of me. It makes the girl who no one ever wanted feel like the woman who has it all. Words of love rise to my lips, threatening to choke me, but I hold them back. It's too soon, and I know instinctively he's not ready to hear them. I'm so afraid they'll slip out in a vulnerable moment, and it will be the catalyst that causes him to leave me.

We stand there for a moment longer, each lost in our own thoughts, before he checks his watch and pulls back. I smooth down the material of the simple linen-shift dress I've borrowed from Rose and square my shoulders. Luc takes my hand and pulls me through the apartment and out to the curb where Sam is waiting in the Mercedes. He straightens from where he is leaning against the car to open the backdoor for us. "Good morning, Lia," he says giving my arm a gentle squeeze of encouragement as I pass him. I hear Lucian exchanging a few words with him before he enters behind me.

Lucian puts his arm around me and pulls me into his side as the car moves through traffic. Neither of us speaks on our short ride to the courthouse, and all too soon, Sam is turning off the engine and opening the door for our exit. "I'll be right here waiting when you are finished," he says. I know this is his way of trying to reassure me that everything will be fine. Impulsively, I turn back, giving him a hug. I can tell he is surprised, but his arms encircle me briefly as he returns the embrace. Lucian takes my hand once again, and we walk up the stairs to the double set of doors where his lawyer Max is waiting.

Lucian's lawyer appears to be in his thirties. His hair is dark, almost black, and neatly styled. Like Lucian, Max is tall and powerfully built. He extends a hand to me. "Miss Adams, I'm Max Decker. Sorry to meet under less-than-desirable circumstances." I shake his hand, liking his straightforward manner. He turns to greet Lucian before turning back to me. "Miss Adams..."

Before he can continue, I hold up a hand, saying, "Please, call me Lia. I have a feeling I'm going to be Miss Adams far too much today as it is."

With a brief incline of his head to acknowledge my request, he continues, "Lia, I realize this will be difficult for you. If it's any consolation, though, I believe this will be fairly quick and straightforward. There is no line of witnesses to go through nor any other testimony besides that of you and your mother, and possibly Mr. Dawson on the rebuttal. There is no jury involved, so the judge will handle the ruling. You will be called to testify first. The purpose is to establish a past pattern of violence and instability. Your mother will testify next and the court will likely break after that. Mr. Dawson will testify after the break, if he so chooses and that should be it.

My body relaxes slightly, responding to the confidence in his voice; if he thinks it's going to be okay, surely he knows better than I do. "You make it sound so simple."

He gives me a look tinged with sympathy, and I decide I quite like Max Decker. It's easy to see why he and Lucian are associates; they both exude the same power and confidence that draws everyone around into their orbit. "The process is simple, Lia, but the reality of what happens in the courtroom is often anything but. Brian Starnes is the prosecutor from the DA's office on this case, and he is a good guy. He'll try to guide you through your testimony as easily as possible. When Brian is finished, Mr. Dawson's lawyer will have the opportunity to cross-examine you."

When he would have continued on, I stop him. "What do you mean, cross-examine me?" I know Lucian has picked up on the quiver in my voice when his grip on my hand tightens.

"Each party has the right to cross-examination. They may or may not use that right. You need to be prepared that Mr. Dawson's lawyer might try to discredit parts of your testimony." I feel the blood drain from my face as the impact of his words hits me. I'm not just going into court to give a simple statement and leave. I've seen enough movies in my time to know I might very well have my entire life ripped apart in front of everyone there.

"But...I'm not on trial. I—I didn't think I'd have to do anything other than testify." By this point, I am shaking and trying desperately to swallow the bile threatening to choke me. If I wasn't so close to freaking out, it would probably be amusing to see two strong men like Lucian and Max so upset over my reaction.

"Lia...I'm so sorry. I assumed you knew that was a possibility. Surely, the DA's office mentioned it to you." He mutters what sounds like a curse word under his breath before adding, "We should have met before now so I could have prepared you. Let me talk to the judge and see if we can get a postponement." As Max starts to walk off, I grab his arm, stopping him.

"No. I just want this out of the way. If I leave now, I will be back in a day, a week or sometime soon. I'll just spend that time dreading this. Maybe it's better this way." Looking down at my watch, I attempt a joke to lighten the mood. "Look, I only have ten minutes left to completely lose it, so I better get started." Max gives what sounds like a reluctant laugh before looking at Lucian, as if silently asking him what he wants to do. Since Lucian is paying his salary, it's probably only fair he get the final decision.

"Give us a minute, will you, Max?" The other man nods his agreement and walks down the hall, pulling out his cellphone to push some buttons. Lucian turns back to me, his eyes full of concern. "Baby, I'm so fucking sorry. I...shit, I thought you knew what would happen today. This is all on me. I should have had Max meet with you days ago. Please, let him try to get this postponed to give you a few days to prepare. I don't want you going in there blindsided."

I step closer to him, resting my hands on his chest. "I don't want to start over again Luc. Yes, finding out I may be cross-examined is a bit of a surprise, and I'm nervous about it, but I need for it to be done. I don't want to leave here today with this still hanging over me. The DA's office probably mentioned it to me, but I just didn't understand." Uncaring of who is watching Lucian cups my face in his hands, looking into my eyes for a moment and seeing the resolve there.

Finally, he expels a breath and kisses me hard on the lips. His kiss conveys his frustration, but the gentle touch of his finger stroking my cheek infuses me with strength. I can do this; I have been through worse in my life. In a few hours, Lucian and I will leave, and it'll be finished. Looking back later, I will realize that believing anything that involves my mother and stepfather could be simple was completely naive. I should have known better.

Max leads the way into the courtroom, stopping by a bench on the front row. "I'll sit first, then Lucian if you'll come next and let Lia have the end." No doubt, he's afraid I will fall on my face if I have to climb over them when my name is called. We settle in just as he requested, and Lucian clasps my hand once again. I look around the room, thinking it looks exactly like something from *Law and Order*. When I make another pass, a woman at the table directly in front of us is staring at us. Shock waves roll over me as I recognize my mother. Her blonde hair is now a dark brown, and she looks fifty pounds smaller than the last time I saw her. Her face is hollow and her body almost emancipated. She looks like someone fighting off a horrible disease.

"Mom?" I whisper, still in shock at the woman looking back at me. She turns fully in her seat, her eyes sliding over me and then taking in Lucian, who, as if sensing a threat, has stiffened beside me. I hate I even cared enough to ask, "Are you all right? You look..."

Her dull eyes seem to suddenly sparkle as the familiar look of malice takes over. "That's real nice, Lia. You take off years ago; don't say a word about where you are, and now you're insulting me. Still just a spoiled brat." I sit there gaping at her then wonder why she still has the ability to surprise me. Have I not heard some version of this crap my entire life? Beside me, Lucian's face has reddened, and he looks very close to completely losing his cool. I put a restraining hand on his thigh, trying to calm him down. I needed him, which means he has to keep it together. I need to show him I can handle what my mother is dishing out. I don't need him to fight this battle; I've done it my whole life.

"Mother, I believe we both know I didn't take off; you kicked me out on the street. And in order to be a spoiled brat, I would have had to be given something in life, and you made sure that never happened." When she would have interjected, I keep going, not giving her time to interrupt. "Now, you want something from me. That's rich, Mother; it really is. I should have went with my first inclination and let them lock me up before helping you in any way, because you never helped me a day in my life."

If the whole white-trash drama that has just occurred wasn't so damned sad, I would probably laugh. She stares at me with her mouth hanging, unable to come up with anything. I have never dared talk back to her, and she is stunned silent. God, if only I had known that years ago, I might have saved myself a lot of abuse. Lucian's big body has relaxed slightly with my words. I was scared he would think me a horrible person for talking to my mother like that, but a quick look at his face seems to show equal parts amusement and pride.

"You ungrateful bitch," my mother hisses before someone at her table shushes her. She gives me a look that promises retribution before turning in her seat without another word.

Lucian leans down to whisper in my ear. "So, I guess we aren't hosting a Mother's Day lunch this year?" Since his words carry over, both Max and I are struggling to cover our mouths and choke off our laughter. Lucian, as always, understands exactly what I need; instead of coddling, he has given me comic relief. Just another thing about the man that is impossible not to love.

As quickly as the smile had come, it is wiped away as my stepfather walks into the room. He hasn't been able to raise the funds for bail, so he has been held in custody prior to today. Instead of the prison-orange I expected, he is wearing a cheap-looking blue suit. Unlike my mother, he looks much the same. Jim Dawson is what some would consider handsome, but to me, the cruelty in his eyes has always been obvious. He always made my skin crawl, and today is no exception.

Court is called to order as the judge enters the room. The case information is read off and before I know it, my name is called. "The court calls our first witness, Lia Adams, to the stand." Lucian's hand tightens around mine before releasing it. I fight the urge to run the other way. Instead, I take a steadying breath as I walk toward the front. I am sworn in and seated in the box next to the judge.

The first series of questions are establishing my relationship and other superficial information. I shift uncomfortably in my wooden chair, feeling the pressure of being the center of attention. "Miss Adams, has the defendant Mr. Dawson ever struck or physically assaulted you?" Even though I knew the question was coming, it still drives the breath from my body. My eyes fly to Lucian who gives me a nod of encouragement.

"Yes...both."

"Miss Adams, could you be more specific as to the nature of the assaults?"

I moisten my suddenly dry lips and clasp my hands together tightly to keep them from shaking. "He...slapped me, choked me, kicked me and...burned me."

"Your Honor, I would like to admit into evidence Exhibit A, showing a scar on Miss Adams' back from a hot iron." Color stains my cheeks as the photo is handed to the judge. Max had arranged for someone from the district attorney's office to come take the photo at Lucian's. I was extremely grateful it had been a woman; something about a man other than Lucian seeing my shame is almost too much to bear. "Miss Adams, can you tell the court how you came to have this scar, please?"

Again, I look at Lucian as I answer. "My mother and stepfather were arguing. I was doing the laundry and couldn't get out of their way fast enough. My mother left the room and I...he was really angry. He took the iron from my hand and tore my shirt. He put the iron on my back and said: 'Cows are always branded so they know who they belong to, and you'll always belong to me.'" Even from across the room, I see Lucian flinch. I have never gone into all the details of what had happened to me, and I realize I should have before today. Regardless of how humiliating this is for me, it's inexcusable that I haven't prepared him better for what he will hear.

The knot in my stomach had started to loosen slightly when the question I had been dreading came. "Miss Adams, did Mr. Dawson ever sexually assault you?" I knew the DA's office already had this information from my deposition, so it's only reasonable they would go over each point for the judge. Unlike my other answers, I can't look at Lucian when I answer this. Why didn't I tell him? God, how could I just let this hit him now? I focus on the paisley pattern on the prosecutor's tie and strive for calm.

"In ways, yes." From the corner of my eye, I see Max grab Lucian's arm, trying to settle him. Before the prosecutor can ask me to clarify, I continue. "He came into my room for months at night. He...he would choke or hurt me until I took my clothes off." I hadn't even realized that tears were tracking silently down my face until one splashed on my hand. "He would touch me with one hand, while...masturbating with his other."

Lucian shouts out as if in agony. Finally, my eyes are on his, and it takes my breath away. His face is filled with naked agony, my words shredding him. My tears flow faster now as my lips soundlessly whisper how sorry I am to him. For someone with his protective streak, news like this is shattering. The prosecutor wisely asks for a recess, and the judge agrees. I have a thirty-minute reprieve, and I need every moment of it to compose myself. As I stand and leave the stand, I am suddenly looking at my stepfather. I'm not sure if I expect some trace of guilt from him, but none is present. He looks at me in a familiar way that makes my skin crawl, as if we share a dirty secret. I turn quickly away and walk toward Lucian and Max. I have almost reached them when my mother steps from behind the table and smirks at me. I feel rage the likes of which I have never felt before. I want to claw her eyes out. She has no shame. She feels not one bit of remorse over not protecting her daughter. She seems to enjoy my pain.

As Lucian walks up behind me, settling a protective arm over my shoulders, she turns her attention to him. He meets her stare, his expression one of contempt and disgust; his opinion of her couldn't be more apparent. He turns me from her without a backward glance, and we walk from the courtroom. He leads me down the hallway and into an empty office, shutting the door behind us. "I'm sorry," I sob into his chest before he can speak.

His arms envelope me, pulling me into his shuddering chest. "Christ, baby, why didn't you tell me what that bastard did to you?"

"He didn't rape me," I whisper against his neck, desperate to get closer.

"Lia, he sexually assaulted you. He may not have been inside you, but the fucker touched you...he fucking forced you to endure that. Goddamn it!"

The floodgates are open, and I am helpless to stop the flow of tears as I sob in Lucian's arms, continuing to apologize. "Honey, please stop saying you're sorry. You have nothing to apologize for. Yes, I wish I had known, but I understand how hard this must be for you." He pulls back, holding me at arm's length. "You know this doesn't change anything between us, right? I'm just blown away by who you are and all that you have accomplished despite what you've had to overcome."

My body sags in relief. A part of me has always been afraid he wouldn't want me if he found out I had let someone do something so dirty to me. In my weaker moments, I second-guessed myself, wondering if he would have really killed me if I had refused. Had I taken the easy way out because of my fear? Didn't that make me a coward? I had no idea I had spoken my fears aloud until Lucian growls.

"Baby, how can you even think that? You, a coward? Shit, that's the most absurd thing I've ever heard. You're one of the strongest people I've ever known. Most people would have given up after enduring what you have. Look at what an amazing woman you are. You refuse to take the easy way out of anything. Hell, you're cleaning my house instead of letting me take care of you like I want to."

I reach up, kissing his throat. "Geez, I needed that." I surprise a laugh out of him, causing me to smile in return. A throat clearing behind us has us both looking toward the door.

Max steps around us, leaning against the opposite wall. "I thought you did well, Lia. We only have a few minutes before we have to go back. Do you have any questions for me?"

"Yeah, when's the next bus run by here?" He grins at me, something I have a feeling he doesn't often do. I think he's secretly relieved I've finished falling apart and am attempting a bit of humor. Something about men being around crying women makes them damn uncomfortable.

"Fair question. I think Luc here will make sure you have a ride out of here at the earliest opportunity. If you are ready, we better get back inside."

Lucian gives me a quick kiss before dropping his arms. "Come on, baby. If we're lucky, we can fit in some more delightful conversation with your mother before they call court to order." I jab him in the side with my elbow, trying to suppress a smile at his words. It's hard to believe I am anything other than a basket case after my testimony, but Lucian makes things better just by being near. I have little doubt this whole ordeal would be much different were he not here with me.

My mother, thankfully, keeps her back to us, and I exchange no further words with her. Uneasily, I let myself look toward my stepfather's table and find him staring back at me. The bastard looks completely unconcerned and almost...giddy. I see him look past me to study Lucian, a frown forming on his face. Something about it makes me more uneasy than having him watch me. I hate exposing Lucian to all the ugliness that is my past, especially my mother and stepfather. I don't want to think of either of them even breathing his name, much less looking at him with interest.

My mother is called to the witness stand next and goes through the same process of being sworn in and giving her information to the court. "Mrs. Dawson, has Mr. Dawson ever assaulted you in any way?"

"No, of course not. He's my husband and sometimes we like things rough...you know, but it's all consensual." Mouths drop throughout the courtroom. Lucian tenses, and my ears buzz. What is she doing? Hadn't she instigated this entire process because he hurt her?

The prosecutor seems to be floundering in shock. Clearly, this is not the response he had been expecting. "Mrs. Dawson, perhaps you didn't understand the question. Has Mr. Dawson ever harmed you physically at any point up to and including the incident that brought us here today?"

My mother looks lovingly at her husband as if such a notion is absurd. "Not at all. That was all just a misunderstanding. I got jealous because Jim was flirting with our neighbor and started a fight with him." She giggles, doing a good job of looking embarrassed before saying, "I was throwing some books at him, and I just fell down, hitting my head on the fireplace. Jim was so worried about me afterwards, but I was still so mad...you know? Our neighbor is a lot younger, and it made me jealous." She shrugs her shoulders as if to say, 'you know how it goes.'

I sit rooted to my spot, stunned speechless. What is she doing? Swiveling my head back to my stepfather, I see him lounging back in his chair, a smirk firmly attached to his lips. His lawyer sits next to him looking stunned. The prosecutor's face is red, and he looks just minutes away from a heart attack. "Mrs. Dawson, I...did you witness any assaults from Mr. Dawson against your daughter?"

My mother looks straight at me and God help me, I know what's coming. This is payback. I dared to taunt her earlier, and she won't let me get away with it. Looking the picture of innocence, she faces the judge. "No, I have no idea what she is talking about. Jim tried so hard to be a father to her, but she rebelled at every opportunity." Giving a dramatic sigh, she adds, "I blame it on myself, Your Honor; I let her get away with everything, trying to make up for the fact that she didn't have a father like other girls. After a while, she had no respect for authority or rules. She resented Jim and was always making up stories to get back at him."

The roaring in my ears grows louder, and I vaguely hear Lucian shout my name. Standing without thinking, I yell, "You're lying, why are you lying!" This starts a fiasco of yelling, gavel banging and movement that makes my head swim. Before I know it, Lucian is leading me from the room with Max following closely behind.

Lucian

"Lia...talk to me, sweetheart." She hasn't said a word since we left the courtroom. We are back in the same office we used during the recent recess. I have taken one of the available chairs in the room and pulled her trembling form down onto my lap. I rub circulation back into her cold hands and whisper soothing words I know are meaningless to her right now. Her mother's testimony had invoked a lot of strong emotions. I wanted to fucking kill the lying bitch; Max was also seething and Lia...she had simply come undone. Her shouts had echoed off the walls, making her the sole focus of the room. At Max's urging, I had gotten her out of there as fast as possible. As I continue to reassure her, Max steps into the room, looking at Lia in concern.

"She okay?"

"What do you think? Her mother pretty much threw her under the bus and backed over her for good measure."

Max winces before shaking his head. "I've met some messed-up people in my time, but that woman takes the cake. There is no question in my mind she was lying through her teeth; hell, everyone in the place knew it. Unfortunately, there's not a damn thing that can be done. Brian is pissed as hell. He's going to have charges brought against her for filing a false police report, along with anything else he can think of. He'll do it, too. He's a good guy, but she made him look like a complete fool in there." Pointing to Lia, he adds, "He feels really bad about what happened to her, as well. Said he would have never brought this case to trial had he known her mother was going to get up there and lie her ass off."

I run a hand through my hair before shifting Lia to a more comfortable position on my lap. "Whole thing blows my mind. That was just pure spite. I can't believe Lia is even related to that woman."

Max and I are both surprised when a voice interjects, "Maybe I was adopted. That would explain a lot. Well...except that I can't see my mother wanting a child enough to actually go that far." She looks at me, giving a half-smile before stretching her limbs. My jaw clinches, and I feel like a bastard for the immediate response of my cock to her movements. There is no way to tell the guy downstairs about bad timing; he doesn't give a damn. When Lia's tight little ass is wiggling in close proximity, all the blood flow rushes down south. I grab her hips, stilling her movements while I fight to control my reaction. I'm pretty sure Max is stifling a grin behind the hand covering his mouth. Bastard, I'd like to see him handle it any better. She turns to look at him, asking, "Can I go now or will I be cross-examined?"

"You're free to go, Lia; that's what I came to tell you. The judge has called it a day, due to the mess your mother's testimony created. Brian needs time to deal with the fallout. I'll give Lucian a call when and if we need to return, but I would hardly expect this case to continue. There is nothing more to be gained from a cross-examination at this point."

Lia slides from my lap, and I discretely button my suit jacket as I rise behind her. "Thanks, Max, I appreciate you being here today."

Max takes my proffered hand then claps me on the shoulder. "Of course. I'll be in touch. Turning to Lia, he says, "I'm sorry again about what happened in there. Just try to put this behind you. As I said, I believe this will be the end." We leave the courthouse and find Sam waiting at the curb with the car. I open the door, helping Lia inside. Sam, always discrete, climbs in the driver's seat, giving us privacy. Max motions for me to hang back, so I close the door after telling her I'll be another minute. "Luc, I'm a little worried about this whole thing. I didn't want to mention this in front of Lia, but Brian will probably have no choice but to dismiss the case against Lia's stepfather. I would expect he will be free within a few days."

"Shit, and now she's back on his radar again."

Max nods in agreement. "She testified against him, tried to put him away. I think the mother was trying to get to Lia, but I believe, in the end, she was also scared to go up against him. He probably threatened her. Just tell Lia to be careful. The usual stuff: walk in groups, check the door before opening it, be more aware of her surroundings, maybe have someone stay with her for a few days."

"She will stay with me." Max isn't blind; he knows Lia and I are involved, but he also knows me well enough to realize I don't have relationships...or haven't in a long time. He is aware of my past; he has helped me legally deal with much of it. So, the surprise on his face at my statement is understandable and almost comical.

"I didn't know she was living with you. That's a big step." I consider Max more than just my lawyer; he is also a friend. As such, he has been privy to much of my sordid past. He is still dealing with one big aspect of that past. Like Aidan, I know he is beyond surprised to find a woman other than a fuck-and-roll in my life. He is also friends with Aidan, so there is little doubt he knew of Lia before I spoke with him.

I shift impatiently, ready to end the conversation before it gets too personal. I'm a bit like a science experiment to those who know me. The question always seems to be, 'how many times will Lucian get knocked down before he gives up?' No one knows how close that has come to happening in past years. If nothing else, though, I have proven to myself that I'm a survivor...thus far, anyway. "She isn't officially living with me but does stay over frequently. With this, though, I need to insure her safety, and I can't do that with her living in her campus apartment."

I know he's dying to say more. The lawyer in him wants to play twenty questions. Shit, when did my friends turn into a bunch of nosy old women? Instead, he simply says, "Good idea. So...how are things with...the other situation? Have you been there lately?"

"Couple of weeks back and nothing new. I believe Aidan is going soon. Anyway, I've got to get going." Yeah, we both know I'm just trying to nip this conversation in the bud. How many years has it been since I've wanted to sit around and talk about the woman who damn near ruined my life? "Thanks for being here today. We'll talk soon." With those words, I join Lia in the car, and Sam pulls away. Lia curls into my side as I settle an arm around her shoulders. "Okay?" She gives me an eager nod, which I know is bullshit, but I don't call her on it.

"I want you to stay in today and take it easy. I have to go to the office, but I'll try to be home early. We can have dinner at Leo's tonight." I lower my head, running my nose against her ear. "The wine there is sweet...and spicy." My words hit their mark, and her face flushes as she remembers our last visit there. She has no idea how close I was that evening to fucking her on the tabletop. Leo, being a lusty Italian, would have probably overlooked the spectacle it would have caused.

She picks up my hand, playing with my fingers in what appears to be a nervous gesture. "Why would a mother hate her child, do you think? I mean...is the hate always there, or does something happen to cause it? Maybe the child cried too much as a baby?"

Here it is; a small window into all the pain I know she is feeling. Reliving her past today was painful; having her own mother completely throw her away is devastating. "Oh, baby, this isn't on you. There is nothing an innocent child could ever do to deserve a parent like that." This whole conversation completely guts me, more than Lia could know. This isn't my first exposure to a situation like hers. I feel just as helpless now as I had the first time I had been faced with the evil a parent can visit upon their own blood.

She continues on as if I haven't spoken, her voice almost detached as if she's reading from a paper. "I tried for so many years to make her love me...or even like me. I kept thinking if I could just be perfect, then she would find something to be proud of. It was never enough, though; no matter what I tried, she hated me.

"I remember when I was thirteen; I got a letter from my teacher about a short story I had written. It was going to be published in the school paper. I thought...here it is...this is the moment that finally connects us." Without interrupting her story, even though it is breaking my fucking heart, I wipe the tears that track down her cheeks and let her continue. "She was in the kitchen cooking, which was pretty rare. We mostly survived on sandwiches or something microwaved. I ran up behind her, waving the letter, excited to show her. I...guess she hadn't heard me come in because she jerked in surprise, causing her to dump the entire box of pasta she had in her hand into the boiling water. It...splashed out on her, and she started screaming. She was so...so mad. I backed away, trying to tell her I was sorry. She took the spatula she was holding and hit me with it over and over. While that was happening, do you know what I was thinking?" I don't answer, knowing she doesn't really want one. "Why was she cooking pasta with a spatula?" Isn't that crazy? She is beating me, and all I can think about is what she is using to do it?" A bitter, almost-hysterical laugh escapes her lips. "I mean, did I really have a preference? When she was finished, she picked up the letter that had fallen on the floor, barely looked at it, then threw it in the trash, dumping the ruined food on top of it. That was it...that was the day I stopped caring about her and started just trying to survive her."

As I struggle for composure, I see Sam's suspiciously bright eyes in the rearview mirror. This beautiful, strong woman in my arms has brought two strong men to their knees with what I know is just one horror story from her past. She was one of the lucky ones, even if she doesn't know it. She has lived through Hell and came out stronger for it. What happened today has knocked her down, but she is far from out. Whether she knows it or not, her hate fuels her need to succeed, and there is not a more-powerful motivator; hell, I know it firsthand.

Hate with a healthy dose of guilt has driven me straight to the top. Cocaine might be my crutch, but hate is my drug of choice. A general hate will distort you, make you weaker, but a focused hate on one person is power. When that hate is born from grave wrongs committed against you, it is an unstoppable train. Lia's hate had been born that day, in that kitchen when her mother severed the bond between mother and daughter.

My hate had been born the day eight years ago when Cassie had attempted to end three lives, only succeeding in ending one. That I was back in this moment again, caring for someone scarred by their past, wasn't lost on me. I felt both the urge to jump from the car and run and the even-stronger desire to shield her from any further harm. I couldn't help but wonder what love between us would do to the hate that had driven us both so far. There were only two possible outcomes I could see: We would either save or destroy each other.

Even as those fears churn through me, I'm powerless to pull away from her emotionally or physically. Instead, I pull her onto my lap, tucking her head against my neck and simply hold on. "You slay me, baby, fucking cut me open." She sobs against my chest, and I let her have that moment without trying to stop the flow. She needs this outlet, the release from the pain. The anger and hate will take over again soon, but for now, she needs to grieve.

CHAPTER FOURTEEN

Lia

Lucian had put me to bed like a child when we had gotten back to the apartment. It had taken a lot of encouragement to get him to continue on to his office as he had planned. I knew he had obligations and truthfully, I needed the space. I needed an afternoon to hold an ugly pity party full of thoughts of my evil mother and equally unsavory stepfather. Facing them both today in the courtroom had been more traumatizing than I had imagined; my stepfather's eyes on me today had made me feel dirty.

When I woke a few minutes ago, I had gone straight to the shower, desperately needing to wash the filth away. His eyes on me brought back memories of all the times he had touched me, defiled me. I scrub until my skin is bright pink. Lather, rinse, repeat, over and over. I sink to the floor of the shower and allow myself one final cry. My feelings of betrayal are definitely on me. Had my mother not proven to me many times over that she has no feelings? She isn't capable of love; she isn't capable of being a human being. I hate her with a passion...I own that. I might loathe my stepfather, but my mother, in ways, is worse. She abandoned me...her own daughter. She is the lowest of life forms. I refuse to let her have another moment of my time. I can only hope the bed she has made with the devil today burns her for an eternity.

Standing, I step from the shower to find the bathroom full of steam. I open the door to release some of it before turning back to the sink. I towel off before applying a layer of the orchid-scented lotion Lucian loves. I drop one of his t-shirts over my head and walk around picking up clothes from the floor. Lucian has gotten more and more insistent about hiring a housekeeper. I stubbornly refuse to relinquish that role, needing to earn the money he has spent on me. He has tried to entice me into a position within Quinn Software, which I refused, as well. I enjoy taking care of him, and I don't want people at his company thinking I have gotten a job there because I am sleeping with the boss. At least with me here, we can have privacy. And, let's face it, it's not like his million-dollar apartment is a pigsty; he is a neat person and always picks up after himself.

I take the clothing I have gathered and dump them into the washer. I am folding the ones that were in the dryer when a pair of Lucian's boxers gives me an idea. Maybe we both need a distraction from the ugliness of the day. Sex might not be the answer to all of life's problems, but it certainly helps sometimes. I jump up, quickly putting away the rest of the clothes before running to the kitchen. In the third drawer, I find what I'm looking for: a pair of scissors. Holding the scissors to the boxers, I hope fleetingly that his underwear isn't as expensive as his suits.

Thirty minutes later and the scene is set. As long as my nipples didn't fall off from lack of blood flow, things will be fine. I have just settled back on Lucian's favorite chaise lounge when the door opens. I have a moment of hoping to God it's not a surprise visit from Sam before my beautiful lover crosses the threshold, thankfully alone. He drops his case on the entryway table before looking toward the bedroom. I know by his intent expression that he is listening for me.

He starts walking in that direction when his gaze flickers to the side, sliding over me before continuing on. My breath catches as he stops abruptly. I almost expect to hear the sound of brakes being hastily applied. Astonishment washes over his face, then desire. I can see the flames flicker before catching fire. Those emotions are tempered by amusement. I am, after all, dressed...or undressed, in a way I'm certain he's never seen before. Crossing my legs at the ankles, I beckon him closer with my hand. "Hey, baby, I'm glad you're home." His eyes blaze at the endearment I so seldom use.

Stopping beside the chaise, his eyes leisurely trace the lines of my body. He reaches out to pinch one plump, erect nipple. "I can see that. I like what you've done with my things." He pulls my ponytail before blinking in shock. "Is that...my boxers?" When I grin, he starts chuckling. I know we both remember him teasing me about my penchant for finding strange things to tie my hair up with. Today, I've taken that to new extremes, and I can tell he loves my creativity. I have a string of dental floss wrapped around one erect nipple, a bread-tie around the other, the elastic I cut from his boxers holding my hair up and his purple silk tie wrapped around my neck as a necklace. He pulls his phone from his pocket, activating the camera. "I promise I'll never share this with anyone." I stiffen for a moment, wanting to refuse, but finally relax back, raising my arms over my head and giving him the shot I know he wants. He clicks twice before tossing the phone on the nearby couch along with his jacket. Before I can offer my help, he has his clothes laying on the floor and his head between my legs, eating me as if starved.

"Luc..." I moan as he thrusts two fingers inside me. His tongue twirls and flicks my clit as he pumps his digits relentlessly. I'm almost there, just starting to crest, when he suddenly stops. "Wh...what. Don't stop!" I shamelessly try to push my pussy against his retreating fingers as he pulls back. He smacks the side of my exposed ass before hauling me sputtering to my feet.

"No orgasm until I'm buried inside you, my little hell cat." I mutter curses under my breath as he takes the end of the tie I'm wearing and leads me over to the floor-to-ceiling glass windows. "Put your hands on the glass and spread your legs, baby." I see the bustle of the street below and look back at him uncertainly. He pushes his big body against mine, wedging his cock between the cheeks of my ass. He nips my ear, causing me to shiver. "What's wrong, Lia? Are you afraid someone might see me fucking you from behind?" He reaches a hand around, cupping one of my breasts before using the dental floss to tug the nipple sharply. Then his hand lowers, sliding through my slick folds to rub my clit. "Afraid someone might see your tits pressed against the glass or your beautiful pussy, begging for more?" At his words, my sex gushes, coating his fingers. He growls, rubbing harder before removing his hand. "You like the thought, don't you, baby? You want someone to see us?" I don't bother to confirm or deny his statement; we both know the truth. My body refuses to lie for me. He kicks my legs further apart and positions my hands on the glass. I push my ass back, begging for his possession. With one mighty shove, he gives me what I've been craving: all of him, buried to the hilt.

Lucian takes advantage of my arms raised high on the glass to grab my exposed breasts. Having him use the dental floss and bread tie to pull on my nipples is unbelievably erotic. The twinge of pain as the restraints cut into my engorged flesh only adds another layer of excitement and soon I'm close, teetering at the edge, just needing his big cock to hit that one sweet spot to push me over. I grind my ass against his base, desperate for the release only he can give me. It's so close, but he's controlling my body, keeping it just out of reach. "Luc...please...oh, please!" At my words, he goes deep...so deep, then takes a hand to my clit, pinching the swollen bundle of nerves. That's all it takes; I'm exploding, flames dancing all around as I convulse around his length. Time stands still; the city below appears frozen, as I stand suspended against the glass. Then suddenly, it all comes roaring back. Lucian's shout of release, the feel of him flooding my insides, our frantic, heavy breathing, and finally the streetlights twinkle as night comes to claim the world around us.

We stand completely nude, and I know someone could be watching, yet I don't care. Eyes peering at us through the heavy glass could never decipher all that we are, all that we feel in that moment. He has taken away my earlier pain and replaced it with love. I have no idea if that is even in the equation for him at this point, but it doesn't matter. He has given me more in a month than anyone else has in my entire life. Because of the man standing behind me, shielding my body with his, I feel hope; hope that someday we can move past all that haunts us, all that torments us and find peace. He is that for me, and I so want to be that for him. After a lifetime of being unwanted, here in this moment, by this man, I am wanted and for now, it's more than enough.

I lean my head back against his chest, enjoying the closeness that only comes from being intimate with another. His arms encircle me, his hands settling on my breasts. I feel his chest rumble against me as he tugs one stiff peak. "I think your nipple is turning blue. We better find something to remove these ties. I'd hate to have to explain your nipple injury to the emergency room." Now that he has brought it to my attention, I notice the pleasure has faded and little needles of pain are shooting through my tethered flesh. Lucian takes my hand and leads me to the bathroom where he finds a pair of clippers. We both appear to be holding our breath as he gingerly snips the dental floss around my sore nipple before carefully untwisting the bread tie. He wiggles his brows as he rubs circulation back into the area. "I think that falls under the category, 'don't try this at home,' don't you?"

Looking at the red circles left behind, I wince. "It sounded like a good idea at the time." My stomach growls as he is turning to set the water temperature in the shower. "I'm starving. Aren't you supposed to feed a girl before you pounce on her?"

Lucian reaches a hand out, pulling me under the warm water. "I think all bets are off when you are naked and wet with all manner of stuff tied to your body. That doesn't say feed me, baby; that says eat me."

"Oh, really," I tease. Wrapping my hand around his rapidly hardening dick, I ask, "And what does this say?"

Digging his hand in my hair, Lucian pushes me until I'm on my knees, my mouth level with his cock. "That says suck me." Taking him into my mouth, I proceed to do just that.

CHAPTER FIFTEEN

Lia

By the time we dress and arrive at Leo's for dinner, I am starving. When we are led to the same corner table we occupied on our last visit, I am shocked to find Rose and Jake already sitting on one side. I whirl to look at Lucian who is smiling in satisfaction. "You said you never see Rose anymore, so I thought this might be a nice surprise." In my heart, I know he wants to show me that even though my mother doesn't give a damn, there are people in my life who do. I throw my arms around his neck, giving him a big kiss in front of everyone in the busy restaurant before turning back to my friends. I slide into the circular booth next to Rose and after a few words with the server; Lucian follows me onto the comfortable seat.

"Girl, where have you been? With you gone from home every night, I've been left with nothing but Jake and his fifteen hands. My hoo-haw is damn near hawed out." Laughter bubbles out of my throat as Jake, instead of being embarrassed, looks strangely proud of himself. Where men are concerned, I would guess being accused of too much sex is hardly an insult. "I need you to come back so I can watch Lifetime and eat a carton of Ben and Jerry's." The

wine Lucian ordered arrives, and we all have a glass. I
blush as Lucian looks at me before rubbing the rim of
his glass. The evil man knows exactly what he's doing
to me as I squirm on my seat. As I look away from
him, I find Rose giving me a knowing smirk. "If you
two are having some kind of silent sex talk, cut it out
unless you want to make it a foursome."

I snort my wine up my nose, almost spraying her as
I yell, "Rose!" She and Jake laugh, but I have to
wonder if part of her statement isn't true. She may
have been unnerved by Jake's interest in anal sex, but
Rose is far from a prude.

Lucian leans around me, putting an end to any
fantasy she may have been entertaining. "I don't
share...with anyone." It may just be my imagination,
but Rose looks almost disappointed for a moment
before rolling out her lip dramatically in a pout.

The rest of the evening is light and fun. Lucian,
although far removed from a struggling college
student, is charming and at times irreverent. He has
Rose and Jake laughing at all his jokes and hanging
on his every word. Any fears I may have had about
him fitting into my world seem silly; we are all
perfectly at ease with each other. When the check
comes, he insists on paying, which ensures that he
moves into hero status.

We are enjoying our last drink before leaving when
the one woman, other than my mother, that I never
want to see stops by our table. Monique -Cruella- is
wearing a fire engine red dress that fits like a second
skin. Aidan walks up behind her, looking at his friend
apologetically. "Luc, I didn't know you would be here
tonight," he says by way of greeting.

Monique waves her manicured nails around the
table, encompassing us all. "It looks like some sort of
romper-room meeting. I recognize Lucy, but who are
your other little friends, Luc?"

Beside me, Rose mutters, "Is this bitch for real?" I see by the slight twist of Lucian's lips that he also caught her comment. He doesn't bother getting to his feet to make the introductions, which I know is his way of dismissing Monique. Instead, he tightens his grip, pulling me closer before speaking.

"Monique, I believe you remember Lia, and these are our friends, Rose and Jake." He then introduces Aidan who shakes hands with everyone, making polite conversation along the way. Aidan invites us to join them, and I'm relieved when Lucian says we were just finishing our last drink before leaving. His meaning is clear; however, Monique is as tacky and clueless as ever.

"Luc, darling, why don't you come back and join us for the evening after you take the...her home? We were planning to stop by Oasis for a few hours after dinner." Giving me a dismissive look, she adds, "They don't admit anyone under age twenty-one." Lucian finishes his drink, and we slip from the booth before he finally answers her snide comment.

"I am taking Lia home...our home. Enjoy the club, though. I don't think you have to worry about being carded." Aidan slaps Lucian on the back, laughing softly under his breath as we pass by. He clasps my hand lightly next as if apologizing for his date. When we reach the sidewalk, Rose flings her arms around Lucian, laughing hysterically.

"I freaking loved that. You. Are. The. Bomb! I always thought just calling someone an asshole was insult enough. But that whole civilized cut-down was epic." Lucian gives her an innocent look as if he has no idea what she's talking about, which makes it that much funnier. Rose and Jake seem to be in a hurry to get home, and from the way they are hanging all over each other, I am pretty sure why. Jake, ever the responsible one in their relationship, drank very little so he could drive home afterwards. When I hug Rose goodbye, she whispers against my ear, "Honey, I'm sorry about today. I'll totally kick your mom's ass; you just say the word, and it's on."

I try to keep it light, not wanting to think about what happened in the courtroom earlier. "Mom? You must have me mistaken for someone who actually has one of those." Rose bumps my shoulder with hers, letting me know she understands where I'm coming from. Jake also surprises me with a hug and a look of sympathy. It appears my family shame is well known by my friends, but I don't mind. Other than Debra, they are the closest I have to family, and today has made that blindingly clear. Suddenly, I have an overwhelming desire to see Debra. I want her to meet Lucian. I asked her earlier in the week not to come to the hearing; I was afraid she would end up attacking my mother and getting locked up in the process. I vow to call her tomorrow and see if she wants to meet for lunch in the next few days.

It's a nice evening outside and even though he argues at first, Lucian finally agrees to walk back to the apartment instead of having Sam pick us up. "Did you have a good time tonight, baby?"

Cuddling closer to his big frame, I sigh. "Thank you, Luc; I really needed an evening just like this. Well...except for maybe the awkward moment with Cruella." His hand rubs up and down my back as he laughs softly.

"Sorry about that. I have no idea what Aidan's doing getting involved with her. There is no way that ends well."

Since he has admitted to sleeping with Monique, I can't resist taking a small jab at his statement. "Isn't that a little pot and kettle, Mr. Quinn?"

"Very funny, Miss Adams. There was never anything between Monique and me other than a quick fuck. That might make me sound like a pig, but it's true." I take a moment to let his words sink in.

Surprisingly, I'm not as bothered by them as I would have thought. I would rather Lucian have never slept with Monique, but somehow him just having sex is much more preferable than him having a relationship with her.

While he is sharing information, I decide to push for more. "Is Monique the last woman...you know...before me?" Is it my imagination or had his stride faltered just a tad at my question?

"No...I dated someone for a few months after her." I stiffen, not expecting his answer. Had I thought I was the first person to spend my nights with him? As if interrupting my silence correctly, he continues. "It was nothing serious. I needed a date for different events and Laurie needed...financial assistance."

"Oh. My. God," I stammer, as I turn to stare at him. "Why does this sound so familiar?"

Lucian stops abruptly, pulling me from the traffic on the sidewalk. "This probably isn't the best place to talk about this, but I don't want you stewing all the way home. Trust me; there are no similarities between you and Laurie. She was a spoiled socialite I met at a party. At the time, I had just made the grave mistake of sleeping with Monique and couldn't get her to leave me the hell alone. Laurie served that purpose. She had expensive taste that she couldn't afford on the allowance her father had put her on. I helped her out with that, and she gave me the illusion of a relationship to hold Monique at bay."

"What happened to Laurie?" I look around almost as if expecting to see her standing behind me. Dear Lord, surely she isn't still in his life; that would be more than I could bear.

"Things are finished with her and were before you and I met. She...wanted more and I didn't." A sudden chill runs up my spine that has nothing to do with the nighttime air. Lucian, feeling my shiver, tucks me back under his arm. "You're cold. Let's go home; we can talk there."

I let him lead me to the apartment, an uncomfortable silence falling between us. My place in his life seems fragile and uncertain. I feel silly that I have even imagined for one moment that Lucian could feel for me the way I feel for him. I am an inexperienced, unsophisticated college student, and he is a rich, successful businessman. What could he possibly see in me? Am I just another way to keep women like Monique from throwing themselves at him? I walk to the kitchen for a bottle of water as he fixes himself a drink. "Can I get you anything?" I ask from the doorway.

"No, baby." He settles on the couch and pats the place next to him. I really want to make an excuse to go lick my wounds in another room, but I know it's childish. If I want Lucian to see me as a mature adult, then I need to act like one. Do I want him to regret opening up to me no matter how much I hated his answer? I sit next to him, playing nervously with the cap on the water bottle. "I can practically hear your mind spinning from here, you know."

"I'm sorry," I say, and I mean it. I wish I could just shut my mind down for the evening and take everything he has said in stride, but the questions loom. "When you said Laurie wanted more, what did you mean? Like marriage?"

Lucian doesn't seem surprised that I have returned to our original conversation; he almost seems to be expecting it. "Eventually, I'm sure that was her goal. She wanted access to more of my life, such as my homes."

"She wanted to live with you? That would make sense."

"No, baby, she wanted to see my homes, spend the night here. Laurie was never in this apartment or my house. She was in my apartment at the office a few times while I was changing for an event, but that's it."

I am completely blown away by his statement. How could he have dated someone for months and never had her here? Of course, would I be here now if not for the fact that I had first walked through the door as his cleaning lady? I am certain the confusion I'm feeling must be apparent in my voice as I say, "That seems strange to me. Didn't you spend the night together...at least some of the time?" I can tell Lucian is getting tired of my twenty questions, but he continues to answer patiently.

"We dated...we had sex at her place, but I didn't spend the night, nor did she spend the night with me...at any time. Lia, you know what happens sometimes when I sleep. I never wanted anyone to witness my...nightmares, so I avoided that risk."

Swallowing around the lump that seems to be wedged in my throat, I ask the one question I need to know, regardless of how badly his answer could hurt me. "What about me? Would I be here if I hadn't forced the cleaning issue?"

He takes his time, not jumping to put my jumble of insecurities to rest. Finally, as my nerves are screaming, he says, "Maybe not as quickly as your first trip, but yes, I feel certain we would have ended up exactly where we are now." He stares at the strand of my hair he's twirling around his finger as if captivated. "From the moment we met, I have been helpless to stay away, even though I should. There is just something about you that draws me in, makes me want to believe in things that scare the hell out of me."

I reach up, cupping his face in my hands and looking into his tormented eyes. "What's wrong with believing in something, Luc?"

He is looking at me but appears to be a million miles away. I rub my finger soothingly on his cheek, bringing his focus back to me. Clearing his throat, he finally answers. "I've done it before. There was a time when I thought all I had to do was believe and things would work out. In the end, that belief forever damaged everyone involved. I just...don't know if I can risk that again. I barely survived it the first time."

I am unable to stop the tear that breaks free and slides down my cheek. I should end the questions now, but I don't...I need one more answer. "Where does that leave us then?"

He kisses me gently, tracing my quivering lips with the tip of his tongue. "I don't know," he groans against my mouth. "I'm trying, baby; don't give up on me yet."

Wrapping myself around him, I give in to all the feelings he invokes in me. "I'm here," I assure him, knowing that no matter how terrified I am of losing him in the end, I can't walk away. He is right; we have been helpless to stay away from each other from the beginning.

Lucian is the type of man any woman would want, but he is so much more than what most see on the outside. The thing that draws me in the most is the troubled man I see glimpses of behind the polished exterior. His words tonight hint at the past tragedy that continues to haunt him even now. I want to push him to tell me everything, but I don't; we both need the peace of communicating without words for a while. I stand, holding my hand out to him. He looks heartbreakingly grateful that I'm still here with him in the moment.

He takes my hand, and we walk to the bedroom. That night, for the first time, we make love. We have had sex many times, but tonight is vastly different from the other times. I feel cherished as he worships every inch of my body with his hands and mouth. No words of love are spoken, but the room is electric with emotion as we come together time and again. Dawn is chasing away the night when we finally collapse into each other's arms, exhausted and content.

CHAPTER SIXTEEN

Lucian

I jerk awake, grabbing my throat as I choke. Next to me, Lia stirs but doesn't wake. My heart is hammering and fear still clutches my insides. Fuck, one night of not self-medicating and I'm right back in Hell. I ease from the bed, careful to make as little noise as possible. Safely inside the bathroom, I go straight to the shaving kit tucked against the back of the cabinet, under the sink, and pull it out. My hands automatically lay out the small mirror and white vial. In less time than it would have taken to find a bottle of Tylenol, I've made two perfectly straight lines of white powder and rolled up a dollar bill into a tight, straw-like shape. A couple of snorts later, I repack the bag, tucking it once again securely out of sight.

The coveted feeling of calm races through my veins, and I'm once again unshakable. The nightmare is fading away, and my world is returning to the upright position. When a knock sounds at the door behind me, I jump guiltily. "Yeah, baby?" I call through the wood as I quickly wash my hands and scan the sink counter to make sure no evidence is left behind.

"Just making sure you are okay. I thought I heard you yell." I cringe at her words, remembering my shout

of relief as the cocaine had made its way into my
system. If she knew my whole story, she of all people
would probably understand my need for relief, but
fuck, I don't want her to know I'm using. I love that
she looks to me for protection, and I'll be damned if I
want to seem like less in her eyes. I am just another
messed-up person who needs a crutch to deal with his
problems, but she doesn't know that, and I want to
keep it that way for as long as I can.

"Sorry, baby. Just...kicked the cabinet with my toe.
Hurt like hell." I wait another moment for the guilt of
the lie to leave my face before opening the door to find
her standing there. She has slipped on my shirt and as
sexy as she is naked, she looks even better wearing my
things.

We had spent a peaceful weekend together. After
her ordeal in court on Friday, we decided to lay low for
a few days. We spent Saturday exploring Biltmore
Village, and Sunday we had returned to my house for
lunch with Aunt Fae and a more PG-rated swim in the
pool. It's early Monday morning now, and we have a
few hours remaining before either of us has to start
the day.

Max let me know on Friday that Lia's stepfather
would remain in jail for the weekend but would
possibly be released at some point today. I have given
her strict instructions that she is to go nowhere
without Sam. I will drive myself to the office this week
so she can have my car at her disposal. Sam will take
her to school and pick her up afterwards. I wanted her
to take a week off, but she is in the middle of finals
and refused.

I have no desire to go back to bed, but I know if I
don't, neither will Lia, and she has exams later on this
morning. I pull back the bed covers and follow her
under them. She turns on her side, and I wrap myself
around her as naturally as if I have been doing the
same thing for years. The routine we have developed

over the last few weeks is both scary and comforting. Our talk earlier has shown me we are both wary and uncertain about what is happening between us. I have let her into a part of me no one has occupied before. I am clueless as to how this has happened so fast.

In truth, my first evening with Lia was for much the same reason as my first date with Laurie-to keep Monique off my ass. Lia was never supposed to be anything other than that. When I met her, though, something stirred to life and that feeling captivated me. My answer to the uncertainty those feelings provoked was to fuck her and get her out of my system.

Yeah, that worked really well; having sex with her only strengthened my fascination. I'm not completely clueless; I know part of the original attraction was the similarities between her and Cassie. Not physically, but their circumstances in life are alarmingly close. Lia, though, is strong and has refused to let life break her. Cassie was broken a long time ago and eventually shattered. Lia is the best version of a girl like Cassie. A girl I loved once, but it was never enough to save her from herself. I have existed in my fucked-up world for so long since that I'm like someone waking from a coma to face the first sunlight they've seen in years. The glare is bright, the world is confusing, and I'm floundering at every turn. However, when I behold the vibrant blue of the day and the fiery glow as the sunsets, I feel nothing but wonder in the moment. That is what I feel when I'm with Lia: awe as each new day dawns with her in my life and fear that one day, the sun will go away again and I'll be back in the darkness, searching desperately for the light...for my Lia.

Lia's steady breathing tells me she's slipped back into sleep; I know I won't be so lucky. The cocaine has brought all my nerve endings to life, and sleep is the furthest thing from my mind. Instead, I pull her closer and breathe in the floral scent of her hair against my nose. My mind gradually relaxes, and I drift in a light doze as sunlight slowly creeps into the bedroom through the tall glass windows. I register the clock moving closer to six and know Lia will need to be up soon; Sam is picking her up at seven-thirty for her early class. I lay there with my morning wood pushing against the delicious crack of her ass, wondering if I'm bastard enough to wake her early. When she wiggles back against me, the decision is made.

Dropping my hand down her body, I slip it under my shirt she is still wearing and cup her sex. She moans low in her throat as I dip a finger into her moist heat; it appears I'm not the only one who woke in a state of need this morning. I leisurely stroke her slit from top to bottom, stopping to apply more pressure to her clit before continuing. The slow pace has her restless. Her hips chase my hand, trying to apply more pressure where she needs it. Just as she is moaning in frustration, I slip my finger in her pussy, sinking it in to my palm. Her breath quickens and I know it won't take much to push her over. I'm selfish, though, and I want my cock inside her when she comes.

Pushing my boxers down, I line my hips up with hers, curving closer to her ass. Before she can register my intention, the head of my cock is pushing against her entrance, and I'm slamming into her from behind. She is tight from this position, and I remain still inside her snug channel until I feel her loosen around me. The urge to start fucking her hard is almost impossible to resist, but I don't want to hurt her, so I let her set the pace. Sweat is beading my brow when she finally starts moving her hips insistently, impaling herself back, begging for it harder...faster. I give her everything she wants, holding nothing back as I power into her pussy over and over. The sound of our flesh slapping together fills the room along with moans of pleasure.

My balls tighten as my release climbs. I grit my teeth, trying to wait for her. "Touch yourself, baby; I need you to come now." As caught up in the moment as I am, she doesn't hesitate. I feel her hand drop and graze my cock as it plunges in and out of her wet sex. She starts to tremble as she works her nub, telling me she is there. I go deep, twisting my hips to hit her sweet spot, and that's it. We both shout as our release races through us. I shoot what feels like an endless spray of cum into her pussy as an orgasm so strong it makes me feel lightheaded blazes through my body. Afterwards, we stay connected, enjoying the moment of closeness before the ticking clock forces us apart.

I take a shower first, giving Lia a little more time to recover before handing the bathroom over to her. Mornings are something I enjoy now. This strange domesticity is foreign, but it makes me feel almost normal as I walk into the kitchen to pour us both a cup of coffee. Lia has been setting the coffeemaker at night, something I never bothered to do.

I am reading the morning news when she walks in later, dressed casually in jeans, a t-shirt, and flip-flops. She looks young and fresh. It's hard to believe she's the same woman I fucked to within an inch of both our lives less than an hour ago. That is part of her appeal, though, her innocence.

"Well, good morning," she whispers against my lips as she leans down to kiss me. She takes a big sip from her now-lukewarm coffee before reading CNN over my shoulder. "Just once, I'd like to see the headline, 'no news to report today, check back tomorrow'." I chuckle in reply, thinking I'd like to see the same damn thing, but it's a fantasy that's never happening for either of us.

Looking at my watch, I know it's almost time for Sam to arrive. She's not going to like it, but it's time to reiterate the rules for today; I'll happily be the bad guy if it keeps her safe. I pull her down onto my lap, kissing the soft skin of her neck. I grin in satisfaction as she shivers in reaction. "Sam's on his way. Remember, he drops you at the front door of St. Claire's and picks you up there, as well. You're not to go anywhere without him until we know what's going on with your stepfather." I work to keep my expression stern, and she pouts like a child.

"Is that really necessary? You need Sam far more than I do. How are you supposed to drive yourself into downtown Asheville today? Have you considered that traffic nightmare?" I am helpless to halt the grin her words bring forward. She's a sassy little shit this morning, and I'm completely charmed, as usual, where she is concerned.

"I've been driving myself around this city for far longer than you have, baby. I'm pretty sure I can handle it. Just do this for me, please. After all, I cannot very well torture my employees and make money while I'm worried about you, now can I?"

Looking completely serious, which I know is a sham, she says, "Good point. I promise to follow the rules, Dad."

I am in the middle of chasing her around the living room, intent on spanking her beautiful bottom, when a knock sounds at the door. As usual, Sam is right on time. Would it have killed him to be a few minutes late, just this once? Lia...the little wench has the audacity to stick her pink tongue out at me as she opens the door. Sam takes one look at our disheveled appearances and shakes his head, muttering something about refilling his coffee cup. I waggle a finger in her face, lowering my voice to promise, "Just delayed, baby, not forgotten."

"I'll hold you to that," she says against my lips as she kisses me before leaving with Sam.

I quickly gather my keys and briefcase. I have a nine o'clock appointment, and Lia is right, the downtown traffic is sure to be hell this morning.

CHAPTER SEVENTEEN

Lia

Sam and I make small talk on the short ride to school. We arrange for him to pick me up at the main entrance of St. Claire's at three that afternoon. Without my car, I plan to remain in the building; I can use the campus coffee shop as a study hall between classes. "I hope having to drive me today isn't messing up any plans you might have had, Sam." I've taken care of myself since I was old enough to walk, so this feels a little surreal to me.

Sam gives me a reassuring smile in the rearview mirror. "Lia, this is no trouble at all. If I wasn't driving you, then I would be driving Luc. Besides, your morning conversational skills are much better; Luc generally buries his head in his computer until we reach the office."

My answering grin says I'm fully aware of how much Lucian loves his morning news and stock reports. The man has a brain like a sponge. After scanning an internet page for a minute, he could probably ace a ten-page quiz on the contents. "Ah, yes, the man does love his technology." Switching gears, I decide I need to get to know the person I will be spending time with this week. "So, how long have you been with Lucian?"

The affection in Sam's voice is obvious as he answers. "All of his life. I worked for his father and then stayed on to help Miss Fae after his parents passed away. When he started Quinn Software, he wanted me with him. Gave both me and Aidan a piece of the company from the beginning. Not many men would do that for an employee. I love that boy like my own."

"If there is one thing I've learned, Sam, Lucian is nothing like other men, so I'm not surprised in the least by his generosity." Holding out a hand to encompass the car, I add, "Just look around. Lucian and I haven't been together long, but he is doing everything in his power to take care of me. Trust me when I say I've never met anyone like him."

"Luc is a complicated man, but you're good for him. Like you, he hasn't had an easy life. For all those people who think money makes everything okay, he's living proof it's not always the case. He's the man he is, though, because of all of those things."

Before I can stop myself, I blurt out, "What happened to him, Sam? The scar on his neck, the dreams? I've heard enough to know it involves Cassie, but she's almost like a ghost. People talk about her, but then act funny when I ask where she is. If you've been with Lucian for this long, you must have known her." I feel guilty when he shifts uncomfortably and falls silent. My God, what is it about that name that brings such strange reactions from everyone? I have my suspicions, but maybe it's worse than even I can imagine.

Finally, Sam says, "Have you asked Luc about her?"

"I have and also his aunt. Both just say she doesn't live here. Well, I already figured that out; otherwise she would be around, right? I gather she was friends with Lucian and Aidan growing up."

"She was...things were pretty bad between the three of them as they got older. A lot of jealousy, misunderstandings, and mistakes. What Luc said, though, is true; she doesn't live here now, and he's better off for it." Sam expels a breath, obviously remembering another time and place. "Lia, it's not my place to tell you about Luc's past. He will, when he's ready. Just give him time and be patient. You're good for him, and I'm happy to see him looking more like the old Luc. Wasn't sure that would ever happen again."

At once, I feel bad for trying to question someone other than Lucian about his past. I am also intrigued about what little Sam has revealed. A few sentences from him provided insight I hadn't previously known. I had already concluded that whatever happened to Lucian years ago involved Cassie. More and more, I feel that somehow it was a love affair gone bad. I'm uncertain, though, about the part Aidan plays in the trio. Was he actually the one involved with Cassie, and Lucian the collateral damage, or was it the other way around?

Thinking through the possible scenarios makes my head spin. If Lucian and I were normal people who were newly dating, life would be so much simpler. Instead, we are two people damaged by our pasts that clicked together like dominoes the moment we met. There seems to be no slow speed in our relationship. Maybe Lucian is correct, and things wouldn't have progressed as quickly if I hadn't been working in his home, but one thing I know for sure, we were destined to end up exactly as we are now. Two lost souls drawn together by the scars of the other. Are we moving fast? Absolutely. Do I want to stop? No. He has become so important to me; I only hope we can both put our pasts behind us enough to have a future together.

CHAPTER EIGHTEEN

Lucian

Hitting the intercom button, I ask, "Cindy, is Aidan in yet?" I shuffle some papers on my desk, trying to make a dent in the work that seems to never end. Since Lia has come into my life, I haven't been working the usual eighteen-hour days, and it's showing. Perhaps Cindy is right; I need to start delegating more work, which is why I'm looking for my right hand.

"No, Luc, he's not back yet?"

Surprised, I ask Cindy to come into my office, which she does immediately, shutting the door behind her. "What's going on? He always comes back on Sunday." I can tell by the worried expression on her face that she's puzzled, as well. Aidan is damn near anal about his routine; deviations just don't happen, especially when it interferes with his job.

"I have no idea. He emailed me earlier to let me know he wasn't back in town yet. He just told me to pass that along but didn't offer any explanations. I forwarded his email to you." I take a moment to check my mail and read the forward from Cindy.

Cindy is right; his email gives no explanations as to his whereabouts, but I know he's been to see Cassie and I worry it's fucking with his head more than usual. I give Cindy a reassuring smile, ready to end her nervous hovering. She is damned efficient, but she worries about Aidan, Sam, and myself too much. She sniffs out problems like a bloodhound. I'm surprised she's never caught on to my coke addiction. Maybe she knows, but I doubt it; she would have kicked my ass first and staged an intervention next. Apparently, Sam does keep some pillow secrets, probably not to protect me so much as to protect himself. He'd be the second one she'd take apart, since he handles my supply and demand.

"I'm sure he just got a late start home. I'll give him a call." Since she's still giving me a nervous look, I decide to give her a mission. Hell, anything to get her out of my office for a while. "Could you go to Madeline's office and see when the quarterly numbers are going to be ready? I'll need those soon to prepare for my meeting tomorrow." I hide a smile as she immediately snaps into bulldog mode. Poor Madeline; Cindy will be on her all afternoon now, and I really don't even need the damn numbers. I stay on top of the finances for my company daily; I don't like surprises where money is concerned.

I click an open line on the telephone and punch in Aidan's number. It rings four times before going to voicemail. I try texting him next, getting no immediate reply. Aidan never falls off the grid, and he damn sure wouldn't on a workday. Fuck. Now, I'm right there with Cindy. Something is going on; I can feel it in my bones. I try to push it aside while I return calls from the previous day.

At lunchtime, I decide to have a sandwich at my desk and check in with Lia. I'm not sure if she's in class or not, so I settle for texting her.

Lucian: Hey, baby.

Lia: Hey, yourself. I was just thinking about you. :)

Lucian: All dirty thoughts, I hope.

Lia: Behave. I have to sit in a boring classroom. I can't be thinking of that...

Lucian: Why not? I'm sitting in a boring office thinking of nothing but that...

Lia: You can show me tonight.

My cock stirs to attention at her teasing words. I hadn't been thinking of sex before our verbal wordplay, but thoughts of fucking her have now moved to the forefront of my mind. I want to continue this teasing conversation, but I don't relish having to jack off in my bathroom after lunch, and that's where it's headed. Practicing a little self-preservation, I change the subject grudgingly.

Lucian: So...you made arrangements for Sam to pick you up this afternoon, right?

I grin, knowing Sam's not far away. I had him stay close to the school today just in case Lia needs him for something.

Lia: Yep, I'm all set. I gotta run, need to grab a drink before my next class. See you later?

Lucian: Of course. See you at home, baby.

I marvel at how easily I refer to my apartment as both of our homes now. This woman has so quickly become my constant. When she mentions staying at her apartment, I firmly nix the thought. I know she doesn't really want to leave my place, but she feels like she should offer to give me space. Strangely enough, though, I don't want that space. I've grown fond of going home to her in the evening. Hell, I've put Cindy on finding us a housekeeper now because I'm tired of Lia insisting on cleaning up after me to pay for her schooling. I admire her independence, but we're together now; I want to take care of her without strings.

Standing, I toss the wrapper from my sandwich into the trashcan and stroll to my bathroom where I keep my workout clothes. I have a workout room adjacent to my office with a treadmill, elliptical, and weights. At some point each day, I run for several miles then lift weights afterwards. It's a good way to stay in shape and relieve stress. Throwing on some basketball shorts, I hit the treadmill, going through a warm-up before my feet start pounding the surface. I watch the news on the television suspended from the wall as I pound out the miles.

I finish my workout and shower quickly before redressing. When I sit back at my desk, I pick up my cellphone, seeing I've missed a call from Aidan. It's about damn time; I was getting ready to send out a search party for his ass. I click to return his call and am pleased when he answers on the first ring. "Luc...hey."

"Hey, man. Where are you? I've barely been able to stop Cindy from hunting you down." Aidan laughs softly, knowing how Cindy is.

"Sorry 'bout that. I'll give her a call next so she won't worry." When he doesn't add anything further, my earlier feeling of foreboding returns full force.

"So...what's going on? We don't usually have to resort to hunting you. Are you back in town?"

"No." Just when I think I'm going to have to prompt him again, he finally continues. "Luc...something happened here. I don't really know what it means, but when I stopped by yesterday on my way out to tell her goodbye...fuck, she knew me. She called my name." I sag back in my seat, weak with shock. Aidan's voice is choked, as if he's overcome by emotion.

"Fuck!" I hiss, feeling a strange urge to end the call and sever the connection. I don't want to hear anymore, but I need to know. "What exactly happened?"

The sound of him taking a breath fills the line. "I—I stopped to see her after I checked out of my hotel, like I always do. I had been there about an hour, you know, just talking about everything and nothing. When I was leaving, I kissed her cheek and told her I'd see her soon. When I pulled back and started to straighten, she...shit, Luc, she touched my face and said, 'Bye, Spence.'"

I take a shaky breath myself, wanting to collapse for a completely different reason. Cassie had always called Aidan by a shortened version of his last name. He was never Aidan to her, just Spence. That she had called him something so personal had to indicate some level of recognition on her part. If she had just said bye, I might believe it was just some kind of reflex action. "What else?" Shit, do I want to hear anymore?

"That was it. Luc, her eyes were so clear for a moment. She seemed to really see me instead of looking straight through like she usually does. I tried to get another response from her, but it was like she had blanked back out almost immediately. I spoke to her doctor, and he thinks it's a good sign. It's the first time in eight years she's shown any recognition toward anyone around her."

It's then that I hear it. My cocky, self-assured friend is crying. The woman he's loved for most of his life...the woman who had a psychotic break after attempting to kill herself...and me-the man she professed to love. That night changed our lives in ways the three of us have never recovered from. On that night, the only person she did kill was my son...my unborn son. And the only other person who was there...who tried to save us all, was Aidan. In our twisted love triangle, Cassie taught me what it was to love and in the next breath, she taught me loss, despair, and finally hate.

I feel the need to cry along with Aidan but for totally different reasons. I don't know if I am ready to handle a world where Cassie might one day be free. I'm just learning to live again with Lia, my beautiful girl. "Aidan..." I begin, just as Max bursts into my office. "Hang on," I say quickly, pushing the mute button. Raising a brow to my lawyer that conveys my irritation at his unannounced interruption, I ask, "What's going on?"

"Sorry, Luc, but Cindy wasn't at her desk. I tried to call you, but you weren't answering. It's Jim Dawson; the court released him a few hours ago. He's out. We should have been notified earlier, but someone fucked up."

"Son of bitch," I snap. "What else today?" Putting the phone back to my ear, I say, "Aidan, I'll call you back. I need to take care of some things here. Just...we'll talk later, okay?" Part of me is just relieved to have a reason to end the call. Communicating with Aidan about Cassie is difficult at best. He loves her and I hate her. At what point could we meet in the middle on something like that? The only way I can have a rational conversation concerning her is to think of her as the girl we used to know and not the woman who had damn near killed me.

By the time I end the call, Max is sitting in a seat in front of my desk. It's never good news when your lawyer feels the need to make himself comfortable. I really just want him gone so I can check in with Lia to make sure everything is okay and also to warn Sam about Jim Dawson's release. "Luc, about the other matter you asked me to check on." At my look of confusion, he promotes, "Lia's biological father."

"Ah, yeah. Did you find something?" I had asked Max to use his connections when Lia told me she'd never known her father. I thought Lia might need the information one day; plus, I like to know everything about the people close to me. I wasn't expecting much after meeting Lia's mother in the courtroom. She was an attractive lady, but what a bitch. I can't imagine that time has changed much there.

Max gives me a look mixed with equal parts amusement and disbelief. "You could say that. Of course, this would have to be confirmed through a blood test, but my investigator has been able to confirm who Maria Dawson was involved with around the time of her pregnancy with Lia. Luckily for us, she didn't have a lot of men in her life, so it wasn't hard to pinpoint it."

When he doesn't continue, I wave a hand, prompting him. Shit, does he think I have nothing else to do today but play fucking guessing games? "I don't need the background right now, Max, just get to the point."

I swear the bastard looks almost giddy as he asks, "You've heard of Lee Jacks?"

Surprised, I say, "Of course, who hasn't? What's that got to do with Lia?" At his look, my eyes widen. "Are you saying...?"

"That's exactly what I'm saying. As far as I can tell, Lee Jacks is the father of Lia Adams. Looks like her mother either had a sentimental or mean streak when she named her daughter Lia."

My head reels as I rub the persistent knot of tension in my neck. Lee Jacks is a real estate developer who owns half of Asheville and its surrounding cities. Hell, I purchased the apartment I call home from his company. I'd met him a few times through the years at various charity events. I figure he's in his late-forties or early-fifties, so it's possible he could have a daughter Lia's age. How in the hell had her mother gotten involved with someone like him, though? "Holy fuck, it just keeps on coming today." I fill him in briefly on my conversation with Aidan, which in turn causes him to look as shell-shocked as I feel.

"Christ, I can't believe that. She's been completely out of it for, what, eight or nine years? Do you want me to check into it?" Max, as my lawyer, handles most of my affairs, including Cassie.

"Let me talk to Aidan again first. Possibly, it was just a one-time thing. Who knows if she actually knew he was there or not. May be just a coincidence."

Max clears his throat as he moves to the edge of his seat. "Luc, I would guess you'll hear from Lee Jacks or someone in his employment. There's no way he's missed the fact I've been asking questions about him; he's going to want to know why. It won't take much digging for him to find out I work solely for Quinn Software...and you. I'll leave it up to you to answer that question." Unspoken between us is the fact we both know Lee Jacks is well known in the area for more than his real estate holdings. It's long been rumored he's well connected on both sides of the law. Undoubtedly, Max is right; a man who rides the gray line as closely as Lee Jacks will almost certainly know when someone unusual is asking personal questions about him.

"Thanks for the warning. I'll let you know if I hear from him." Max stands, taking my words for what they are-a polite dismissal, for now. "I'll call you later after I speak with Aidan." As he shuts the door behind me, I am already dialing Sam. I need to update him on Lia's stepfather.

Lia

I set my pencil on my desk, fighting the urge to do a fist pump. My last test of the day is complete, and I know I did well. I had easily known the answers to the majority of the questions, and I am finished well ahead of schedule. I quietly make my way to the front of the classroom, handing the test to my teacher, Miss Riddle. She gives me an absent smile and waves me toward the door. I have almost an hour before Sam is picking me up. I look around the empty halls for a moment before heading toward the courtyard and the coffee shop. I'll kill some time by having a frappe while I wait. I know he would drop everything and come early, but I don't want to put him out; he's already doing enough by driving me everywhere I need to go.

I text Rose when I get settled with my cold drink-hoping she's finished early, as well-but know when there's no immediate reply that she's still in class. As I take the first sip of my drink, I accidently squeeze the cup too hard and the top pops off. "Shit," I gasp as the cold, icy liquid splatters onto the front of my shirt, making an ugly stain right over my left breast. I dab it with a handful of napkins, but the stain only spreads. Just great. Now I'm stuck sitting here, or worse yet, walking around for forty-five minutes looking like I have a leaking nipple.

My bra is now uncomfortably wet and sticky, and I can't fathom having to meet Sam looking like this. Suddenly, it hits me. My apartment is only a block away. I need to get some more clothes to take to Lucian's anyway. He'll be pissed if he finds out I've gone by myself, but if Sam mentions it, I'll just say I met up with Rose. If I hurry, I'll be back in plenty of time to meet Sam. Standing, I hold the still-messy cup far away from my body and throw it in the trashcan on the way out the door. I walk through the back gates of the university, skirting the delivery trucks coming and going.

When I reach our apartment building, I feel a touch of nostalgia. I have hardly been here at all the last few weeks. For all intents and purposes, I have unofficially moved in with Lucian. I'm also still cleaning his apartment, despite his various and vocal protests. I thought men liked it when women took care of them? He seems to feel guilty every time I wash a dish or a load of laundry. It's really nothing new to me; I have always taken care of myself along with being my mother's slave for years.

I miss the girl-time with Rose, sitting around watching a Lifetime movie while gossiping. I love going to sleep and waking up with Lucian each day, though...and the sex. Oh, my, the sex. Lucian likes it a lot, and he needs very little recovery time between. I feel my face heat just thinking of the way he touches me, possesses me. Just one look from him and I am melting in a puddle at his feet.

My face is stretched into a sappy, goofy grin, and I thinking of nothing but him as I enter our building. I stop by the mailboxes, finding mine is overflowing. As I sift through the pile, pulling out the junk mail, I am surprised more than alarmed when arms come around my body and a hand clamps over my mouth. My first thought is Rose or even Jake, though it is hardly his style to manhandle me. Lucian even runs through my mind. Maybe he's found out I walked home and is here to give me hell over it.

When the arms tighten and I am bodily-dragged across the floor toward the now-open door that leads to the tenants' storage lockers, I start to panic. This isn't right. Lucian, nor any of my friends, would do this. Whoever is holding me is far stronger than Rose and taller than Jake. I am struggling now in earnest, knowing instinctively that something bad is going to happen if I am pulled through that door. My foot stomps down, connecting with the person's foot that is holding me. I hear a grunt and then curses. "You'll pay for that, cunt."

The strength suddenly leaves my body. I sag weakly against my attacker as he pulls me through the door and shuts it behind us. Oh, dear God, I know that voice. Please, oh please, let me be wrong. As I am shoved roughly against a wall, a rag smelling of gas is shoved into my mouth, almost immediately followed by a wide, silver piece of tape over my lips. In my panic, I can't breathe. I move my hands to claw at the tape, but they are wrenched above my head, restrained tightly together with the same silver tape. Stars dance behind my eyes as I start to hyperventilate. My face is roughly pulled up, forcing me to look directly into the eyes of my captor. Jim Dawson, my stepfather, stares back at me, looking triumphant. "No," I mumble around the rag in my mouth. The spinning, black void rises to claim me, and I slump limply to the floor, barely registering the pain in my head as it connects with the metal corner of a shelf. Oblivion is what I need now, and I go into it willingly.

CHAPTER NINETEEN

Lucian

"Sam, how long until you pick up Lia?" As soon as Max leaves my office, I pick up the phone to call Sam. He needs to be updated on Lia's stepfather.

"I'm picking her up at three. I'm here now waiting for her." I take a quick look at my watch, frowning when I see it's now ten minutes past that time.

"That was ten minutes ago. Is she in the car or isn't she?"

"No...she's not here yet, Luc. I'm out front now, walking around the courtyard. Maybe she got held up in her last class."

"Fuck," I hiss; can't anything go smoothly today? "Listen, Sam, Lia's stepfather was released from jail earlier. I don't have any reason to think he'd come for her, but we need to be on our guard. Head to the office and talk to Mrs. Phillips. Tell her I need to know Lia's schedule today and then track down her last class. I know Mrs. Phillips' husband, so she'll give you the information. Call me as soon as you have something." Without waiting for a reply, I end the call. Running a hand through my hair, I kick the side of my desk in frustration. Today has been nothing but one big clusterfuck; nothing has gone as planned from the moment I walked through the doors this morning.

Cindy sticks her head inside my office, probably alarmed by the sound of me blowing off some steam. She knows me well. She gives me a silent look that asks if I need anything from her, I shake my head briefly, and she pulls the door closed behind her. I pick up my cellphone and dial Lia's number. It goes straight to voicemail without ringing, as if it's turned off. I try to assure myself it's just because she's been in class all day. Of course, she'd have her phone off; she wouldn't want to get any calls during her exams.

I fire off a text:

Lucian: Baby, where are you? Sam is looking for you.

A long few minutes pass with no reply. I quickly tap out another message.

Lucian: Lia, answer me or I'm coming to find you.

Again, there is no reply. By this time, I'm pacing the floor. When my phone rings, I answer without looking at the caller ID.

"Lia?" Even I can't miss the quaver in my voice.

"No, Luc, it's me." Sam says. "I just left Lia's last class. Luc, she's been gone from there for over an hour. The teacher said the test was short, and Lia was one of the first people finished. She turned it in, and the teacher dismissed her."

"Goddammit!" I roar. "Where the hell is she then? Go back out to the car and see if she's there now. Maybe she was just sitting somewhere near until it was time for you."

"Luc...I am outside. It's pretty much cleared out

here now. There are only a few people standing around and none of them are her. How about that friend of hers she lives with? Do you think she's with her?"

I relax slightly, thinking that's probably exactly where she is. I don't have her number though, shit. "Sam, go back inside and have Mrs. Phillips pull Rose's file and give you her number."

"And her last name is?"

Damn..."MADDEN! It's Madden." Thank fuck I've listened when Lia talks about her best friend. Of course, in a school as small as St. Claire's, Mrs. Phillips could no doubt make the connection without the last name. "I'm heading that way now. If you find her, put her in the car and don't move. I'll be there in twenty minutes. Keep me updated."

I grab my keys off the desk and almost run over Cindy on my way out. "Luc, is everything all right?"

"I have no idea," I answer truthfully. I continue past her; there is no time to stop and explain. Cindy, no doubt, will know what's going on very shortly; she seems to have a pipeline to Sam at all times. I check my phone again as I turn the ignition of the Rover. Still no text from Lia. *"Oh, baby, where are you?"* I ask the quiet phone as if expecting an answer. I pull out into traffic and press the gas pedal to the floor when I hit the open highway. The sense of foreboding I've felt on and off all morning has returned in full strength. Much the same way as I'd known something was going on with Aidan, I know something has happened to Lia. The last time she didn't answer my calls, she was sick. My phone rings again and Sam picks up our conversation in almost the exact place we left off.

"I spoke to Rose. She hasn't talked to Lia since this morning. She said she had a missed call from her around the time of her last class but was taking her exams and had her phone off. She has been trying to call her, as well. She's going to their apartment now to make sure she didn't go there."

"All right, just stay near the car in case she shows up looking for you. I'll stop by her apartment to see Rose." I end the call and break a few more traffic laws before skidding to a halt outside Lia's apartment. I take the front steps two at a time, running into the lobby just as Rose comes running down the stairs, waving something in her hands.

"Lucian, Lia's not in the apartment and it doesn't look like she has been." Audibly swallowing, she holds out what I now see is mail. "Our neighbor handed these to me when I was leaving. She said they were lying on the floor below the mailboxes." Her hand is shaking as I take the envelopes and see Lia's name on them. "Where is she?" Rose asks, looking on the verge of full panic. I put one arm around her shoulders, trying to calm her as I reach for my phone to call Sam. There is a sudden commotion to the right of the lobby. I hear shouts of alarm and cries for help. I take off toward the noise with Rose following closely behind. A tall, thin girl with very short, brown hair comes running through a doorway in the corner, near a bank of mailboxes. Rose grabs her arm as she goes to pass, us asking, "Ashley, what's going on? Are you all right?"

The girl stops as if she's seen a ghost. She is breathing heavy and in obvious distress. I look around, still trying to discern the source of her anxiety, but see nothing amiss. "Rose, oh God, Rose...The door was jammed, and I needed my golf clubs." By this time, she is panting and every word is gasped out. "Lia...Lia..."

I take her arm, shaking her lightly. At the mention of Lia's name, I feel my own anxiety climbing. Something is badly wrong, and this girl has the answers. "What about Lia? Where is she?" I practically shout. I know it's not wise to yell at someone so close to the edge, but I need fucking answers. Rose is shaking her, as well, both of us talking at once.

"Lia's down there...Me and Mr. Leslie found her. I need to go for help. She's not moving!" I drop Ashley's arm and run for the doorway she came through. I see nothing for a moment but wall-to-wall lockers. Then I hear a voice yelling from the left and take off in that direction. What I find at the end of the aisle has me staggering unsteadily on my feet.

A pair of bare legs and feet are partially obscured by the elderly man kneeling next to them. I catch a glimpse of blonde hair and stumble, overcome with fear. Rose screams, sobbing Lia's name. The man on the floor spins around, looking like he's on the point of a nervous breakdown. "Please, help her," he yells. "I just found her and she's not waking up!"

I run the rest of the way to his side...and then I see her. "Oh, my God," I whisper as I fall to my knees beside her. I barely hear Rose's screams above the roaring in my ears. Something foreign and unfamiliar drips down my face, and I'm shocked to realize it's tears. As I stare down at the broken body of my beautiful girl, the fear I'm doomed to lose everyone I love pierces my soul.

To be continued...

Lucian and Lia's story continues in Winter 2014 with Fractured.

ABOUT THE AUTHOR

Sydney Landon lives in Greenville, South Carolina and has spent the last twenty-five years working in accounting. Sydney met her own prince charming in 2000 and received the most romantic proposal on a pier in Myrtle Beach, South Carolina, thus creating her eternal love for the city. The fact that her future husband was a fellow computer geek completely sealed the deal for her. She credits him with keeping her calm and rational while also understanding her need for a new pair of shoes every other week. They have two children who keep life interesting and borderline insane, but never boring.

The idea of the Danvers' Series popped into her head and refused to go away. She started writing the first story never imagining that it would ever be finished. Three months later it turned into her first book, Weekends Required. Within a few months, it had quickly made the best-seller list on Amazon, and went on to make the New York Times Best Seller List. Barely taking a breath between books, Sydney followed up with the second book in the series, Not Planning on You. Within the first month, this book also became a best-seller. The third book in the series, Fall For Me was released in February 2013 and became a New York Times Best Seller. The fourth book in the series, Fighting For You released in paperback in February 2014. Sydney is currently working on the fifth book in the Danvers' Series and the second book in the Lucian and Lia Trilogy. When she isn't writing, Sydney enjoys reading, swimming and being a mini-van driving, soccer mom.

ACKNOWLEDGEMENTS

Many thanks to Becky with Hot Tree Editing. Also, to Jenny Sims with Editing 4 Indies. It was a real pleasure working you ladies.

Thanks to the wonderfully talented Kimberly Killion with the Killion Group who took my vision and made it into such a beautiful, sexy cover.

To my wonderful friends Lorie Gullian, Amanda Lanclos, Lisa Salvary, Teresa Alverson, Shelly Lazar, Marion Archer and Heather Waterman. Thanks for all of your help!

A special thanks to Allison Quattlander, you rock!

CPSIA information can be obtained at www.ICGtesting.com
Printed in the USA
BVOW02s1122041015

420895BV00002B/212/P